THE BRIDGE TO
REMBRANDT

First published in The Netherlands by San San, 2021

www.thebridgetorembrandt.com

San San B.V.
Voorhaven 58,
1135 BS, Edam
The Netherlands

A catalogue record of this book is registered with the Koninklijke Bibliotheek.

ISBN 978-90-9034589-5

This novel is entirely a work of fiction. The names, characters and incidents portrayed, while at times based on historical fact, are the work of the author's imagination.

PART I

"Who the hell was that?"

CHAPTER ONE

The abruptness of the abuse was more surprising than alarming. It was supposed to be a peaceful morning for Robert, enjoying a coffee break at one of the many terraces in Amsterdam. The assault on him was thankfully verbal, rather than physical, but he felt the legs of the chair shake under him, as if he were sitting too close to the bass speakers at a festival. Or was it his own legs shaking?

"Here, what you looking at, mate?" said a deep voice.

Robert had been in one of those trances, staring at nothing in particular, deep in thought. He was jolted into life by a person he had never seen before, inches away from his face. He felt the warm breath. As he focused his eyes, Robert found himself nose to nose with a sorry apparition who looked like he had just come from another century, with plump cheeks and ruffled hair protruding from under his black beret. He had an unwashed aroma to go with the look and was unsteady on his feet. He was leaning on the table with a soiled hand coated in what looked like paint remnants.

"Pay no attention to me," answered Robert. "Or have I missed something?"

"What you staring at? Listen, I have a lot of problems and I don't need people like you making me feel worse," replied the stranger.

"Sorry, if you thought that. I really wasn't looking at you; I was miles away."

The stranger seemed torn between pushing his anger further or lapsing into despondency. The despondency won.

"Maybe you'll be hearing more from me," he said, and resumed his travels, pushing his ancient and unusable bike, which seemed to be loaded with his only possessions. Robert sighed. He never felt he was in any danger, but it had certainly woken him up. He knew he had been in a world of his own. His attention was on the girls in their summer clothes, not the wanderer. He watched as the owner of the booming voice and strange gait disappeared from view, wondering why he had picked on him. Just for staring?

It was nice, warm, pre-summer weather and everyone had a spring in their step, especially the girls. Before he was disturbed, Robert's thoughts were bouncing awkwardly between the girls on the street and his marriage. He was happy – no, comfortable – but the excitement was gone, and he had little idea how he could get that back. Right now, he was playfully contemplating how he could travel back to his student days, a time he felt he was more in control, even if it was control of a more chaotic life. He wanted his past back. In the meantime, he was playing with fire and the fire's name was Saskia.

The day dreaming was over. As he was about to leave, Robert eyed a coin that had been left on his table. He had no idea how it got there, but he was pretty sure it wasn't there before. He picked it up and saw that it was very old, rough around the edges. It looked silver, but he didn't know what it was made of. It appeared to depict an armed figure holding a sword and a coat of arms; the date looked like it said 1660. It was clearly not a current currency, so he put it in his pocket for later investigation. Strange morning, thought Robert.

Robert was a picture of health. He lived a good, if complicated, life close to the centre of Amsterdam, in a leafy part of Java Island, just on the northern edge of the city. He recently made his life more complicated when he started juggling too many things at the same time.

Saskia was one of these things, but so, too, was his decision to embark on a new business venture with one of his best buddies, Mark. On paper that gave him two jobs, but he thought he could handle that with relative ease. His main employment was the business of organising music festivals, but because that was seasonal it gave him ample time to explore other opportunities. His friend Mark was in the

3

business of selling high quality paints for artists and had stumbled upon some of the artist collectives in China who specialised in copying old masters. One thing led to another and after much brainstorming they started a webshop with the name *Masters in Paint*, offering 'original' hand-painted copies of old masters and, later, even copies of any painting that anyone wanted. It wasn't limited to the famous old masters like Rembrandt, Vermeer, Constable, or Monet.

Mark was a British expat who had been living in Amsterdam for a while. While Robert was full of ideas, Mark was the one who moved things along with a typical British can-do attitude, one that Robert was sure had landed them in the trouble.

Mark had all the right contacts in China, and they had front-loaded their website with hundreds of sample paintings so that potential clients could see and choose from a library of images. It didn't matter that these paintings were not part of their stock, it was just a part of their marketing strategy. Each order was unique, so all they had to do was wait and let the orders come in, without holding any inventory. For Robert, the business was a no- brainer.

One of the more immediate complicating factors was Robert's wife, Belinda. Unlike him, she was the conservative type, and did not share Robert's enthusiasm for new ventures that might disrupt their steady suburban life. She already had to live with the vagaries of Robert's festival business and, without knowing why exactly, she didn't like the sound of a business that copied other people's paintings. The Chinese already had a bad reputation for copying intellectual property, and to her this was even more "in your face" than a hectic festival. She was not happy about it and she made sure Robert knew.

"Isn't it time you started thinking more about your family than new businesses? Especially risky ones," she would say.

Robert, in turn, tried to head his wife off by answering, "I think I am doing this for the family." He emphasised the word family. "You know the festival business is somewhat unpredictable and insecure, so it's only right that we have something to fall back on. Mark knows his stuff and we have all the right contacts in China. It's not a huge investment because we only need a website, some good marketing, and a generous dose of common sense. The bottom line is that it gives us some extra income. For the family."

"I still think it's risky. What happens if you get caught selling copies? I mean, your website will be easily traced."

"No, no. You don't understand. That's not an issue. It's all perfectly legal. If the artist has been dead for more than seventy years, then it falls into the public domain. Then anyone can copy the painting. You just can't try and pass it off as a genuine article."

"But still…"

Robert immediately added, "And the margins are good."

"Robert, it still doesn't change my opinion. You're already away a lot, and now you're adding all of this, so how do you think that's going to help our already rocky relationship?"

"I had hoped it would. Yes, I am doing this for me—but also for the family. And I think you'll warm to it, eventually," Robert finished hopefully, adding, "And I think you should meet Mark. He's a bit of a charmer, but I'm sure you'll like him and maybe it'll make you feel more comfortable about the business. And, like you, he's English."

"I'm not going to be a part of it. It's your thing. But be careful. I'm sure I'll meet Mark one day. Then I can give him the same message I'm giving you."

Belinda's lack of interest in her husband's entrepreneurial instincts had become more and more frustrating for Robert, and he was sure that she felt frustrated too. Robert wondered where this would lead. In the meantime, he carried on with his two jobs and, in his own opinion, finely managed the balance between them and his family.

That included his two kids, Daniel and Maxine, who were thirteen and eleven respectively. Even if the children could now look after themselves, Belinda was the brooding type, continually worrying about every little thing, and she expected Robert to be the same. That wasn't working either, as Robert was much more inclined towards a *laissez faire* existence. He was a freewheeler who wanted to see his own children stand on their own two feet and not be fretted over.

Belinda's fears about *Masters in Paint* were about to become reality. On their website, Robert and his partner Mark had decided to include an option that allowed users to select any painting they wanted to have copied, regardless of whether or not it was in their portfolio. They didn't say anything about the rules of public domain, but it was addressed in the frequently asked questions.

The result was that there were people who wanted more than just a painting from a long dead master. They started receiving requests for works of art from well-known painters who were still very much alive.

"Now what?" said Robert to Mark.

"As I see it, we have two options. One is to simply say 'sorry, we cannot do this,' but then we're turning away good business. The other is to ask for assurance from the buyer that it's for personal use only and will not be used in any public place. I favour the latter," said Mark, who was surprising Robert more by the day. He steadily became more assertive, more of a risk taker. For Robert's part, the rattling cogs in his brain were reminding him of Belinda's warnings.

"Are you sure we're not running any risks?"

"No, not if the buyer is using it privately."

"Yes, but we're just going on his word. That's not safe."

"Robert, look how many requests we're getting. I think it's something we can safely do. And other sites in other countries offer the same, at least from what I can see."

"OK, but let's make sure we get it in writing from the buyers."

"Agreed, but, technically, that is not protection. You know that?"

"Technically, yes."

After that, *Masters in Paint* started accepting orders for living artists, and it slowly became a sizeable part of their small business. Everything had been running smoothly, but that smoothness was interrupted when they received a cease and desist letter, and a claim. The letter came from the lawyers of one Emerson Parker, a well-known Brazilian-American painter who normally enjoyed sales of his work in the low millions. The letter made it very clear that there would be financial consequences.

Robert was stunned when they received it. He was in the small office he had set up with Mark, where they fielded customer enquiries, managed the website, and even did some framing for clients who wanted a finished product. The paintings normally arrived as rolled canvases from China.

After the inevitable arguments with Mark had died down, Robert began pacing the office and went on like that for a while.

"Will you stop that 'ijsberen?' It's driving me insane," said Mark, who had used the Dutch word for pacing. Literally translated, the word turned the noun polar bear into a verb, "to polar bear." Robert was often like a pacing polar bear. He always thought it was one of those Dutch words that aptly described the feeling of frustration.

"I'm going to continue my 'ijsberen' outside. We can talk about this later."

The fact that Robert now had a major problem on his hands—and was in the middle of the festival preparation season—meant pressure was mounting up. He needed some immediate down time and Saskia was the comfort he craved right now. It had been fifteen years since he first got together with Belinda, and eight years since they had married. Saskia offered him the refuge he needed, when he needed it, but Robert was aware that he was walking a tightrope. Sometimes he asked himself whether he was exploiting Saskia's kindness and affection for him without giving much in return, though he did think that his sexual prowess was a bonus.

Saskia was in her mid-forties and she had had some tragic moments in her life. The worst was the loss of both of her parents in the MH 17 plane crash over Ukraine, along with more than one hundred other Dutch citizens. As a result of this tragedy, she had received an inheritance which enabled her to lead a more relaxed life than others around her. Saskia would often remember the repatriation of the bodies, arriving at Eindhoven airport followed by the precision of a convoy of over seventy hearses, all black, driving over more than 100km of motorway lined with clapping onlookers. Her personal tragedy played out as tear-jerker news on all media channels and around the world.

She had been married very briefly, and had one daughter, Lynda. She was the product, if you can call it that, of a short but intense relationship when Saskia was in her early twenties, long before marrying her husband. She enjoyed motherhood and looking after Lynda, but the relationship with her partner at the time was always doomed. Lynda was now twenty-one, no longer at home, and studying at the University of Bristol in the UK.

It was one of those impulsive on/off relationships that started at the height of youth; but, when Saskia became pregnant, she dearly wanted to try to make something of it, if only for the benefit of Lynda, and maybe for any other children she might have. It didn't take long for her to realise that this was not going to happen and there was clearly no future in trying to hold the relationship together. This relationship cast a shadow over her future love life. Her new partners were never settling companions, and she had difficulty juggling the dating scene with being a single mother. She was happy with the place she was in now. Despite the lack of a father figure, her daughter had both feet on the ground, and she was proud of how things had worked out. The father was nowhere to be seen or heard from, which had been a tragedy.

More recently, Saskia had had her own personal setback. Medical this time.

She had never been one to grumble or rush to the doctor at the first sign of something. She was also not one to pay much attention to inspecting her own breasts on a regular, or even irregular, basis. She was still relatively young.

Breast tumours were known to be deceptive. They hid, like snakes under a rock. Saskia didn't find her snakes until it was almost too late, only turning over her rock after the tumours had been germinating for several years. They were small but malignant, so had to be removed, and the surgery was complemented with a round of chemotherapy. Fortunately, breast cancer treatment now had a remarkably good track record for recovery, but the scare was there, and remained a constant reminder. The snakes could come back. But she was not worrying about that now.

At home, Saskia heard the doorbell ring and knew it was Robert. She lived on the bottom two floors of a house on the Herengracht canal in the heart of Amsterdam. There was hardly a nicer place in the city to live, unless you needed a lot of parking space, which simply did not exist in Amsterdam. The house was a traditional "heren" house, the type of house that would have been home to a gentleman of the city many centuries ago. Now, the houses were occupied in whole or in part by the established rich as well as the millennial rich. The house was part of the inheritance which Saskia, an only daughter, had received after the plane crash.

Saskia liked Robert, whom she met a few years ago. His surname was Dekker, which Saskia thought was a little pedestrian compared to some of the weird and whacky names that many of the Dutch have. She did allow herself the thought that it would be nice if he had something a little more colourful. In Holland, you would only have to open the now non-existent telephone directory to discover the range of wonderful surnames; Throw-a-Coin (Muntjewerf), Born Naked (Naaktgeboren), Thunder Shop (Donderwinkel) and many more. The story, or myth, went that when the French occupied The Netherlands, Napoleon was frustrated that no one had a surname and if he wanted to collect taxes and draft new soldiers for his army, he needed some form of identification. So he instructed the Dutch to create surnames for themselves. Not taking this particularly seriously, the Dutch developed names to amuse themselves and confuse their French occupiers as much as possible. They also thought it would be a temporary measure, but the names had stuck and been passed on from generation to generation.

Robert was a powerful name in its own right and fitted her Robert well. Two strong syllables, and plenty of precedent, with names like Robert the Bruce, Robert Kennedy, Robert de Niro, Robert Redford. On the other side of the coin, Robert Mugabe might not be a shining example, but he also belonged to a powerful, if questionable, elite.

Saskia met Robert quite by accident. One day, he was driving down the Herengracht canal at the same time as Saskia was going back into her apartment loaded with bags and boxes. Her trip was only from her car further down the road, but she was being a little too ambitious. Robert, who had an impulsive streak to him, pulled over into the miraculously free parking space behind and offered his help. With some hesitation, Saskia accepted. Robert stood out in a crowd and her curiosity got the better of her.

Robert grabbed a couple of the boxes from her arms and followed her up the short flight of steps to the front door. Once inside, they went down the narrow hallway to the back of the house where there was a large kitchen and living area that opened onto a large inner patio. There were double doors opening from there back towards the front of the house, where there was another large room, primarily used as a den and an office for Saskia. There were high ceilings, which was typical of the old houses, and Robert noticed that his new acquaintance's place was exceptionally "gezellig," the all-encompassing Dutch word for cosy, and the apartment was blessed with some stunning paintings. One in particular was a very large and striking abstract painting that looked much like wheat fields, dominating the kitchen area with many of tones of yellow.

"Hi, my name's Saskia, and thanks very much for helping me," she said before Robert headed back out.

No problem at all, I enjoyed it. I'm Robert," he said as he presented a hand to her.

"I have one more bag in the car, front seat, I mustn't forget."

"Do you need help with it?"

"No, no. You've already done enough, thanks."

Robert started heading for the door but turned just before leaving.

"Can I be ever so rude and ask to use your bathroom?"

"Oh, is that why you wanted to help?" she quipped. Robert ignored it with a big smile.

"The toilet is down there on the right. Yes, that's it."

Saskia followed Robert out of the house as she went to retrieve her last package.

"It was nice meeting you. It's a small town, so maybe we'll see each other somewhere, sometime," Robert said, trying unsuccessfully to elicit a positive response.

A few months later, more or less, Robert finally "met" Saskia at a reception for people in the events business. It turned out that Saskia had her own business, designing and arranging sets for theatre and occasionally product launches, but she preferred the former. After the excitement of the first few months, and as they became closer, it was clear Robert's marriage was not a deterrent to Saskia; she was not in search of anything lasting. She did have her reservations about the secrecy, however. She didn't want to be responsible for any break between Robert and Belinda.

It didn't take long for the two of them to be physically attracted to each other. In fact, that was the easy part, much like covalent bonding between two chemicals. Their characters also matched well. Both were freewheeling types with strong independent tendencies, with a good dose of intelligence and a grounding of common sense, even if having an affair was a deviation from that.

Today, Robert had arrived at Saskia's by bike because he knew that it was highly unlikely he would find a parking space for his Volvo estate. Unlike many others in the city, Robert was not a fan of the bike, considering it merely a necessary evil. With more bikes in Amsterdam than inhabitants, if you couldn't beat them, you had to join them.

He had had to cover some five kilometres from the *Masters in Paint* office, which also meant navigating what could only be described as a gridlock jungle, despite all the dedicated bike lanes.

Robert's journey to the Herengracht canal meant he had to deal with a mix of the local car and cycle traffic and the horror of tourists. One group knew exactly what it was doing and disobeyed every road rule known to man; the other had no idea what they were doing and were a hazard to themselves and others. Robert knew what he was doing, but didn't enjoy it. He knew the city and could easily avoid the worst hotspots, but there was always a hothead who was not paying attention, on their phone or listening to music on headsets.

Saskia's house was generally their meeting place, as they both preferred not to take the risk of being seen together in bars, restaurants etc. Amsterdam was a small city, and if you were in the bombastic festival business, or the more pedestrian theatre business, you could generally assume that everyone knew you and you needed to know everyone.

Robert arrived, not exhausted but hot. The weather was already getting warm. The day's events had not left him in a good mood, but he summoned up some level of frivolity when Saskia greeted him at the door with a simple kiss and hug, supplemented by a tug at his bum.

"I do like that bum of yours. Always have," she said.

Robert followed Saskia down the narrow stone hallway to the back of the house, which opened onto the inner garden via the patio, a large wall of glass windows, and a small flight of steps. Saskia's bum was also a sight to behold, and she knew it. Today she was dressed in a tight, revealing jogging outfit with colour highlights in all the right places. Robert could not resist a quick grope as they proceeded to the back.

"And I am jealous of yours as well. How do you keep it like that? At your age."

A quick but friendly slap followed. Saskia worked hard to stay in shape and took the compliment as it was intended. She was not tall, but also not small. She had a nice figure, with only a bit of weakness developing in the stomach area. Her hair was black with highlights that enhanced her face and gentle skin, which had a very slight hint of olive. She was the product of a Dutch father and an Italian mother, and it was clear that the prevailing genes had come from the maternal side. She was in top form.

It was only mid-afternoon. And it was almost as if the two already had a muted regimen together. There was no hot pursuit of a sexual encounter, nor any plans for one. Saskia had recently arrived back from the gym.

"I have to take a shower. I know this is no way to greet you. If you'd like a drink, why don't you grab something and come with me?"

"Sure, I'll be there in a sec."

Saskia headed downstairs to the bathroom, which adjoined her bedroom in the basement. It was not a basement as most people would understand it to be. It opened onto the garden at the back, so got plenty of light. It was a sunken part of the house that ran from front to back, and for Saskia it was home to her two bedrooms, a bathroom, and some utility space for things like bikes, a washing machine, and an old wooden chest of drawers; a chest that looked odd because it was not symmetric. Her own bedroom had French windows which could open out to the garden. She had a large shower, as well as space in the bathroom to accommodate a whole family, if you wanted to. She turned on the shower, disposed of her jogging clothes and jumped in. Robert came downstairs, with a beer, bottle of wine, and glasses in his hands.

"I brought you a wine."

"Isn't it a little early for alcohol?"

"Believe me, now is a good time for alcohol. I need it."

"Something happen?"

"Yes, but I'll tell you after you've had your shower. I'll just sit here and watch."

That statement in itself was enough to excite Saskia. She decided to play up to the situation, with a lot of soap and much overstated caressing and limb movement. Robert knew what was coming, but that was part of the game. Just the stimulus and excitement that he was looking for, remote foreplay. He put down his glass. As much as he would have liked to walk into the shower fully clothed, he was realistic enough to know that would have raised another dilemma. Instead, he undressed and joined Saskia in the shower and immediately took over the task of gently caressing her body. Saskia enjoyed the attention to all parts of her body. Water and soap was just as sexy as massage oil and without going any further than the shower, they entwined under a stream of water that drowned out their respective climaxes. It was what Robert needed, but Saskia felt he was rougher than he normally was. Robert felt better, blissfully unaware of any change in himself.

An hour later, they were both on the patio in the garden, this time with a couple of wines. As it was pleasant weather, Saskia had put on one of her favourite floral dresses that ended just above the knees, revealing shapely legs and, especially, that sweet spot visible along the outside flank when a woman sits cross-legged. Robert knew he needed to get back home soon. The phone was in his pocket on silent mode, but he could feel the buzz of WhatsApps that came in.

"So, tell me, what's stirring in you? I can feel it?" Saskia asked.

"Yes, I'm sorry if it's so obvious. I've had a shitty day, really shitty."

"Tell me, if you want. I can't help you if you don't tell me."

"I know, but I'm not sure you can help me anyway, apart from being here."

"Well?"

"It's the painting business. We've received a threatening letter and a claim from a lawyer representing a living painter."

"But you don't copy living painters' paintings. You told me that."

"Yes, but we changed our policy, provided it was for personal use only and not hung in public. Other sites offer something similar."

"Robert, you're an intelligent man. That wasn't a wise thing to do, was it?"

"That's what I thought too," Robert said, "but Mark convinced me, so now I don't know what we're going to do. The worst thing about it is that if it comes to a serious claim, then I am personally liable. I don't have *Masters in Paint* protected as a limited company. And Belinda will kill me if that happens. Or I'll kill myself."

"I'm going to stay calm, but I think we can agree that was very naive of you. With any luck, they're just making an example of you to warn off others and it will blow over. But you will need to be very apologetic. Time to grovel."

"I know. I haven't really discussed it with Mark yet. I was too pissed off to be around him."

"So, you came here?"

"Yes, I'm sorry. That was unfair of me," said Robert.

"No. In a way, I'm flattered, but I can't always be your bolt hole when things are bad; or even good. Which brings me to the subject."

"Which is?"

"You know, I've been thinking, we've been going around in"— and at this she hesitated—"very enjoyable circles for a couple of years now. You know I love you coming here, and I love being with you, but it's no longer as rewarding as it was."

"Eh?"

"No, don't get me wrong. That didn't come out right. I mean I still love seeing you, I still love the sex we have; but our relationship is potentially heading up a cul de sac, don't you think?"

"I haven't really thought about it."

16

"Exactly my point. Robert, sometimes you're in your own world and you lose sight of the people who are important to you. Me, for example. I don't know that I can go on like this forever without some prospect of a future. And it's not going to be a future which has you just turning up when it's convenient for you."

"Wow, two low blows in one day."

"Yes, I'm sorry, our chat just led into it. I hadn't planned it for right now. But I had been meaning to talk to you one of these days. Maybe it's for the best. This way you have one really bad day instead of two."

"But I thought you liked your freedom and independence?"

"I do, that's me to a tee. But with you I feel I'm moving on from my past, even if you're not the most attentive of men. I do think you have it in you, and that's the you I would like to get to know. And I fear I'm the one who gave you the wrong idea. Yes, I once told you that the one marriage I had—and any subsequent relationships— didn't work out because I liked my independence. Maybe that gave you the wrong impression?

Robert seized on what little defence he had and answered, "Yes, I think maybe you did. I do remember he was a First Officer on a cruise ship, he had a glamourous life on board, and you also got what you wanted; time to yourself and time with him."

"Yes, two months on, two months off. What I had not counted on was that the two months off for him, was two months on for me, literally and figuratively. It became suffocating. But it's not the same. And I am older now. More mellowed, don't you think? And I'm not looking for a repeat."

"Absolutely, but I think you are sending me mixed messages."

"No, I'm just reinforcing the message you don't seem to be picking up on."

"That's clear," Robert said. "I used to think you didn't even know what you were going to do tomorrow, let alone next week or next month. I guess that's changing?"

"Now you got it." And then a pause. "No, I didn't mean it like that. Robert, all I am asking is that you think about where you want to go with our relationship. There's no rush. I don't want to burst the bubble we're in, I just want it to be bigger than this house."

"Alright. Please, give me time. As you can see, I'm juggling just a few too many things at the moment. And maybe I should compare my marriage to a cruise ship. Once it gains momentum it takes forever to bring it to a stop."

Saskia ignored this.

"You've forgotten your wine. Take a few slugs. You'll feel better."

There was a bit of a pregnant pause. Then the two of them moved onto less touchy issues. They talked about Robert's other work with festivals, Saskia's own work, and rehearsed standard grumbles about the Amsterdam council, traffic, tourists, and other mundane matters.

At about 6 o'clock Robert left to head back home so he would be there in time for dinner and help with some homework for the kids. It was the same hectic story on the bike ride back, this time even more so because of the rush hour. Robert had the opportunity to get rid of some of his frustration by yelling at other cyclists and pedestrians who got in his way.

Fortunately, his day didn't get any worse, but he did call Mark and suggested that they let the copyright liability matter sit until after the weekend. It was going to be dragged out anyway.

CHAPTER TWO

It was a new day, a Saturday.

Robert had just returned home from a visit on his own to his parents in a town called Alkmaar, about a half hour to the north of Amsterdam. The journey gave him time to contemplate how he was juggling too many things at the same time, and how they were getting in his way.

"I'm back."

No response.

And then louder, "Hello, anyone at home?"

"Up here, we're all upstairs. In Daniel's room."

Robert climbed the stairs and proceeded to Daniel's bedroom. As with any adolescent, it was a mess, though there appeared to be an attempt to bring some order to the chaos. Daniel had a closet for clothes, but the rest of the ailing and failing IKEA furniture conveyed a sense of poverty. Everyone knew and loved IKEA, but their furniture didn't wear well. From experience, Robert and Belinda knew that IKEA was the place you went for the ultimate test of your relationship. The flat-pack packaging was a genial invention that led to the love–hate relationship with the Allen key, and a lot of domestic arguments.

"We've decided that it really is time for action, so this is just the start," said Belinda. "Since you left, we have been hard at work, but I have to admit most of the time has been on *Marktplaats*." *Marktplaats* was the eBay of Holland, where you could find almost anything anyone was trying to get rid of.

"I'm not sure I like the sound of that," said Robert. "Jesus, what have you guys been up to? I can't even see the bed… I guess it means we are considering secondhand furniture of some kind or other. I'm not disagreeing, just wondering what we can find that Daniel will like, and fits."

"We're ahead of you. One nice thing about kids their age is that they have an inbuilt online affinity and, if they know they are going to get something, have inexhaustible patience to find what they want. Look at your son. All day on the computer!"

"Yes, but did he find anything?"

"Of course I did. The intelligence agencies are no match for me," Daniel responded. "Dad, there's this great chest of drawers painted in a pastel blue, so a little beachy. It looks old, but it's the right size and would fit great in that corner. Here, take a look. And only twenty-five euros."

Daniel picked up his featherweight laptop with stickers all over the front and showed his father the *Marktplaats* site with a picture and details of the chest.

"Looks great," said Robert. "But it's already reserved."

"Yep, that's us. We already called and came to a deal."

"OK. I guess you don't need me then."

"Yes, we do. You and Mum are going to pick it up tomorrow morning. I've got football."

Belinda then added, "And you and I are also picking up some other things I think we could use. The owner of the chest is getting rid of an almost new Kenwood food mixer. And they have a nice mirror we could use downstairs, or even here in Daniel's room. All good stuff."

Robert laughed. "If it's not one thing, it's another, eh?"

"Don't laugh at your wife's choices. After all, you're one of them," Belinda cracked back with a smile.

"OK, point taken. Sounds like a plan. I hope the chest is not too heavy, and it fits in the car."

"Don't worry, already figured that one out."

They all proceeded downstairs for dinner in their large open plan kitchen, where there was more than enough space to land an aircraft on the cooking island in the middle. For Robert and Belinda, their kitchen was the nucleus of their life at home.

As always, preceding a meal, Robert had to give himself an injection of insulin. Robert didn't hide his injections, not in front of the family. The children didn't really understand it, but Daniel was becoming more curious and asked.

"Dad, if you have diabetes, am I also going to get it? I still don't really understand it."

"You and the rest of the world," replied Robert, sarcastically. "No, but seriously, with LADA diabetes—Latent Autoimmune Diabetes in Adults—there is an assumed genetic relationship, and it may run in some families. But it's not likely," he said, reassuringly. "I can't promise that it won't happen. What I can do is comfort you by saying that the doctors have come a long way in the last few decades and you can easily live with the disease. There is no cure."

"So, you could die if you didn't take insulin?" said Daniel.

"I guess the short answer to that is yes, I would. If I didn't have access to insulin, my internal organs, like my kidneys, would eventually fail. But we don't need to discuss that. Your Dad has easy access to insulin and I fully expect to live a full, normal life. Shall we eat?"

Daniel wasn't finished yet, but he did start eating. "Yes, Dad, but can you please explain what diabetes is. In a way I, and Maxine, can understand."

"I'll try. You make the assumption I know, but I'll try," Robert replied. "Let's see." He took a while to think and eventually started:

"First, you need to know that sugar, or glucose as it is called, is very important for our bodies."

"I like sugar," Maxine interrupted.

"No, well, it's not exactly like that, but that's too much detail. You get glucose from all types of food. For example, pasta, like we're eating now. The glucose from that is converted into energy, and fat, in our bodies."

"I don't like fat," interrupted Maxine again with a smile. Robert continued:

"OK. Now imagine you're in a hotel. For this purpose, a large hotel with long corridors where there are rooms on either side. Got it? Can you picture it?" Robert asked rhetorically and proceeded when he got some nods. "The corridor represents your blood veins. After you eat, the corridor fills up with people, as if they all just came out of the lift. These are the glucose molecules."

"What are molecules, Dad?" asked Daniel.

"Don't worry about that right now," answered Robert. He continued:

"The glucose people are travelling down the corridor. On either side of the corridor, you have doors that lead into the rooms. Now these rooms are your cells, where the energy is created, and the people, the glucose, need to get through those doors. But you don't have a key, right?" Robert looked at his audience to see if there was any sign of comprehension. They were still nodding, even concentrating.

"If everything is normal with your body, an organ called the pancreas sends out something called insulin." Robert held up his insulin pen as an illustration and proceeded. "The insulins are like keys. They open the doors so that the glucose, the sugar, can get into your cells. If you have no keys, then the glucose stays in your blood and will just build up and build up. That is very dangerous. So, imagine that the insulin is a key, and it opens the doors and lets the glucose get to where it needs to go. The pancreas is like the hotel reception, and they normally give you the keys, right? So you need reception to be open all the time; and working."

There was still silence, but they appeared to be listening.

"So, now to me. Like everyone else, I have hundreds of thousands of corridors in my body and even more rooms. The problem is I have lost most of the keys and I need help from outside. So, this little pen here is my substitute for the keys and it keeps me going. Every time I eat, like now—which is why I inject myself before a meal—I need to have more keys to compensate for all the glucose that comes from the food. Does that make sense? Does that help? I'm not sure if I can find another way of explaining it."

Belinda was impressed.

"Now I understand it even better. That was revealing. How did you come up with the analogy of a hotel?"

"I don't recall. I remember someone once talking about doors, so I made it a hotel. Diabetes is a very complex disease, so I hope this helps—right guys?" Robert saw more nods and continued, "staying with the analogy, I guess you could say that Type 1 diabetes is a disease where the hotel reception is closed and permanently gone home. Type 2 diabetes is where reception is open but not very efficient at handing out the keys, and the doors are hard to open. The LADA diabetes is bit of a combination of both, with reception taking more and more time off as time goes by. And the hotel is old!"

Belinda decided to make a point here as she saw an opening. "See, your father is not all hot air!" she said with a smile. "Please take note, life doesn't always revolve around Google, a laptop, or smartphone.

Granted, Google is good, very good, but your Dad has just shown you how story telling can change how you understand something very complex. You understood, right?"

"Yes, yes," both kids acknowledged. But Daniel had further questions.

"But you haven't told us what happens if you don't manage your diabetes."

"That's true. This story was more about the science behind it. Indeed, the consequences of diabetes can be dramatic. Now, it gets complicated again, so I'll resort to another analogy. This one comes from my doctor, who told it to me a while ago. You need to know that there is something in diabetes called a 'Hyper' and a 'Hypo'. These are manifestations of the poor management of your diabetes."

"What are manifestations?" interrupted Maxine.

"Good question. That was maybe too obscure. Manifestations are the consequences or symptoms that show if you are not managing the disease properly. A 'Hyper' is if the sugar, or glucose, in your blood is too high. A 'Hypo' is if the glucose gets too low. If you are too low— a 'Hypo'— then you need to eat sugar or something that will convert to sugar. If you are too high, a 'Hyper', then you need to take a shot of insulin. Those are the ground rules."

"But I'm still not following," said Daniel.

"I'm getting there," answered Robert.

"Now, imagine you're in your car driving up a narrow mountain road. There is a steep rock face on one side, and a ravine on the other. You are scared, so to be on the safe side you drive very close to the cliff and you keep scraping the car on the rocks. Imagine that is a 'Hyper.' In other words, the car is your body, and every time you damage the car you're accumulating more damage to yourself, but you don't really notice it, because you're protected by the car's bodywork. Over time, it could threaten your life as you get more and more damage. If you have a 'Hypo', then that is more sudden. You may not know it is coming and you run the risk of driving over the edge and into the ravine. With a 'Hypo', if your glucose goes too low, you start getting symptoms of dizziness and weakness and could fall into a coma, hence the ravine. Get it?"

The kids nodded. "I prefer being safe in the hotel," offered Maxine.

Belinda then intervened, hoping to get a message across. "Thank you, Dad." As she looked at Robert with some affection. Then to the kids, she said, "Don't be afraid to ask us, or your teachers, like Daniel did. Google is not God. It's just a service algorithm. Now, off you go—if you want."

They both got up, grabbed their smartphones, and ran off into other parts of the house, one of them saying as they went.

"Let's watch old fashioned television."

Robert turned to Belinda and said, "You know. Most of our television programmes have subtitles. If they turned the sound off, then we could say they were reading. Right?" Belinda smiled. It didn't require an answer.

CHAPTER THREE

As normal, Sunday followed Saturday, and the family went about their business. Daniel to football, Maxine to a music lesson. Robert and Belinda were due to pick up the chest before midday from an address in the city. First, they needed to sort out their people mover, a Volvo estate, so that there was room in the back. Down with the seats and a couple of protective blankets, just in case.

Robert wound himself into the driver's seat, Belinda next to him. As always, he had to do this gently because he was very tall. Even a large Volvo estate was not ideal for Robert, and even less so as a form of transport in the smaller streets or canals of Amsterdam. It did serve well as a donkey for transporting items.

Robert drove through the old harbour part of town towards the main railway station, following instructions from Belinda. Much like in Rome, driving in Amsterdam is an art form, because you generally have to deal with forces beyond your control. The bicycle was one. More recently, the new menace was the horror of the courier van stopping at every second door to make a delivery from one or other online webshop. They had absolutely no sympathy for anyone waiting behind them as they went in hunt of someone who was actually home. Today was a Sunday, so it was not so bad, but even Sunday was no longer as hallowed it used to be, and deliveries were the order of the day.

Robert was eventually told to turn left onto a canal called Singel. They were now in the heart of old Amsterdam, the part where all the canals and roads form a crescent as they circle around the city. Someone once compared Amsterdam to the rings of a tree. The city got older as you got closer to the centre.

Belinda instructed Robert to go down one of the connecting streets between the canals until they reached the Herengracht canal. Robert's heart skipped a beat as his mind turned to where Saskia lived, but that was still a way away. Belinda did indeed ask Robert to turn onto the Herengracht, just on the side he would have preferred not to be. They were still some way from Saskia's house, but their final destination could have been any one of these houses. "So don't fret," he thought. But he did, because they started getting closer and Belinda was staring up at the house numbers. Robert didn't even dare ask which number.

"Park somewhere here. It's that house," she said, pointing at number 87.

Robert's heart sank. It was the house right next door to Saskia, uncomfortably close. What if she opened the door or came back right when they were busy loading the car? Robert was sweating, and not just because of the heat.

"Are you OK?" asked Belinda.

"I've had better days. It's really hot."

They both got out of the car and proceeded up the small flight of stairs to the door on the right. Belinda pressed the doorbell and waited. After a short while, a woman, about sixty, appeared at the door and greeted them. She was expecting them, so immediately ushered them into the house. It was almost a mirror image of the one next door, but a bit bigger and with a larger expanse of windows. Robert could hardly say anything. He was just relieved that he was now out of sight, if only for a short while. There was still some noise to be made moving in and out of the house with the furniture.

The lady of the house, whose name was José, had already collected the goods she was selling in the back room. On seeing them, Robert concluded that it would be no problem getting everything into the car. They settled their debt in cash, and Belinda and Robert started with the chest, painted in a washed-look pastel blue. They carried it outside, down the stairs to the car. Robert hid his head low, just in case, and did not look at anything other than the chest. It was a solid looking chest, but Robert noticed something strange. It was asymmetrical. Or rather, it was lopsided by design. On the left the chest had a nicely rounded turned twirl. On the right, there was nothing. Just a direct line from top to bottom. "Odd," he thought, "but it is what it is."

After the chest was safely loaded, Robert rushed back into the house to pick up the mirror, also fairly antique, and Belinda took the food mixer, which was bright red.

They thanked José and headed out, almost as quickly as they had entered. Robert was beginning to breathe a sigh of relief as he rounded the car to arrive at the front door. Still nothing from number 85. They both got into the car and sped off.

"Robert, this is not a racetrack, you know," Belinda said, with the emphasis on the two syllables of his name.

"I'm sorry, you're right," he said, as he slowed down to a more normal canal driving speed. He had relaxed and was getting back to his normal self. That had been uncomfortable.

The pair drove back home and unloaded the car. They took the chest to Daniel's room, the food mixer to the kitchen and the mirror to "storage," a corner where things went to be decided upon later.

Not long after they had settled down to a coffee in the kitchen, the familiar sound of Belinda's ring tone, the soundtrack to *The Good, the Bad and the Ugly*, pierced the air. It was José.

"Hi, this is José from the Herengracht. You were just here. I'm afraid I forgot to give you all of the accessories for the food mixer. I have them here now if you would like to pick them up."

"Oh, thank you. Yes, they are important. We can come over in the afternoon if that's OK with you?" said Belinda, looking at Robert but not consulting him.

She put the phone down and mentioned to Robert that they had another errand.

"You don't need me for this," said Robert.

"Oh, come on. You're not doing anything, and I'd like you to keep me company. And you know I don't enjoy driving that monster in the city."

"You underestimate yourself."

"Robert." Again with the two stressed syllables. "I don't ask much of you, so please let's just get this over with. I'm not exactly asking a lot and you're not doing anything."

Robert felt the walls converging on him, but he agreed to take Belinda. He would simply stay in the car while she picked up the accessories. Robert knew that Belinda still didn't really like driving in the city.

Back at the Herengracht canal, Robert was sweating again. He did not need this stress. Despite resisting, Robert didn't stand a chance when Belinda told him not to be impolite and to come with her. They got out of the car and rang the doorbell. José opened the door, and they again went to the back of the house. There was a box on the kitchen counter with the accessories. It was bigger than Robert expected. They didn't stay and left the same way they came in.

At the front door, as they were leaving, Saskia was also exiting her house, together with a man. Robert and Saskia exchanged knowing, piercing glances, but no smiling. Saskia knew full well that the woman with Robert was likely to be his wife. Robert, however, had no idea who this man was. And what was he doing leaving Saskia's house on a Sunday morning? Robert's head started spinning with all sorts of speculation.

There was a very pregnant silence on the plateau of the two front doors as the two couples exchanged nods of the head. Nothing more, but Robert could feel Saskia's eyes following him.

Robert and Belinda headed to the car in silence. Once in the car, Belinda asked why Robert could not have been a little more polite, but then passed over it as not important. Robert was wondering who the man might be. Not a brother, because Saskia was an only daughter. He also knew he had no right to be judgmental. Nevertheless, he had an uncomfortable feeling in the pit of his stomach, and even this gave him some cause for concern. He had no right to have any thoughts of exclusivity, especially after their most recent conversation.

They went home.

For a while, Robert engrossed himself in the murky business they had got themselves into at *Masters in Paint*. His relationship with his partner, Mark, was being tested, but they remained civil, and consulted with lawyers in an attempt to find a way through the mess. Further research revealed that most of their competitors seemed to be doing the same thing. Nevertheless, they were still on shaky ground and the struggle would likely drag on for a long time. In the meantime, Robert didn't say a word about it at home to Belinda, as he was still hoping it would all blow over.

Robert turned his attention to his festival projects. He had to, because the season was fast approaching, and he had to cope with all the strange requests he started getting from artists.

Robert was not the owner of the festival company, so he would not be the one staring down at the bottom of the bank account if it all went pear shaped. Still, it was his life, and he couldn't imagine doing anything else. *Masters in Paint* was just a profitable hobby. Festivals allowed him to feed off the creativity and excitement of organising something for thousands of party-going visitors—a younger generation that was looking for a life experience and less interested in owning assets.

Robert couldn't concentrate. Not only did he have serious problems with one of his business interests, he was not yet resolved on what he was going to do about Saskia and, by extension, Belinda and his family. He found his attention gravitating towards his relationship issues, which were taking precedence over everything else. One way or another he had to come to some resolution.

He decided on a walk, which turned out to be a long one around the harbour island they lived on. Robert felt he was being boxed into a corner by Saskia when all he really wanted was the status quo. He also didn't like the thought of abandoning his family. He decided would go and see Saskia. He was going to use his problems with work to try and push this into the long grass, if he could. It wasn't neat, he knew that.

When he got home, Robert sent Saskia a WhatsApp:

Everything OK? You around today?

If you were under the age of 30, you might reply in a half hour; if you were under the age of 20, maybe 10 minutes; if you were under the age of 17, then that was more likely to be measured in seconds.

For Saskia, who was 46, there was silence for a long time. After a few hours, there was the familiar ping of a message on Robert's phone. It was Saskia. Like Robert, she did not say anything about the chance meeting on Sunday. Why should she? She answered Robert though:

All fine here. Sure, I'm around and not doing much. You want to talk?

Robert thought that was an ominous answer. It told him it was going to be more than a social visit. Still, it was an invitation, even though Robert suddenly felt anxious about it.

It was a weekday, so not a great deal was going on. It was grey and grim, with low clouds and the ever-present drizzle associated with such weather. Much like any other day, thought Robert.

The grim weather was an excuse for Robert to choose the car again. He decided to first change into something a little better than jeans and a T-shirt, and settled on a dark blue jacket, short-sleeved blue polo shirt, khaki trousers, and brown shoes. He looked in the mirror to make sure he was at least presentable, not that he was going any further than someone else's house. At the last moment, he picked up the curious old coin he had acquired and put it in his pocket.

31

He wound himself back into his Volvo and headed once more in the direction of the main ring of canals. Living on an island meant he had little choice in how he drove, but now there was more apprehension in his driving. There was no real reason for him to be concerned. Saskia probably had a good explanation about who the stranger was, but he also knew he had no right to even ask. Maybe the best strategy was to stay silent and not even bring the subject up.

His journey was broken by the ping of a WhatsApp on his phone. At the next traffic lights, he took a quick peek to see if it was important. He wished he had not done this and pulled over onto the curb. The text was from Mark and said:

More from the artist's lawyers. They've indicated what we should expect in the way of a claim. You don't want to know.

After a few choice swearwords, Robert decided not to answer Mark. That would come later.

He headed down the road that ran alongside the harbour and went under the railway station tunnel, where he then took a left turn under the railway lines and into the ring of canals. There was not much activity on the roads, or even on the canals, because of the miserable day.

He turned onto a canal called the Brouwersgracht, or Brewers' canal, and then at the end he turned the car left and over a bridge. It was one of those classic hump bridges, a bit shallower than many others, over about seven metres of canal. It had iron railings on the side, and the name in the middle on an iron plaque "*West Indische Brug.*" There was a sudden jolt as the car reached the apex and then continued onwards. Robert momentarily blacked out but was back almost immediately, staring at the road ahead of him, which was suddenly under clear skies and sun. The warmth of the day had attracted more people outside.

He stopped. "What the fuck is this?" he asked himself as he took in what was around him. He just couldn't understand how the weather could turn like that. It couldn't. His surprise grew enormously when he turned his attention to the front of his car. It was no longer dark blue, but a deep Bordeaux red. Despite the change, it was still the distinctive shape of his Volvo. "That can't be," he thought. "What's going on?" Then he realised the inside also looked different, and he started fiddling around with the controls, the central console, the glove box, and looked in the back. "Holy shit! This is my old car."

PART II:

"Rembrandt seems to be following us around"

CHAPTER FOUR

Robert pulled over where he could and got out of the car. He walked around, taking in what he already knew, kicked the tyres a few times for no particular reason, and swore even more. The skyline, roads, and everything else all looked the same. But why in the hell was he back in his old car? That didn't make sense. His trousers were khaki; the shirt was blue. That all fitted. He even had his mobile phone, though it looked like it was in better shape than he remembered. He sat for a while on the side of the canal as he took it all in—except he couldn't.

There was no point in staying where he was, so he got into his old car and headed over to where Saskia lived. The car purred, the day was bright, but why was everything so different? He should have taken the bike, he thought. As he turned onto Saskia's part of the Herengracht, he started looking for a parking space. He could see Saskia ahead of him trying vainly to get as many of her bags and boxes from her car to her front door.

It was automatic. Robert pulled up behind her, just as he had a few years ago.

He got out and yelled her name: "Saskia!"

The response was a stare, as if he was out of his mind. "Do we know each other?" Saskia asked. "How do you know my name, that's creepy?"

Robert was lost for words. He had to think quickly. It was one thing to find yourself in your old car, but now he really was beginning to worry about his sanity, or the sanity of the situation.

"Um, I'm sorry, I'm just not having one of my best days and frankly I'm still a little lost. I was pretty sure we knew each other, but you just pricked that balloon. Are you sure we've never met?"

"Doubly sure. Believe me, I remember people, and I'm pretty sure I would remember you. But you called me by my name. How's that possible?"

"If we've never met, I don't have a good explanation. Some form of premonition? But while I'm here, and you seem to be struggling, perhaps I can give you a hand with those bags. A handful has its limits."

Saskia hesitated, then accepted, and Robert followed her to her house, up the small flight of steps. On the pavement outside, the neighbours appeared to be preparing a chest for painting. The chest looked very familiar, but Robert did not make any immediate connection. It was a nice day, so it looked just the place to do the work—keep the dust from the sanding out of the house. Robert could see from the pot of paint that it would become blue and started to wonder whether or not the chest they had bought was the same blue.

They entered the house and proceeded down the hallway to the back, just as he had done before. Once in the kitchen area, Robert looked around, taking in the space and décor, which was a little lacking in colour, very different from what he was used to.

"What a lovely place you have, plenty of room, and all these big walls. Great space for some standout art," he offered as he noticed that the walls were devoid of the art he was familiar with.

Robert saw little point in hanging around. He was already feeling uncomfortable. But there was something exciting about it, as if he were meeting a new woman even though he knew her. It was uncanny. Without thinking, he once again asked if he could use the bathroom.

"Sure, it's down there' second door on the ri…" —The remainder of Saskia's sentence was left hanging as Robert already had the door half open and went in— "…ght." She completed the sentence as he closed the door behind him.

Once Robert was finished, he headed towards the front door, turning towards Saskia. "What date is it today?"

"Strange question. Er, 7th April, I think."

Robert then opened the front door, which had already been left ajar, and stepped out. Saskia thanked him for his help, but he responded mischievously, "Don't forget, you still have one more box in your car... front seat."

Again, Saskia was taken aback. First the bathroom, now a box in the car. None of this made sense, but what questions could she ask? Robert was already halfway down the street and was smiling wryly. He enjoyed the moment of leaving Saskia in some doubt, but he realised now that there was something seriously wrong. Or different. He had a date to work on, but not a year. He got into his car and pulled out his mobile phone. Sure enough, 7th April, but the home screen never tells you what year it is. So he pulled up the calendar and on the top he read to himself 2...0...1...6. Three years earlier. "What in Christ's name happened to 2019?" He rested his head on the steering wheel, but not before banging it a couple of times.

Robert pulled gently out of the parking space and started driving in no particular direction, taking in the surroundings. If it really was 2016, then surely there would be signs? Everything looked more or less the same. The roads, the buildings, the bikes, the trams. The billboards didn't help either. Everywhere in the city you could see posters announcing dates for one or another art show, concert, or festival—but no year.

Robert pulled the car onto a curb and went into a local magazine shop to buy a paper. The best way to get ultimate confirmation he thought. He picked up a copy of *De Telegraaf* but was only interested in the date. 7th April, 2016. Now he had this sorted out, and he knew he was healthy and not mad, he began to think about why he was back here. How had it happened? And why, if he had to be a time traveller, had he only gone back three years. It was like they said, if you are going to rob a bank, rob a big bank. Why couldn't he go back to sometime really interesting? Not that he really wanted to, but the thought crossed his mind.

Robert started heading back home in his new "old" car. He knew he and Belinda still had the same maisonette in 2016. He drove straight there. He parked more or less where he usually did and used the same key to open the front door. It seemed strange to be thinking that way, but the same key was his reassurance that nothing much had changed, apart from time. Belinda was there, as were Maxine and Daniel. They were younger than when he last saw them. His immediate thought was the horror of having to relive three years of pre-puberty. They greeted him as if it were just another day.

It was evening and Belinda was busy with a dinner for everyone. As if nothing was any different, Belinda asked, "How was your day? Anything exciting?"

How do you answer that when you feel like you have just been kicked up the backside? And bundled back three years. There was no way he could convincingly explain what had happened, so he said.

"It's funny you should ask."

"I often ask."

"I know you do. I have had one of those uneventful, yet very eventful days. I know that sounds contradictory. It is. It was uneventful because I really don't think I accomplished anything, but I'm also willing to call it eventful because I had a eureka moment.

"What could that possibly mean?"

"You know, when you have one of those enlightening moments that is going to help you get a better perspective on your path forward."

"You're still talking in riddles."

"I know, I know. It's better to call it an epiphany. You've seen *Back to the Future*, the film, right?"

"Of course. Who hasn't? But how could that possibly be relevant?"

"Do you believe in time travel?" Robert asked.

"No. That's just stupid."

"Well, let's just suppose it could happen, it would be an eye-opener, right? So, if I told you I felt, today, as if my body was transposed to another time period, would you believe me?"

"Is that your revelation? You've been to the future and come back in time for dinner? Are you sure you're alright?"

"I'm fine, but yes, something happened."

"As much as I love you, you don't need to fantasise and assume the role of Marty Mcfly. Fine, if it helps you find a theme for your next festival, but don't go weird on me and bring it home. Though I quite like the idea of a festival based on time travel. You could invite David Bowie, or his *Ziggy Stardust* persona."

"Nice idea, but he just died. Remember?"

Belinda had no chance to reply. At that moment, her mobile rang, and she switched her attention to answering it and began a long chat with one of her many friends, as if to say that she had had enough of Robert's bizarre thinking. The discussion about time travel was going nowhere, and Robert just let the matter slip. If he found another opportunity, he might address it again, but Belinda was getting a bit snappy with him.

When Belinda was finished on the phone, he asked. "On a totally unrelated matter. How long have we had the car?"

"I don't know. Cars are not something I pay a great deal of attention to, least of all how long we've owned one. Let's see, say five years, more or less. Why?"

"Oh, I was just wondering. Volvos are like family tanks, but maybe it's time to upgrade to an SUV," said Robert, allowing his thoughts to run wild and trying to elicit a response.

"We don't need another car. Well, maybe we do, but not yet, and certainly not an even bigger one. Here, have a drink." Belinda gave him a wine in the hope that he would settle.

Robert's thoughts drifted, and as best he could he went back to his life of three years earlier. Frankly, not much was different. It was not as if his life had been in disarray. He still had his family and job. And he appeared to be back on better terms with his wife.

Had his transportation to another time period been about sending him a message? And what about Saskia, whom he had just met again for the "first" time? He knew the 2019 Saskia well, he knew the 2016 Saskia well, but now there was a second 2016. Would things be different, a second time around?

Robert had to get used to the idea that he was about to revisit a part of his life. Would everything change? And indeed, what did he remember? History could not be altered. He knew that, but surely there would be the extra benefit of hindsight as he manoeuvered his way through the processes of work, school, family life, friends—and Saskia. Three years don't change much, but from what he knew now, it would be highly likely he would be reliving previous experiences, one of which would be getting to know Saskia, again. The thought did occur to him that maybe he shouldn't even do it.

But history doesn't work that way, Robert thought; it doesn't have a pause button. Maybe the history wouldn't change, but he was the one in control of his emotions. That thought excited him. In the big picture, nothing would be different, but he would know, she wouldn't.

One day he might get back to a present that had not changed. He put that aside for the moment.

Robert resumed his life as best he could. He started reorganising festivals he had already organised. Not surprisingly, the second time round seemed much easier. He already knew who he was going to invite; he knew how much they would accept for performing; and he knew the quirky requests they all seem to come up with. He used the time travel "licence" given to him to make small tweaks where necessary.

At home, he also started helping his kids with their homework. This time he knew exactly where their weak points were. Maxine for example, had just started biology. The subject at hand that day was understanding cells and cell division. This was something which Robert was comfortable helping with. Before he moved into the festival business, he had started studying pharmacy, but he never finished. The festival business was far more exciting.

Despite how busy it was, Robert registered for one of the occasional seminars about events. In reality, this would be nothing more than a one-day seminar where people in the business exchanged views and experiences on matters like security, design, insurance, royalties, employees, and so forth. The day normally concluded with a buffet reception at an "interesting" location in Amsterdam. This year, the choice had fallen on the Marriott Hotel for the seminar and the famous Rijksmuseum for the evening reception, almost next door.

Robert knew that this was where he first spent time with Saskia, and he was hoping for the suspense of three years earlier. He felt a sense of excitement as he dressed in the morning, his mind wandering back and forth, thinking about what the encounter had been like. He didn't want an exact repeat. In his mind he was now three years more mature, and he wanted to avoid some of the pitfalls of his first attempt in 2016. Middle age had mellowed him. Now he had the opportunity to steer the relationship differently, more delicately.

The Wednesday of the seminar came, and Robert left the house early. The talks were due to start at 8.30 am. Definitely no car today. Parking all day in the centre of Amsterdam would be an extraordinary expense, and he would most likely be drinking in the evening. He exchanged one lethal weapon for the other, his bike.

Robert had a bit of distance to cover, and it took him about twenty-five minutes to be at the hotel. The hotel was on the edge of the centre, very close to the Rijksmuseum. He entered and followed the signs to the seminar on the first floor. There were about 100 people attending and Robert picked up his name badge, which was waiting for him at a reception desk managed by a very attractive lady. He briefly thought he would have remembered someone so attractive, but he let the thought slide.

There was coffee and croissants for those who had missed out on their breakfast at home, but he went immediately into the room where all the presentations were to take place. It was being held in a plenary format, so there were no breakouts that he would have to choose between. It was just a straightforward day of presentations, not all of which interested him.

Just like three years earlier, there was no sign of Saskia. Not yet. There was a simple explanation, which he knew; arriving on time was not one of her strong points.

The first session covered contracts, royalties, and payments to artists, including the peculiarity of "riders," when artists make demands well beyond simple payment for work. It always made for an amusing sideline to a serious topic. Robert's festivals were not generally at the top end of the market, where a performer's star rating got the better of them. The case of the rock star Van Halen was classic. He reportedly insisted that the organisers provide M&M's, but that they remove all the brown ones. Adele demanded Marlboro Lights, presumably to help her already powerful voice, and only the very best quality wines. Madonna wanted her dressing room to be a mirror image of her home. A lot of alcohol in the rooms seemed to be the

42

common denominator. One thing Robert had experienced was that many of his artists tended to eat the same thing. There was little variation in their diet, at least during a festival.

There was a break at 10.30am and still no sign of Saskia. He mingled with other delegates and chatted with one of his own colleagues. He was responsible for the ancillary services, such as catering, security, and the part that no one liked, the mass sanitary facilities. They returned to the room for the session that would take them until lunch. As Robert headed towards where he had been sitting with his colleague, he saw Saskia, already seated two rows behind him. She had no idea he was there—why would she? He made some obvious movements by turning in her direction. She had no choice but to look briefly into his face. Immediately, she noticed Robert's familiar features. It was not recognition exactly, but she acknowledged with a nod that they must know each other from somewhere. They settled into a presentation and discussion about the architecture and design of décor for stage events. Lunch followed. Robert knew they would connect.

Lunch was typically Dutch. The Dutch were not like the French or Italians, who gravitated towards a warm meal and took their time. A standard lunch break in any Dutch company or organisation was no more than a half hour, a case of eating quickly and eating simply. A sandwich or roll of some sort met the needs of most people. Maybe some fruit. Lunch that day was a stand-up affair with so-called "broodjes" or rolls, milk, juices, and some small sweet nibbles. The drinking would be done later.

After the session, Robert headed towards the lunch area, knowing he would bump into Saskia at some point. He was keeping a close eye on her, so that the bumping into her was more than just coincidental. Eventually, he succeeded. As their glances connected, there was a measure of recognition from Saskia and once they were closer she said:

"Oh, you look so familiar. Do I know you from somewhere?"

Robert wasn't quite expecting that. He thought he had made more of an impression when they last met, albeit briefly. Somewhat mischievously, he tried a dangerous tactic:

"Do you watch porn?"

She did not flinch. "Should I know you from something? Do you have a speciality I should know about?

It was Robert's turn to be surprised, but he played along. "No, not really, but maybe this helps: The tongue is one of the strongest muscles in the human body, and it never tires." And, after a pause and a smile, he said, "No seriously, we met briefly a while back when I helped you with some boxes from your car."

"Of course. How could I forget? You were the one with a premonition. That I still had another box in my car after you helped me. Remember? I never figured that one out."

"Spooky, eh? Yeah, I've been visiting clairvoyants."

Saskia ignored this and continued, "What brings you here, to this seminar?"

"I work for IDM. We organise a few open-air festivals each year, ranging from homemade Dutch music to Latin sounds. How do you fit into this motley mix of people?"

"I'm a theatre set designer, so, unlike you, very much indoors. I'm actually a freelancer, but I work with various theatre groups and theatre building companies to propose and design sets for their productions."

"So, you're an artist? I'm envious," said Robert, putting Saskia more at ease, and staring more intently into her big brown eyes. She was wearing smart blue jeans, a cream linen blouse, and a red jacket. Her reading glasses were still perched just above her forehead on her rich head of black hair, which showed some highlights. The meeting was no different from four years ago, except for the conversation. Robert offered to get her another roll, and a glass of orange juice.

"I wouldn't call myself an artist, but I have found a niche for myself. I am first and foremost a designer, and I know my way around CAD systems, enough to be able to put my design ideas into 3D and for them to be interactive."

"Sounds very imaginative. And complicated. So you spend a lot of time on your own behind a computer?"

"Not at all. I make a point of getting out and about to absorb inspiration from things around me, and of course other theatre settings. And that can be here in Amsterdam, or wherever it takes me. In fact, I've just come back from Budapest. I was there being very vain and getting some facings done on my teeth. I'm so happy with the result." She said this with a big smile, showing off her new teeth. "And it's so much cheaper, and all very professional. It does mean you have to stay in the city a while, so I took the opportunity to hunt down new ideas. Fascinating city. Do you know Budapest?"

"No, I don't. One day, I hope. You can be my guide," answered Robert with a smile and some uncertainty.

It was uncomfortable to revisit a flirtation that he embarked upon three years ago, but there was also an unexpected exhilaration as he explored new ways of doing the same thing. The environs were all the same, the seminar was the same, but he was experiencing it again as if it were the first time. How could that happen? He had no idea, but was sensing that it was not a certainty that things would be the same. Would he learn from the seminar? Would he get the girl? These were all passing thoughts, but he knew the answer. Not much would change. The road forward would be the same, the emotions might be different.

Robert and Saskia nibbled at their lunch and talked a little more, also with colleagues and others they knew. Although the normal

Dutch lunch was very short, an event like this would schedule in time for mingling. Networking was what it was all about. Once lunch was over, they both ambled back into the session room and took their respective seats, the same ones as before. It seemed strange to Robert how people always gravitated to the same seat, it was maybe a hangover from the days when you always stayed in the same seat at school.

Robert didn't really know why he was staying for the next speaker, but he liked the idea of being in the same room as Saskia. The next talk sounded, on the face of it, as dull as could be: fire prevention and protection measures for indoor events, but the speaker had given it a provocative title *Where There's Smoke There's Fire*. The presenter was not Dutch but a Brit who had been invited because he had a track record in fire prevention in theatre and other environments. In fact, the smoke and fire of the title was because the talk was about fire curtain systems which contain smoke and prevent fire and smoke from spreading, so people could escape. The speaker, a certain Andrew something or other, was probably on the wrong side of 65, not tall, and very comfortable around the waist. He had a round face and an engaging manner, which made a potentially dull subject more interesting. In fact, he clearly enjoyed speaking to an audience and made a point of injecting anecdotes about things that had gone right and wrong in the fire testing and, slightly more worrying, in real life. Andrew pointed out that it was difficult to make fun or joke about fire, but he somehow managed to make it very practical, and entertaining.

Robert was absolutely fascinated by the presentation that followed, which was about sound effects. In fact, he didn't even know such an industry had been created around the concept of sound effects. There was even a noun for it, *Foley*, named after the sound effects artist and creator, an American from New York. There were now artists known as *Foley* artists, who worked in *Foley* studios, and whose sole role was to add to the enormous digital database of sounds that filmmakers and theatre directors can use in their productions. It made Robert wonder how he might be able to introduce something playful like this into the transitions during his festivals. Maybe he could even make it interactive.

A presentation like this was a speaker's dream, because you could give any number of examples and anecdotes, with video of the actual making of the sound and the end result; and all that happened in between. So, for example, walking on creaky floors? Use an old shipping pallet; horses' hooves would be a coconut; and breaking bones could either be a carrot or celery.

The end of the day rolled around. The plan was that there would be a break of about one and a half hours before they would all go to the Rijksmuseum next door for a buffet dinner and a wander around parts of the museum which would be kept open for them.

Saskia had disappeared without a word. He wondered if she might not come.

CHAPTER FIVE

The Rijksmuseum was Amsterdam's preeminent museum and stood proudly at the head of the Museumplein, or Museum square. This was a large open greenfield area surrounded by other cultural hotspots, and often home to big celebrations such as the winning of a championship by the local football team, Ajax; or returning Olympic medal winners.

The entrance to the Rijksmuseum was under a long archway which was a well-known cycling "freeway," so you really had to be careful not to be knocked over by a bike, or even knock over a bike. Momentum and centrifugal force from a physical confrontation with a pedestrian can have a devastating effect on a cyclist, most often grazed arms or legs, or both—and Dutch cyclists generally didn't wear helmets.

At this time of day, the entrance hall was empty. In the middle was a large information desk which, at this late stage in the day, was now only staffed by one attractive looking receptionist. Robert's attention was drawn to the scene because he recognised the familiar broad shoulders and long hair of his friend Mark, his partner in *Masters in Paint*. It came as no surprise to Robert that the conversation with the receptionist looked more like flirting than any business discussion. Mark was leaning demonstrably over the counter and there was a lot of smiling and laughing. This was the friend he knew, the charmer in chief.

Robert still had a big bone to pick with him, but he knew he was in the wrong year for that. Nevertheless, he approached him from the side in the hope that Mark would catch sight of him coming. But no, he was too absorbed in his flirtations and only reacted when he felt a tap on his shoulder.

"Robert. What are you doing here?"

"I'm off to a reception, here, upstairs." Robert pointed to a sign that indicated where he would have to go.

"It's good to see you. And it's uncanny that it is here, in the art temple of Amsterdam. I have been meaning to call you."

Mark then turned to the unknown receptionist. "My apologies, please excuse the rudeness of my friend for interrupting our conversation. But I do need to talk to him for a moment."

Before Mark could start, Robert said, "What are you doing here?"

"I come here more often than you might think. Although most of what you see here in the museum are finished paintings, there's still a lot that goes on behind the scenes. And I like to think I have some of the best paints to help them. And they're very scientific about making their choices."

"Good for you. And the receptionist here helps you, no doubt."

Mark ignored that with a big smile and continued, "Robert, you know me, always full of ideas, eh? And, I have been mulling over a new business idea which I have been wanting to talk to you about."

"I know."

"What do you mean – I know?"

"Oh nothing, just a hunch," Robert said with a smile. "I know you can't stay still at the best of times."

"Well, this is not the place to talk in detail, but the Rijksmuseum is definitely a good location to get the ball rolling and I think you and I would make great business partners. I now have good contacts in China, and I think we should get into the business of copying old masters for the consumer market. It's perfectly legal. And dead simple."

"Ever the optimist, eh? With hindsight, which I have in spades at the moment, my polite answer is likely to be a simple no. I don't want to get sued by some guy for copying his paintings.

"Robert, I'm not following you. But I'll take your intimate knowledge of the subject as a positive sign. I've got to run now, but I'll call you to make an appointment so we can talk about it in detail."

"If we do ever do anything together, I can assure you that my ground rules will apply," answered Robert knowingly as he accepted he was never going to be able to change what had already happened. If he could, there would definitely be new rules which would reign in some of Mark's more impulsive actions.

"If we do ever go into business together, I will be watching you very closely," said Robert as he watched Mark go back to the information desk and he followed the signposting showing him where he should go.

Their reception was in an open area overlooking the square and the Rijksmuseum's own gardens. It was nothing more than stand-up party tables covered in those tight black twisted drapes you often saw. The real party piece of a reception in the Rijksmuseum was the opportunity of visiting selected areas of the museum, in particular the Dutch masters' paintings. There would be the chance to see the Rembrandt paintings, including the *Nachtwacht*, or *Night Watch*.

Robert first headed to the toilets. He needed to give himself a shot of insulin before eating. Quite often, he would inject himself in the company of people he knew; but, as this was a professional environment, he sought out a more private spot. Insulin shots in the twenty-first century were easy. Compared to the horrible long needles of yesteryear, nowadays you had a syringe pen which contained the insulin, and a tiny delicate needle was then used to inject what you needed. You barely felt it, though it could leave isolated hemorrhages in the pin cushion called your stomach.

Most of the people from the seminar were already there, and the wine and beer were already flowing. Robert headed towards the table with the white and red wine. He selected a white, not paying much attention to what it was. His focus was on seeing whether Saskia was there. Why in hell was he worrying about it? He knew she would be.

She wasn't—at least not yet. This bothered him.

He was still at the wine table when the British speaker on fire prevention came to help himself to a wine. Robert turned and said, "I enjoyed your presentation. How on earth do you turn such a dull subject into something so interesting?"

While it was a compliment, it was typical Dutch. Straight to the point but in harmony with congratulations to soften any blow. Andrew took it as it was intended, but he didn't see the subject as being dull. He had lived his life around dealing with fire and smoke prevention.

"Thank you, but I think you'll find that the subject has more going for it than you might imagine. You only need a few scary incidents, and that focuses the minds of the best of us to find solutions." He continued, "But was what I said of any help for you with your business?"

"To be honest, no. I am at the softer end of the business, finding and contracting artists for big outdoor festivals, so we're not really in the business of worrying about indoor smoke prevention. Still, I enjoyed your stories and the way you tell them. How did you get into the business?"

"Well, it was a long time ago. A really long time ago. I went to work in my father's sun-blind business, which was not having the best of times. In fact, your country is a good case in point; selling sun blinds to the Dutch is like selling coals to Newcastle. Do you know the expression?"

"No, sorry, I don't."

"Well, you only have to drive around Holland and all you see are sun blinds, every apartment, and every house. They all have one, so there was really no market for us here. Newcastle in the north of England was famous for its coal mines, so the expression means that there was no point in selling coal in Newcastle because they already had so much of it."

"Ah, I see."

Andrew continued, "The blind business was quickly going nowhere, so one of our clients one day approached us with a dilemma about holding smoke back in the event of fire. Now I like a challenge and an engineering conundrum, and this turned out to be the turning point for our company."

"You're an engineer, then?"

"God, no. I am one of those amateur engineers that never got a qualification, but I had the good fortune to hit on a solution to what grew into a large business."

Robert changed the subject to something he could have a little fun with. "So, what's it like being in the UK right now, in the middle of all the Brexit campaigning. I followed it…sorry I am following it on the news here in Holland, and it's very passionate, especially those who want to leave the EU."

"Passionate is too diplomatic. The Brexiteers are inflamed and will break our country apart if they get their way. I'll be honest. I absolutely hate it—and that idiot Cameron, our prime minister, was a fool to even suggest a referendum. Now he has got himself into a real bind. It's also going to do wonders for those who want the whole of the United Kingdom to split up. One joker summed it up. An Englishman, an Irishman and a Scotsman walk into a bar. The Englishman didn't want to stay, so they all had to leave. Sends the right message, eh?"

"And what do you think will happen?"

"Oh, I'm pretty sure people will come to their senses and we'll stay in. The polls say it's close, but the so-called remainers seem to have the advantage. No, it will all blow over and we'll laugh about it afterwards."

Robert could not help himself. "I don't know. If I was a betting man, I would put money on the Brexiteers getting their way and once that happens there will be a lot of navel gazing as your country struggles to keep itself together."

"You seem to be pretty confident?"

"Oh, just a hunch," Robert replied, "and, when you do leave, we will wave from the beaches."

"You may. We won't. We'll be drowning our sorrows in the pub, not waving back. See, the pub is our sunscreen."

Robert laughed and was then interrupted. It was Saskia.

"You two took like you're having fun. Am I interrupting anything?"

"No, not at all," answered Andrew quickly. "This gentleman here—I am sorry, we haven't introduced ourselves yet."

"Robert," Robert interjected.

"Robert seems to think that the UK will vote to leave the EU in the referendum in a few weeks' time. He's even prepared to put money on it… I guess we always knew the Dutch were confident people! What do you think?"

"Hi, I'm Saskia. I enjoyed your talk this afternoon. No, I think the UK will come to their senses and we'll be happy bed partners again. You know, we depend on each other more than you might think. We don't want you to leave the marriage, but divorce is always painful. No, I don't even want to think about it."

Andrew interceded and addressed Robert, "And I guess the next thing you'll tell me is that that idiotic, monosyllabic Trump will become the next President of the US?"

"Now that you mention it, don't be surprised if he does."

"Now you are going a little too far. What do you know that we don't? We know Americans often live on a different planet to the rest of us, but that would be taking their own stupidity one step too far. Trump is only after two things. Power, which he would not know how to use, and self-adulation. Can you imagine him even being diplomatic?"

Robert knew any conversation about Trump could go on forever, and in reality, of course that was exactly what had happened. He therefore changed subject:

"Tell me, Andrew, do you enjoy coming to Holland?"

"Please call me Andy," he said. "Absolutely, I come here quite regularly at the moment. I am having a modest boat built in a place called Monnickendam in the North of Holland. When it's ready, I will keep it in France."

"Why France, when you live in the UK?"

"Do you know how expensive it is to live in the UK? And to keep a boat there. It is much cheaper in France, and nowadays just as easy to suffer a horrible Ryanair flight for an hour. And, of course, the weather's generally better in France, so that kills two birds with one stone."

At that point, there was the recognisable clinking of cutlery on glass. The Chairman of the meeting was trying to get everyone's attention, and he came perilously close to using too much force on the glass. When it was quiet, he introduced Maria, who was standing next to him. Maria was an art historian and specialised in giving tours of the Rijksmuseum. Today she was going to only do a brief tour of the parts of the museum which accommodate Vermeer and Rembrandt paintings, the so-called Gallery of Honour. She was all too aware that her audience were not people who were here to really see the museum, but she hoped a few would tag along and at least give her the respect her knowledge deserved.

Maria had a powerful voice. And no microphone. She immediately picked up where the Chairman left off, otherwise the room would have immediately descended into chaos again. She began in Dutch:

"Hello everyone. And welcome to the Rijksmuseum. I understand that almost everyone here is Dutch, so you will be more than familiar with the Rijksmuseum – at least I hope so." Switching quickly to

English, she continued, "I also understand that there are a couple of non-Dutch speakers here, so I will ask them to stay close to me so I can also help them. For those that wish to join me, we are going to gather by those big double doors over there. I will then take you through to see the Vermeers and Rembrandts, the two preeminent Dutch painters," she said, adding, "Oh, by the way, you cannot bring your drinks with you. I don't need to explain why."

Some smart arse from the back shouted, "Please do," but received no response.

Saskia looked at both Robert and Andy. "Is anyone joining me? And she looked invitingly at Robert.

Andy responded immediately, "I certainly am. I'm not exactly a culture bum, so I need to take every opportunity I'm offered."

Saskia kept her eye on Robert to see what he was going to do. He had no doubt in his mind. Saskia had obviously gone home in the interval and changed from her jeans into something more appropriate for a reception in a museum. Or maybe to impress? She was now dressed in a stunning red dress and was carrying a relatively large, dark blue handbag on a long strap. It was a wrap dress that closed on itself, about 10 centimeters above the knee. It wasn't an evening dress but had enough going for it to get anyone's attention, certainly when there was a sexy body and a sexy swing in the step. Saskia knew she had that.

Of course, Robert had noticed, and he said "Sure, I'd love to come with you," as they all gently shuffled towards the double doors, putting their drinks down somewhere on the way. No doubt all the half-filled glasses would be gone by the time they got back, and the museum caterers could start over again. And charge accordingly.

They were already on the first floor and walked through into the main gallery area which housed the famous painters from the so-called Golden Age, the prosperous period for Amsterdam in the seventeenth century.

Maria maneuvered everyone into a group. Because there were no tourists around, she did not have to worry about lone wolves joining her group. She started:

"We are, as you know, in the Rijksmuseum, Holland's premier museum and home to thousands of works of art, but primarily the paintings of the well-known Dutch masters. The museum was closed for many years to undergo complete renovation and reopened in 2013. So, what you are now seeing is the result of ten years of hard work to restore it, inevitably a lot longer than they intended. Isn't it wonderful?" she asked rhetorically.

"We are now in the Gallery of Honour, which is home to Vermeer, Hals, Rembrandt, and many more. But these are probably the three most famous painters in Dutch history. We will start with this one, Vermeer's *Melkmeisje* or *Milkmaid*. As you can see, Vermeer was a painter who paid attention to soft focus. The subject is generally easy to understand. The light-fall highlights where the painter wants you to focus your eyes, in this case the upper torso and the flowing milk. Vermeer's most famous painting is the *Girl with a Pearl Earring*, but you need to go to The Hague for that."

The group wandered slowly from one painting to another. Robert kept close to Saskia, not talking. Now and then he took the opportunity of gently grabbing her by the upper arm, just to guide her in the right direction, or to point something out. A whisper in her ear had two objectives. One, to show her that he knew a little about the masters, but also for her to feel his presence.

Maria now started to concentrate on Rembrandt:

"Here we start our very brief tour of Rembrandt paintings. Rembrandt is Rembrandt van Rijn, Holland's most famous painter. He was born in 1606 in Leiden, and was one of ten in his family.

Relative to those times, he enjoyed a comfortable upbringing and started painting in Leiden, under the tuition of a certain van Swanenburg. He started painting on panel board and then moved on to the more expensive canvas as he grew in stature and could afford it. After a couple of years, he moved to Amsterdam, where he was a quick learner under another artist, Lastman. In those days, the sign of a good learner was to be able to copy the works of the master, to the point that you can barely tell the difference between the two. So much for creativity. Rembrandt was more than a good learner and he eventually moved on to establish his own style, one which has stood the test of time and is still an inspiration to today's artists."

"On the personal front, Rembrandt had a mixed life. On the one hand, he was remarkably successful, but his life was punctuated by disappointment and tragedy. Disappointment because of the ups and downs of relationships with his clients and the church; tragedies with the loss of the women in his life, and almost all of his children. Rembrandt told the stories of his relationships through his paintings, and you will see much of this here in the form of self-portraits, and paintings of two of his loves; his wife Saskia, and the mother of his last child, Hendrickje, who died in 1663. The missing woman in his life is Geertje, but there is no record of any painting depicting her."

Robert leant over to Saskia and quietly whispered, "Nice name, Saskia!"

"Of course." She smiled back.

Maria went on, "Rembrandt's career progressed remarkably quickly, and he eventually got the attention of the Prince of Orange and other notable gentlemen prospering from the trade that allowed Amsterdam to dominate in the Golden Age, roughly the period between the end of the sixteenth century and late seventeenth century. As we can see here, Rembrandt's style is unique. He was devoted to an extreme attention for detail, which acknowledged human imperfection if needed. He portrayed people as they were, and he departed from the long-held view that the subjects should be religious figures. For Rembrandt, normal people made for a better, more viable choice. His paymasters were the well-placed and wealthy, so that's why most of his paintings represent subjects with status. Nevertheless, Rembrandt still painted as he saw the characters, which sometimes upset his clients. Here in this room, we have *De Staalmeesters* or *Drapers Guild* and at the end of course, his most famous painting, The *Night Watch*."

Again, Robert gently touched Saskia as they moved towards the *Night Watch*. Andy came alongside, as they walked at the back of the group.

"I'm so glad I have to stay close to Maria, he said, "Look around you"—he indicated with a sweep of his hands that there was no way he could see over the heads of the group, or even their shoulders— "Even the women are taller than me in this country!"

They all gathered in front of the *Night Watch*.

The *Night Watch* was a very large, imposing canvas. It began at the floor and stood majestically tall. When she had everyone's attention, Maria began to explain:

"This is Rembrandt's masterwork and the one for which he is most well-known. It was done at the request of what can best be described as local militia, or vigilantes. Maybe a better description today is local enforcement, since they were not military, but they were armed groups who 'looked after' certain neighbourhoods. These were 'schutters' armed with muskets, and the name of the game in those times was to show off how respected you were. This masterpiece, with the principal characters, their dog and a spot-lit woman, who is said to look very much like Rembrandt's wife, was commissioned by the musketeers, and was given a long and cumbersome title, which I won't bother you with. Over time, as the painting became darker, it looked more like it was a night scene. It got its nickname in the mid-nineteenth century, the *Night Watch*. And that has stuck ever since."

Maria continued, "The painting was controversial not because of its subject, but because of the way Rembrandt depicted the group's members. Rather than giving each of them equal prominence, he created the painter's equivalent of a snapshot: a group of militiamen who have just moved into action and are about to march off. You can see that Rembrandt is trying to tell a story. It is highly likely that it upset a few of the militiamen when they saw it, but they would be enormously proud today to know that their status really has had a long life."

Maria came to the end of her speech, "Before we conclude, if there are any questions, just let me know. I will also be staying for a drink." There were none, at least not publicly.

The group moved back towards the reception area where they mingled again with the guests who stayed behind. They loaded up on fresh drinks. Saskia and Robert were now alone together.

Saskia opened the conversation. "You know, I get so depressed when I hear and see stories of how life was centuries ago. Can you imagine? Rembrandt losing three of his children, almost all at birth, and his only son later to the plague. Horrific. There's nothing worse than having to say goodbye to your kids before you go on your own last journey."

Robert knew what she might be referring to, but now wasn't the time to bring up the subject, so he answered, "Right. Just the thought. I wouldn't ever want to imagine it for my own kids. God forbid. But fate has a horrible way of intervening. Other than the plague, even simple things, like childbirth, were perilous in those days. For both mother and child."

This gave Saskia the opening to move onto more personal questions. "So you have a couple of kids of your own?"

"Yes, two in fact, a son and daughter. Best of both worlds. They are now thirteen and eleven... sorry, ten and eight."

"That's a big difference. Don't you know your own kids' ages?"

Robert partly ignored the dig. To avoid any further confusion, he added, "I know, early dementia."

He told Saskia, "We live on Java Island and my wife is British, but she has become native pretty quickly. She has learnt how to become just as direct as everyone else, even if she does sometimes feel guilty that she is being a little rude. Strange how the rest of the world can't see the difference between direct and rude?"

"So true. I have a daughter, and she lives in Bristol. Occasionally I have her on the phone telling me how funny it can be, especially with the English. There have been countless times when her directness has been taken for being impolite. Where she might simply say 'no' to a request for a favour, the English embark on a long dialogue to first establish whether the favour is likely to be an imposition, something like, 'are you really sure this is not an inconvenience?' If the Dutch say 'no' it doesn't mean we're not friends anymore."

"So, you have a daughter?" said Robert, directly. "More than one?"

"No, just the one. Lynda. She is now 21 and at university in Bristol, studying veterinary medicine." And anticipating the next question, she replied, "Her dad is no longer on the scene. In fact, he never was really on the scene and neither of us know where he is now. We are abandoned puppies."

"How awful for your daughter, Linda, right? Not to have a father in her life."

"Yes," she replied, "Lynda, spelt with a 'y.'"

"Any reason for the 'y?'"

"No. It just seemed right. Maybe rebellious."

"Oh, OK, that answers that one. But it must have also been very difficult for you?" said Robert, probing further. "Does that mean you brought Lynda up on your own, or does she have a stepfather? If I may ask?"

"Of course you can ask. But it doesn't mean you'll get an answer," she replied with a smile, and then continued, "I guess it was a blessing in disguise. Yes, Lynda misses having a father, but it did mean that we developed a very close bond, and we still have that today. We speak to each other regularly. I go to England regularly and she comes here. For a short while I was also married; to a First Officer on a cruise ship, but that didn't last long. Thereafter, Lynda got used to one or two new partners of mine – well maybe more than one or two – but nothing ever stuck for the long term. We all have stories to tell," Saskia said, invitingly but rhetorically.

"Yes, we do. But that's for another time." Robert changed tack, By the way, I do want to apologise for my unrefined introduction this afternoon. It was not really appropriate." He wanted to undo the harm he might have done with his introduction, and he didn't want to fall back into the old Robert.

Saskia looked at Robert quizzically. Then she realised.

"Oh, you mean that. Your porn skills. To be honest, I had already forgotten about it, but I agree it was different, even amusing?"

"Yes, but still inappropriate."

"Oh, I'm sure I'll get a laugh out of it when I tell some of my friends. And I haven't forgotten your answer to my question."

Robert blushed.

Saskia continued, "If that was indeed impulsive, then you're probably one of those types where jokes come naturally, and you can hold your own in a café with an audience."

"I'm not uncomfortable in a café setting," Robert said with a bit of a laugh. "I view it as a part of my job, hunting down new talent for one of our stages. So, when push comes to shove, I can hold my own, if I have to."

"OK, enlighten me with one of your jokes."

"This isn't really the right setting. Maybe later," said Robert, not really knowing what he meant by that statement. He already knew there would be a later, but he did not quite know the path he was going to follow. He could not explain the feelings of exhilaration he was experiencing, as if it was all the first time around.

"OK. I'll tell you what we'll do," said Saskia, taking control, "I'm done here, and going to head home. If you like we can have another drink on the way, assuming you are going in the same direction."

"Sure, that's a nice idea. I'm on the bike. You?"

"I'm walking."

Robert's eyes moved to look down at Saskia's footwear, relatively high heels. Not the most comfortable for navigating Amsterdam's cobbled streets and canals. Saskia noticed his glance.

"I come prepared," she said. "This bag may not exactly be the norm for a party, but lo-and-behold."

Saskia pulled a pair of red sneakers from her bag and waved them provocatively in Robert's direction. She lost about 10 centimetres in height as she removed her shoes. For a moment she stayed rooted to the floor in her bare feet, which was enough to awaken Robert's senses even more. Saskia had beautiful feet and ankles.

"Ah hell," he mumbled to himself. He was winding himself into more lustful knots.

"Well, I know where you live," Robert said, "so let's head in that direction. I can either walk the bike or you're welcome to jump on the back."

"Let's just walk. I was never one for having my bones shaken to bits on the back of a bike. I like to keep them in the same place."

They both put down their drinks. Saskia quickly bent over to tie her laces—straight from the hip, no bending her knees. She must be fit, Robert thought as they headed out to where his bike was housed, under the archway to the Rijksmuseum. They started walking toward the Leidseplein where Robert had been before the reception started. They walked, or rather strolled, until they joined the Herengracht, Saskia's canal. They found a small café next to one of the bridges with some outside seating overlooking the canal.

It was still relatively early, still light, still warm, and the streets and canals were full of people, especially the canals. In the spring and summer, Amsterdam's canals were home to hundreds of boats cruising back and forth with no particular destination in mind. Robert looked at the passing "sloeps." Each one of these boats likely hosted a small party. Young people passing an evening with music, food, drink, and as many friends as they could accommodate. Robert heard the engines hum, sometimes even growl, as they passed by.

The waitress came out to greet them and asked what they would like. Robert looked at Saskia. "Wine?" "Red?" he asked, and she nodded in agreement. The waitress picked up on the message and said, "Two red wines then?" "Does the size matter?"

"Of course size matters," Robert said smiling, "No one wants a small glass of wine."

Saskia also smiled at this and was coming to the conclusion that Robert had the occasional mischief in him. So, she pushed him on it.

"Right, now we're in a different place. Let's see how accomplished your jokes are?" began Saskia, "Only one."

"Do I have to? I'm not used to an audience of one. And I get nervous."

"I'm listening."

"OK, one. It's clean," Robert answered and continued, "There was a really old pirate who wanders into a café. Well, he didn't exactly wander, he limped into the café. He was the complete picture of what you would expect of a pirate, a wooden leg, a hook on the end of one arm, and a patch over one eye."

Saskia smiled at the thought but stayed silent.

"There are two men sitting at the bar enjoying their beers. Needless to say, they looked up from their beers when this apparition turns up in the bar. One of them asks 'Wow, it's not often that we see people like you. If I may, how did you end up with so many injuries?'"

In the best pirate accent Robert could muster, he continued, "'I'll tell ye if ye buys me a beer.' And, once the beers arrive, the pirate says, 'It was the year of our Lord 1785, and t'was storming like you've never seen it. T'was at the same time we was busy boarding another ship. My leg gets stuck between the two ships. Then, there was a huge wave and a big crack. Leg gone. You know, I had bad insurance, so I end up with a wooden leg. And we moved on.'

"The man at the bar looks at the pirate, and says, 'Yes, but what about the hook?'

"'Ja, t'was another year of our Lord, 1800, and another heavy storm. We were fighting a Spanish ship and fighting with our swords. I slipped and caught my arm on a post. Ja, the Spaniard with the sword hacked my hand off. Ja, you know, bad insurance, so now a hook. And we moved on.'

"The man at the bar observes, 'You've really been unlucky and had it tough. But what about the eye patch?'

"'Ja, it's still our lord's year 1800, and not long after. Beautiful weather, not a cloud in the sky. A seagull flies over my head, then craps, just like that, right in my eye.'

"The man at the bar says, 'Yes, but you don't lose an eye from a little shit.'

"'Na, but I'd only had the bloody hook for one day.'"

Saskia was smiling all along as Robert continued with his Caribbean interpretations and laughed.

"Very nice. And clean. I assume you have more?"

"Yes, but not today. And they can get raunchier."

"Well, I guess we'll have to try and find other opportunities. Sometime."

"I'd like that."

Robert and Saskia chatted for another hour or so, jumping back and forth from work to travel, and eventually back to family.

"I haven't told you everything, said Saskia, "The stories tonight about Rembrandt brought it all back for me, but that wasn't the place to tell you."

Saskia chose to tell Robert about her own tragedies, "All the stuff with my ex-partners and my daughter, that pales in comparison to what happened to my parents."

Not knowing that Robert already knew, Saskia explained the whole story about the MH 17 disaster and how she lost both her parents in the plane crash in Ukraine. She told the story in some detail. The emotion was clear to see when she came to tell how she experienced the day of the return of her parents' remains. It was particularly painful for Saskia because she had to go through the same process twice. Her mother's body parts arrived on one of the first flights, her father's, later. The multiple funerals and the constant reminders in the media still hurt.

"I know I said earlier, back at the museum, that it must be horrific to lose your children before you bite the dust yourself. But to lose my parents like that. They weren't old. They still had much of their life ahead of them. I shudder every time I think about it and feel guilty it was them and not me. I know I am the child here, even so, they were robbed of their life too young. And for no reason. I'm now in survival guilt mode."

Robert looked quizzically at Saskia, as if to ask what survival guilt was.

Saskia picked up on it. "Guilt is something we all have to live with, even if some are much better at it than others. The example I gave you about Rembrandt is classic, losing most of your children before you die. It's not your fault, but the guilt still remains, deep inside. And, with MH17, there were a lot of parents who lost one or more of their kids, even worse than my situation. Teenagers on their way to Asia for the experience of a lifetime. Imagine their pain. And it lives on for the rest of their lives."

Saskia continued, "I even read up on the subject. It's more of a scientific subject than you might imagine. Survival guilt has been around for a while, but more recently it has been folded into the more recognised terminology of PTSD, Post Traumatic Stress Disorder. This is primarily associated with military combat, natural disasters and so on, but in fact it has a broad range. Sorry, bear with me, because I really looked into this, and it has been studied using examples from other events. Typically, you have three types. First the guilt of staying alive while others died. That's me. Then there's the guilt of failing to do something, for example, to save someone's life. And the third, also a horror scenario in hindsight, those that run to save their own skin and don't try to do their best to save others. That mounts up. In Rembrandt's case, his troubles just kept on piling up, but he was the one who survived. Because it was such a common occurrence then, I wonder if he had the same empathy about it that we do today. What about you, no tragedies?"

"No, in all honesty. None. My family is all healthy and well, and that also includes my parents and my in-laws." Robert decided to continue on the family theme so that Saskia was fully informed. "I have two healthy kids, Daniel and Maxine, who are just reaching their teens, my wife is British, and my parents live close to Alkmaar. Sorry, not very exciting really." Robert noted to himself that he had not mentioned Belinda's name but decided not to correct the mishap. He continued, "I'm now 43 years old and I left it quite late before I got married. I actually met my wife many years earlier while backpacking in Australia, but we didn't really get together until a lot later when she was still living in the UK…"

Saskia interrupted "—And does your wife have a name?"

"Mea culpa… Belinda," he said, "We had kept in touch since Australia, and I was often in the UK, so we got together frequently. It's probably clear from what I'm saying that it wasn't exactly love at first sight. But that developed over time. We found ourselves doing more and more together. And it felt right. I had the fortune of having to go to the UK often, so one thing led to another, and Belinda came to Amsterdam about fifteen years ago. But it still took us a while before we got married. I particularly like the mix of cultures in our life, and we are naturally bringing our kids up with both languages. That's easy in this country."

"I don't sense a lot of enthusiasm for married life?"

"Partially true. I dwell on this often. We have the best of everything, especially two wonderful kids—who can sometimes be a pain in the arse, like most kids… After so many years, yes, there is a bit of a stalemate." Robert was now in two minds, bouncing between the Belinda he had left in 2019, and the friendlier one he had reencountered in 2016. Where was he exactly, he asked himself.

Saskia looked at Robert with eyes that simply said, "and?"

"There's not really much more. Don't get me wrong, I'm happy with where I am, but you're right, the excitement and enthusiasm have been dampened, and I guess it's fair to say we rumble along from one day to the next."

There was a pregnant pause as Saskia took this in. She was beginning to like Robert, not just because of his looks and presence. He was easy to be with, intelligent, and had what appeared to be an impulsive and independent spirit which she was attracted to. He was married, but that hadn't stopped her in the past.

Robert was looking down at his watch. "I really should be going," he said, "It's already nine thirty and I will be expected home at some point; don't you think?"

Their drinks were already finished, so Robert went inside the bar and paid. He collected his bike from the other side of the road and they both started heading in the direction of Saskia's apartment, further down the Herengracht.

It was not unusual in Amsterdam for the roads to be uneven in places. After all, they were brick roads and each brick was literally laid one by one, by hand. The soft and unstable earth under the bricks meant that they moved and shifted over time. That's what made walking in high heels in Amsterdam a dangerous undertaking. Saskia wasn't in high heels but that didn't stop her stumbling briefly; but even with a bike in one hand, Robert was quick to prevent a complete fall. It felt good to feel Saskia's flesh as he grabbed her upper arm and immediately righted her. They both stared at each other, and a warm rush came over Saskia. She wanted to see more of this man.

At the house, Robert stopped at the bottom of the steps and there was a brief silence. Saskia broke it.

"Would you like my telephone number?"

"I already ha…" Robert started, but did not finish as he mumbled and tried to lose the rest of the sentence.

"Yes, please do. I would love that."

Saskia then provided her number, which Robert typed into his phone. Since he already had the name Saskia, he designated the new number Saskia 2016, for want of a better name. He would probably change it later, but it would do for now. Robert also briefly glanced at the other "Saskia" number. They were indeed the same.

They both moved closer to exchange farewells. It was the usual three kisser, which the Dutch are very accomplished at. They don't have a patent on it, but unlike most other European countries, they have adopted the three kisses with verve. Robert and Saskia also included a hug, but it was more of an impassioned hug than the normal Dutch variant. While the Dutch kiss with abandon, their hugs are a more modest affair. You could sometimes drive a coach through the gap. This wasn't the case with Robert and Saskia today.

CHAPTER SIX

It was just after 10pm by the time Robert got home. The kids were already in bed, and Belinda was on her laptop, enjoying some chocolate and finishing a glass of wine.

"Mm, nice combination, chocolate and wine," observed Robert.

"Maybe in your book," answered Belinda. "Look at me. My heart says chocolate and wine, but my jeans say, 'woman eat a salad.'" She pulled at the waist of her jeans.

She asked him, "How was your evening?"

Robert moved closer and gave Belinda a peck on the lips. "Actually, the whole day was interesting, and we had a nice dinner reception at the Rijksmuseum, with a guided tour."

"That's just up your alley. Did you meet anyone interesting?"

Robert didn't say anything immediately but was then caught in guilt. He knew that in 2019 he had said nothing about his relationship, now he had a sudden urge to rectify that by at least saying he had met Saskia. If he did, then back in 2019—if he ever got back—he thought he would be partially cleansed of that guilt even if it is only to say, "I did tell you we had met."

"Yes, several interesting speakers and the occasional chat with other delegates." No mention of Saskia, so the status quo continued.

Robert resumed his work and life at home in his new time dimension. Although he seriously contemplated resigning himself to staying where we was in 2016, and leaving the problems of *Masters in Paint* behind him, he knew he had to figure out what had happened. First things first, he thought, to get on with his life. Part of that would include Saskia. Not only did he know that wouldn't change, but he didn't want it to either. His feelings for Saskia were just the same. He was just embarking on a new path and journey which had suddenly become all the more exciting. He was reliving it, not repeating it.

"And, maybe I'll be adding three years to my life," he thought.

Robert left it a couple of days before contacting Saskia, just to add a little to the tension, if there was any. He then WhatsApped her

Hi Saskia. It was so nice meeting you, this time properly, without loads of bags. I enjoyed our evening together.

Nothing more than that. It was to see what type of response he would get, if any.

It came after a while, but Robert was made to wait.

Me too

That wasn't really helpful. But positive. And playful, Robert thought. He dwelt for a while on how to answer, but he had a plan and an idea. He was not sure how it would be received. He started typing.

Saskia

He purposely began with her name:

I have maybe a bizarre suggestion.

Would you be interested in coming to London with me for a Bruce Springsteen concert? I am in fact going to listen to a support act I am thinking of booking for one of our festivals. We cannot afford Springsteen!-

Robert sent it like this and then followed with:

I would like that. But I fully understand if you think otherwise.

After a few minutes.

Wow, I would love to go to a Springsteen concert. But let me think about that. When is it? And how does that sit with your wife?

Robert was half expecting that.

That's great. It's midweek, two weeks on Wednesday. Let me know. My wife knows I will be in London. She is used to me going on exploratory trips to listen to bands.

Robert was amused that he used the word "exploratory." It would be true in more ways than one. He also knew that he hadn't really addressed Saskia's question about Belinda, but he would wait and see if Saskia pushed him for a clearer answer. Robert preferred to avoid the subject.

Saskia took her time to respond, but when she did it said:

Again, lovely idea, and I accept. But let's discuss on the phone because this is too much for WhatsApp.

OK, call you tomorrow.

To that, a smiley was appended.

Robert dutifully called the following day.

"Hi, good morning, it's Robert. How are you?"

"Good, thanks, you?"

"Mm, fine, just busy today with sorting out some admin at work. It's so nice that you can come to London. It gives me a little more prep work to do once we agree on how and where. The concert is at the O2, so a big indoor stadium. But I thought we could stay in the Kensington area. Much nicer there."

"And I will book two rooms," Robert added.

"Good idea. I've always wanted to go to a Springsteen concert, so this will be a real treat."

"Prepare yourself for a late night, because Springsteen is one of those performers who doesn't have an off switch. He can go on for hours."

"Great. Looking forward to it. On the practical side of things, how are we going to get there and when?"

"I suggest I book flights for the Wednesday morning, and then we still have plenty of time if we're delayed. There's always lots to do in London. I generally book easyJet to either Stanstead or Gatwick."

"Sounds good. So long as it's not Ryanair. I wrote a memo to myself never to fly Ryanair again."

"Don't worry, not Ryanair."

Saskia then told Robert. "Just so we are on the same page, I will pay my fair share. That's one thing you need to know about me. Let me know which flights and I will book my own tickets. You book the hotel, but I will pay my bit when we are there."

"Are you sure? I'm happy to cover it."

"No, no. It's just one of those things about me."

'OK, perfect. I'll book two rooms and let you know." And Robert continued. "It would be nice to get together again before we leave, but I'm not sure I have the time."

"See how it goes. Let's first put the plans in place... I've got to run now. I might call or WhatsApp you later if any questions crop up."

Saskia hung up and Robert switched from his office admin to looking into flights and hotels. He opted for an easyJet flight to Gatwick and a hotel in Kensington called Jury's.

They didn't meet up, but a couple of weeks later, Robert connected with Saskia at the railway station in Amsterdam. Once again, Robert could not avoid admiring Saskia, who was again smartly dressed, almost all in denim, with a yellow blouse, figure-hugging blue jeans, and black sneakers. Robert was also in jeans and wearing a leather jacket. Both trailed their obligatory cabin luggage on wheels behind them, while Robert had a small backpack for his laptop.

The train to Schiphol airport, was uneventful, as was the check in and security. Once they had settled for a coffee, Saskia said.

"Why me?"

Robert looked puzzled.

"The invitation. Here. You know."

Robert had an emotional battle of his own going on inside him. He would have loved to tell Saskia the truth about his distortion in time, but he knew this would never be believed. And, if he was in Saskia's position, he would never believe someone telling him they were a time traveller, even one who had only travelled three years. He was too sober in his thinking to raise the subject. Instead, he answered.

"I feel I know you," he said, and paused, "very well."

"I know you know me, but you certainly don't know me well. And certainly not very well. At least not yet."

"Yes. That's true. Generally, I'm not a sentimental person, but although we've only seen each other a couple of times, it's left me with a warm fuzziness, a kind of affinity. Maybe that sounds a little clumsy. No, it is clumsy, but I enjoyed your company then and I hope to still. I also thought you would enjoy a Bruce Springsteen concert."

"Well, you're definitely right on the second part. I don't think I've ever had someone describe a feeling for me as warm fuzziness, but I am touched... I think. And I like the clumsiness of it. As long as that sits well for you on the home front?"

"Yes, yes, I'm comfortable with it... I hope you will be too. As I said before, my wife is used to my travel and knows where I am going. In the interests of complete transparency, I will admit that I didn't tell her I invited someone else."

"You mean me. Another woman."

"I work with a lot of women and also travel with women. Fortunately, I don't have to defend myself about who my travel partners are."

"OK, as long as we're on the same page. Let's just enjoy a fun couple of days."

Saskia wasn't entirely sure, though she had an inkling of what she was getting into. Naturally, she didn't know that Robert knew what was happening all the time. Even Robert harboured doubts about whether this was the right thing to do, but his heart, and his biology, were beginning to rule his actions. It was no different than before.

Eventually, the flight was called, and Robert and Saskia made their way towards the easyJet gates. There was no rush, but it was still a long walk, one Robert was used to. He admired the way Amsterdam's Schiphol airport, housed in a city of only some 800,000 inhabitants, was so vast. You could easily get your day's exercise by just walking from security to your gate.

They arrived at London Gatwick more or less on time. Robert had been here many times and always regarded it as one of the ugliest airports in Europe. Not only did it have one runway, and therefore a lot of queueing on taxiways, it had a patchwork of terminals linked together by whatever weird and wonderful route the architects could think of. The route from the easyJet gate took Robert and Saskia on yet another long walk, up and over a very high bridge, where they stopped briefly to watch a plane move gently beneath them. They continued through the jungle of different buildings until they reached immigration. Robert often arrived at Gatwick "at the wrong time," meaning he would then be welcomed by the chaos of the British immigration system, but not today.

Robert and Saskia acknowledged the courtesy of the immigration officer as he smiled and waved both of them through. It was a welcome change from American immigration, for Robert, the world's most unwelcoming border. There, even a smile could send a threatening message.

They proceeded on their way to the railway station linked to the airport. Yet another conjugated route, this time by shuttle. They took the Gatwick Express to Victoria Station, in the centre of London, and on to their hotel in Kensington.

Jury's was a Georgian hotel, set in the heart of London's museum district. It offered the feel of a mix between a restored London mansion and a modern private members club, lots of leather chairs in the lobby, and velvet lined hallways. All very eclectic, thought Robert.

It wasn't busy at the red marble top reception desk. Robert and Saskia introduced themselves and the male receptionist immediately pulled up their reservation.

"I have you down for two rooms. I assume you would like to be close to each other, so I have put you both on the same floor. I take it that's OK?"

Robert and Saskia looked at each other, smiled, and said in unison, "Sure."

After the receptionist had explained how to get to their rooms, they navigated the various lifts and corridors that took them up and down different levels, with the incessant fire doors that were unique to the UK. Robert realised that this was another example of buildings that were the result of gluing individual houses together to make one hotel.

They reached their respective rooms and agreed to see each other in the lobby in a half hour. Robert was there first, together with his ever-present backpack. He sat down in one of the leather Chesterfields and pulled out his laptop. Once he had logged onto the WiFi, he pulled up his emails and browsed quickly to see if there was anything important.

"Of course," he mumbled to himself, quietly. Then he read the email, which he had been expecting. The caption said, "Bruce Springsteen concert postponed." It didn't say "cancelled," and Robert read on. The message announced that Springsteen was suffering from the tail end of a little laryngitis—the throat being somewhat important for a singer—and they had decided to postpone the concert until the following day. The organisers, and Springsteen himself, were confident that things were heading in the right direction. Robert knew only too well how frail singers could be, but this was Springsteen. His body was like a rock; indeed, he put the rock into rock and roll. Robert was in no doubt. Things would quickly right themselves. But he still had the problem of what to do. He could easily manage an extra day in London, but he didn't know about Saskia. He sat and contemplated next steps while he waited for her.

Saskia wandered down, fashionably late, but looking refreshed. She was still wearing the same clothes and looked prepared for an afternoon of sightseeing.

Robert motioned her to sit down.

"Aren't we going out? Late lunch first, then maybe a museum… Or shopping?" she asked him.

"Not just yet, I'm afraid, we need to talk."

"This sounds serious."

"Yes and no. I was just checking my emails and there's one saying that tonight's concert has been postponed till tomorrow. Springsteen has laryngitis, but they are confident that all will be well tomorrow."

"Fuck. I only packed for one night!" said Saskia, ironically. "No, I also mean that's awful for Bruce Springsteen. And pardon my French."

"Well, I guess from that answer you're OK if we stay an extra night?"

"Absolutely. I am not tied down to anything at home."

"Phew," said Robert. "I was hoping you would say that, as it would be a real pity to miss it."

"Oh, if I had had to go back, you could have stayed. No problem… But this is actually great. We can find more things to do in London."

"Now you mention that… While I was waiting, I started Googling, but I have to confess, I was looking to see if there were any major

77

football matches on. I always enjoy the English game: fast, aggressive, and generally more exciting than at home. Dare I ask, do you like football?"

"I've been to a few games, but I'm not sure I would call myself a fan. I don't go regularly, but if you guarantee it will be worth it, I am open to the idea."

"I guarantee nothing. The last one I went to was a 0-0 draw, so it can only go up from here!"

"That's comforting."

"If I can get tickets, the home team is Queens Park Rangers, or QPR, and they're playing Leeds United. Leeds used to be one of the giants of English football, but now languish with QPR in the second tier, in what's called the Championship, as opposed to the Premier League."

Robert continued, "So, we're on, if I can get tickets? He looked to see Saskia nodding. "It's the end of the regular season and there aren't many games mid-week. So, this would be best, and it's not far away. Bear with me a second."

Robert got up and headed to the reception desk. The nice gentleman who had helped them earlier asked, "Can I help you, sir?"

"Yes, please, if you can. We'd like to get two tickets for the QPR match tonight and I see you offer a ticket service," said Robert, taking the easy way out. He could have done it online, but elected to make use of the hotel service, even if they charged an admin fee.

"That's no problem, sir. We'll see what we can do. Can you give me about ten minutes?" He retreated into a back office.

Robert returned to his seat on the Chesterfield with Saskia, who was now deep into the messages on her mobile. Robert did the same and took the opportunity to send Belinda a WhatsApp to tell her what had happened. Belinda's reply was a little disgruntled, but she knew these things happened sometimes. Still, Robert thought, they add up. Each time he seemed not to prioritise Belinda or his family would get her thinking harder about whether their marriage was really working.

After a while, the receptionist came over waving two pieces of paper with a barcode, and the QPR crest on the top.

"Success. We got you two tickets for the Loftus Road entrance, seven thirty kick-off." He handed over the pieces of paper.

"Perfect, thank you very much. We appreciate it."

"I'll add the cost to your bill?" the receptionist added.

"Absolutely, that would be great. Again, thank you."

"Enjoy the game, I am sure QPR will win. They rarely do, but the Gods will be on their side today."

"You know for sure?" quizzed Robert, wondering for a moment if he wasn't alone in a time warp.

"No, I have no idea, just a wish. I'm also a QPR supporter."

"Shall we?" Robert motioned to Saskia as he got up and headed towards the door.

CHAPTER SEVEN

Once out on the street, Saskia turned to Robert:

"I don't know about you, but I am famished, so let's eat… something healthy. And, as we are going to football tonight, let's make a deal. No museums. It's a nice day, so we could go shopping, but we need to figure out where to go."

"Ah, you spoilt my plan for this afternoon," Robert said sarcastically. "I was hoping to shut myself away with you in a stuffy museum." He continued, "Of course, that's a good plan. Let's find the nearest bistro and have something to eat and we can explore where to go so we end up in the right place for tonight."

Robert started taking big strides in a northerly direction and Saskia immediately had to shout.

"Woah, tiger. Not so fast. I may have legs to die for, but I can't match that speed."

Robert immediately reduced speed and bowed towards Saskia with a 'namaste' apology, holding the palms of his two hands together. They turned a corner and immediately found a cute bistro which served their purposes. It was warm enough for them to sit outside. Once settled, Robert pulled out his mobile and called up Google maps. He was already pretty familiar with the area but wanted to plan an afternoon that would give them some window shopping and places to see. He was hoping for window shopping but was not sure what "shopping" meant for Saskia. They had dabbled in some shopping together, but not much.

"Do you really mean shopping or are you just curious to see what there is?" he asked.

"I don't know. I never know. We'll see," she said teasingly.

"So, how then do we plan for the afternoon if you don't know?"

"Let's not plan, let's take the shops as they come."

Robert was getting a little frustrated, but he tried to push a bit of his own agenda, so they at least had a goal.

"This is what we'll do," he said firmly. "We are now here." As he pointed to a small spot on his screen. We'll continue to head north, up past the Albert Hall and on through Hyde Park until we reach Notting Hill. That's our first port of call for shops. Do you know the area? It is like a village within a city. Famous for its road full of antique shops, and other quirky establishments. Notting Hill, as in the film of the same name."

"Heard of it, but never been there. Sounds good."

"We can do all of this by foot. Then we'll walk in the direction of the QPR ground, which will give us some exercise.

"I'll follow. But moderate your steps!" said Saskia as she stood up, ready to go.

"Hang on one second," said Robert. I have to go to the bathroom.

"Again? You just went, when we arrived. Are you OK?"

"Yes, yes, it's just that I forgot something."

"You forgot something, in the toilets? How can that happen?"

Robert was in a corner. He preferred to excuse himself when he needed a shot of insulin, especially in the company of people he didn't know well. He should have done it when he first went to the bathroom, but forgot. He decided to tell Saskia.

"I'm a diabetic, actually—only very recently. And I forgot to inject myself."

"Really, Type 2? You don't look like you would suffer from diabetes."

"No, I'm fit enough, but it is a late diabetes in adults. It's a Type 1 diabetes. It's just one of those things. Probably genetic, though neither of my parents have it. I need to take a few units of insulin every time I eat. And I forgot when I was there earlier."

"But why do you need to do it in secret? I have a friend who has had Type 1 since she was very young, and she is all out in the open when it comes to injecting herself," said Saskia.

"I've only had it for about a year, so I guess I'm still in a denial mode. There's nothing for me to be ashamed of, but I still struggle with it in front of other people."

"Well, let's start by me helping you. We are together for the next couple of days, and there's absolutely no need for you to rush off to the bathroom each time. If I could help, I would," Saskia said. "But I can't, I don't think. Do you also have to prick yourself in your fingers?"

"No, thank God. Not anymore. I've just started using a brand-new device that constantly measures my glucose. Here on my arm." Robert tried to manoeuvre his sleeve up, but he couldn't do it with the long-sleeved shirt. "See, you can just see a small bulge." He squeezed the cloth of his sleeve to reveal a barely noticeable bulge.

Saskia moved closer and put her hand on Robert's arm so she could feel the sensor. "Wow, that's cool. How do you use it?" Robert felt her warm hand.

"It really is fantastic. No more pricking in the finger—which hurt. Now it's just a question of running a scanner, mostly my mobile, over the sensor—like this—and it gives you a result. Based on that, you can better manage your diabetes, either with food, or insulin. Now I average about 30 scans a day. Compare that to the three to four pricks a day before, at best."

Robert showed Saskia the screen of his phone, which read 12.6. "Too high," he said, "So, I need to take some insulin."

Robert ignored his original desire to go to the bathroom and extracted his fast-acting insulin. He injected just a few units into a fold in his stomach and they went on their way. Saskia gave him an admiring glance, but no words were said.

They headed up Queens Gate until they hit the main road running alongside Hyde Park. As they turned to head towards the Albert Hall and the entrance to Hyde Park, there was a lot of tooting and rumble of noise as a fleet of vehicles passed from left to right, heading towards the Albert Hall. In the middle was a huge red double-decker bus. It wasn't a regular routemaster bus. It was still a double decker, but it was the *Take Back Control* battle bus for the Brexit Leave campaign.

"Mad," said Saskia. "The British have lost all sense of reality. How could they have ever reached this point? I only hope that they'll come to their senses. Empires are a thing of the past, and the older generation could ruin it for the younger ones. I once heard a journalist interviewing a pensioner, and she said, 'they should make the referendum just for those under 60, because we are voting on their future.' And that from a pensioner. Bless her."

Robert added, "Just keep watching. They'll build their campaign up to a fever pitch, promoting how good it was in the 'old days.' Don't be surprised if they get their way. And even after any decision, there will be a political circus as the decision sinks in. Mark my words," Robert said.

"I'm getting used to your predictions."

They watched the bus turn into the circle around Albert Hall. Clearly, the vast flock of people waiting there was the intended audience for the next stop of their Brexit bus. Robert and Saskia ignored them and headed across the road into Hyde Park. They paid a brief visit to the Albert memorial, an imposing pavilion with a statue of Prince Albert in the centre, and then onto the Princess Diana Memorial Fountain, their next brief stop.

"This park seems to be a favourite site for royal memorials," said Saskia.

The remainder of the walk through the park was uneventful. There were joggers, walkers, couples in the grass, and even horses on the special track around the park. They exited to the north and into the east side of Notting Hill. Robert's objective was Portobello Road, which he had been to before, but would be new to Saskia. They meandered through the very nice residential area alongside the park, using Google to help them navigate to Portobello.

"Shops at last," Robert said cynically.

"These are not shops. Well, they are, but they also spill onto the street, so we have a market. Just my thing."

Robert feared what was coming. He looked at his watch. Plenty of time he thought, as he settled into his "got to be patient" mode. He knew enough about Saskia and suspected she would take forever browsing, as if shopping was like getting the last drop of petrol out of the tank. So they idled their way through the market, looking at shops with antique clothes, boutique clothes, bric a brac, posters and art of all kinds; and there were plenty of places to imbibe a drink or two.

Saskia, as Robert had already seen, even on their few brief outings, had a knack of losing him. Not intentionally. She was simply in her own world, and Robert could not keep track of which shop or stall she was in, because she had the infuriating knack of retracing her steps. He decided to plant himself at one establishment and ordered himself a cappuccino. He found Saskia in time to tell her where he would be. She just nodded. A half hour later, he was still sitting there. He wasn't bored. There was plenty to see, and May's early summer weather was made for "Girls in their summer clothes," as Bruce Springsteen would sing. Fifteen more minutes and he was still alone. And he couldn't move because this was their intended meeting place.

"I'm done," Robert heard Saskia say from behind him, "Shopped out."

"But you're empty handed."

"I know, but shopping is a journey, not a destination."

"No, no, that's not right. You need to be focused, otherwise you will lose all sense of purpose."

"That may be your approach, but I'm afraid I like to lose myself in the experience, the journey. And if there's something I like and want, then I'll buy it… If I can afford it."

"Even if you don't need it."

"There are always ways of justifying your purchase. I believe they call that cognitive dissonance."

"That is very scientific."

"I studied—remember."

Robert got up, briefly took Saskia by the upper arm, and guided her out of the immediate stalls as they headed towards White City.

"We are heading in the direction of a place called Westfield. It's a huge shopping mall not too far away from the football ground, but it's not our destination, just a landmark. Just so you know. We need to meander our way through these streets in a westerly direction and we should bump straight into it. You can't miss it."

"I'm ready. Lead on."

They were at the bottom of Portobello Road and turned towards the west, through some very pleasant residential crescents. After a short walk, they found themselves walking through an area of social housing, which was a complete contrast with what they had just been through. It wasn't depressing, but you could tell the difference, brown block gallery apartments, and tall non-descript tower blocks, confined living.

Robert didn't really know where they were, other than he was confident they were going in the right direction. He stopped suddenly, and gazed up in awe, and horror.

Saskia was still walking and hadn't noticed Robert had stopped. Eventually she did, turned and asked, "Is something wrong? You look like you've seen a ghost?"

Robert had just passed a sign which said Grenfell Tower, the block of flats that was to dominate the news in the UK and around the world. It was naturally all still intact, but he momentarily had an image of the enormous inferno which was to overwhelm the tower in a year or so. He couldn't remember when it was, but he knew what was coming. He felt awful that he couldn't do a thing.

After a long pause, he answered Saskia, "In a way, I have. Can you imagine, living like that in an enormous square block, no balconies. It just gives me the shivers." He purposely avoided any reference to a fire. That would just put him in a position to answer more questions.

"Let's move on," said Robert, as he briefly and gently took Saskia by the arm. They went underneath the tube line, which was now above ground in this part of London. Eventually they saw the Westfield shopping centre looming in front of them and proceeded around the front towards Shepherd's Bush with its abundance of multicultural businesses. This was to be their stopping point to get something to eat and drink, so Robert headed into the nearest pub and came outside with a wine for Saskia, and for him what the British like best, warm beer. They found a small spot on the pavement where they could use someone else's windowsill to park their drinks.

"We have a little time before the game, so shall we also get a bite to eat here?" Robert waved his arms in the vague direction of the whole square, which was actually a triangle.

"We have an abundance of choice. Turkish pizza? But it will be here, standing room only."

"Fine by me, it's not as if we're on a date—or are we?" she said teasingly.

Robert smiled, but he was confident in his answer. "Yes, this is a date. It may not be the most romantic of settings, but frankly I had expected to be elsewhere at this time." They should have been headed towards the O2 for the Springsteen concert, not having a pizza and pint on a pavement before a football match.

The message was not lost on Saskia. She laid her hand on his.

"That's sweet of you. If this is a date, then I can't think of any better way of spending it with you and thousands of other men at a football match." Saskia smiled.

"You'll be surprised. There'll also be a lot of women there as well."

"I know. Seriously though, I've been with married men before, but I'm not proud saying that. It has happened, sometimes it was just a lustful interlude. If I'm attracted to someone, then I'm attracted, and I won't let precedent and norms get in the way. But I will be realistic, I won't get in the way of someone's family. Full stop. I like you, Robert, from the beginning when we first met, but this boat— by the way you're the boat—has a long way to go before reaching port… And the port is what you're thinking of."

Saskia removed her hand and took a sip of wine, looking deep into Robert's blue eyes and wondering what response she would get.

"I'll be honest. I'm just as confused as you are. Even our first meeting on the street in front of your house—which I think you've forgotten—was memorable for me. Do you remember? You with your boxes. It was very brief, but it had an impact. So, meeting you again a few weeks later was like the cherry on the cake," said Robert.

"That's very nice, thank you. And as I recall, I was wearing cherry red that day," replied Saskia. "And yes, I do remember, but for me, I will admit, our meeting did not scale the same height as your cherry."

"That's OK, I'm just happy that we can have this conversation. Let's get our pizzas and then move on. It'll be crowded at QPR."

Once they had finished, they left the square and headed on down the Uxbridge Road. All of a sudden you could not escape men, women and kids all adorned with blue and white scarfs heading in the same direction. Even if Loftus Road was small compared to other London stadiums, it was still big. The crowds grew heavier as they approached the ground and walked towards the entrance indicated on their tickets. It took a while to squeeze through the narrow turnstiles, but they eventually became settled and took in the swelling atmosphere of beer smelling men and intense rock music from the speakers.

When the teams came out, the home crowd immediately started a chorus which Saskia could not understand.

"Do you know what they're shouting?" she said.

"As it happens, yes. QPR is colloquially known as the Hoops, because of the blue horizontal rings on their shirts. That's what they're cheering—not shouting!"

"Ah, makes sense. I suppose."

From an excitement point of view, it turned out to be a seesaw of a game. Extremely exciting even. Leeds were in their usual all white outfits, shirts, shorts, and socks all white. In some cases, also white boots. Today, while it was a fairly even contest, Leeds suffered the ignominy of a late winner from QPR, making the final score 3-2 in favour of the home side. Everyone on the home terraces left happy. Both Robert and Saskia felt the same way as they got carried away with the fans of QPR, literally and figuratively.

When they had been swept out of the stadium and got away from the crowds, Robert asked, "Do you want to walk back, or take a taxi, or tube?"

"Walk, I think. We've walked a lot today, but I can manage a bit more."

"I reckon a half hour or so, and we can always stop, no, we will stop on the way if and when we see a pub with some action. OK?"

"I'm ready. We have just been sitting for 90 minutes."

Robert and Saskia headed back towards Kensington. Robert didn't know the way exactly, so used Google maps to plot out the shortest route. This took them through some of the nicest areas of London, including Holland Park with its imposing houses. It was approaching 10pm by the time they came to a place called The Bolton Pub, not too far away from their hotel.

"Shall we?" Robert motioned to Saskia.

"Why not, good a place as any?"

They entered through the double doors on the corner of the building. From the outside it looked very much like a classic English pub, but it was more like déjà vu as they stepped into what seemed to be a very smart Dutch café. Ahead of them behind the bar was a huge reproduction of Rembrandt's *Night Watch*. There were other reminders that you were on home turf, pictures of Dutch-English naval battles, and Delft blue tiles on the walls.

"Nice. So much for taking in the local watering holes," Robert said sarcastically.

Robert noticed that the Bolton Pub also had a suffix name, the Rembrandt Proeflokaal, or tasting locale. So, that explained the art. In fact, it was a pleasant mix of classic British pub interior with a tip of the hat to the Dutch. It also boasted hundreds of European beers, especially Belgian beers. They both avoided the beers and went for the red wine. The pub was comfortably full, but they found a place for two at the end of a long table in the middle of the pub. A sign on the table announced live music, but not today, only weekends. Today it was a fairly loud mix of canned popular and soul music. Everyone was either deep in conversation or absorbed in their mobiles. So much for social interaction.

"Rembrandt seems to be following us around," stated Saskia, as she pointed at the art.

They sat silently for a while, as they took in the bar and all the activity. Then Saskia asked:

"Why and how did you get into the festival business?"

"Well, I sort of fell into it really. When I was at university, I started off by studying pharmacy, which sounds like a strange choice for me now you know what I do. In retrospect, I felt I was coerced into it a little by my parents, who were doctors. I tried, I really did, but it was not the life I was looking for. Too sedate. I stayed in Groningen and moved on to study communications, but in the meantime I also got heavily involved in the music scene around the city. I'm not a front man, but I can play a mean bass guitar."

"You play the guitar?" Saskia interrupted. And added, "I'm envious, I wish I could play a music instrument."

"Yep, believe it or not. Frankly, I don't play much anymore, but it's there if I ever need it. Anyhow, that's what rolled me into the festival groups, because occasionally we would play a small festival here and there. It wasn't until I moved to Amsterdam that it really turned into something more concrete and I met and got to know the guys who ran a company called IDM. In this business, you don't really apply for a job. It comes to you by way of showing your enthusiasm and doing small bits and pieces on an ad hoc basis. After all, most festivals grow from small beginnings, and they rely on volunteers and enthusiasts to get the ball rolling. Nowadays, there are just too many festivals in Holland, so there may well be a culling in the coming years."

"And now?" Asked Saskia.

"It's been hectic as we prepare for the summer, but I also have another business, which is my insurance for times when festivals won't be what they are now, and for the off season. It's called *Masters in Paint*, and we offer customers the opportunity to have original copies made of some of the old masters, like our friend Rembrandt here. Made in China, no, painted in China."

"You're kidding. Is that legal?"

Robert explained the law relating to copyright to Saskia, but he realised that he was telling her about a business he had in 2019, not 2016. It didn't really matter right now, but if he couldn't get out of 2016, how was he then going to explain a non-existent business?

Robert changed subject. "Funny we should also be following your namesake around, eh? Remember, the Saskia in Rembrandt's painting. Now she's staring down at us from behind a bar."

"Probably very appropriate," said Saskia. "She had such a tragic life, and now she's condemned to watch over other people's enjoyment. Wouldn't it be nice if she could just step out of that painting and into our time?"

"I think that would be too much of a shock," Robert replied, "Three hundred years is not a long time in human history, but it's still going to be much more of a shock for someone jumping ahead in time, than going backwards. Don't you think?"

"Undoubtedly. I don't think people from the seventeenth century could ever ground themselves. The list of what we have achieved in those years is endless. And the human race is literally just a miniscule spot in history. Literally. I once heard a scientist say that the full stop at the end of fourteen volumes of encyclopedia represents the time that we humans have existed."

"Wow, just a pinprick! That's all?"

"Yep. That's all we are."

They both had another wine and concluded after a while that they had had enough for the night, and it was time for them to head back to the hotel. Before they did, there was a large crashing sound coming from just behind them. Robert looked over at the bar to see bodies tumbling from a couple of bar stools. Panic ensued.

Robert and Saskia took in the scene. It looked like a young couple, probably only in their early twenties, had both fallen from their stools. Saskia intervened to tell Robert—who had not seen— how it happened.

"The boy suddenly had convulsions and grabbed at the girl's arm to stop himself falling, but they both went flying."

The barman, who was not young, came around to help, as did a few others. Robert looked on but took no action. The boy was on the ground, still convulsing but now losing consciousness. His girlfriend was panicking more and more, while the barman was also trying to get information from her.

"I've only known him a few days," she tried to get the words out.

"Does he suffer from epilepsy?" he asked.

"I don't know. I don't think so," she replied.

The barman went back behind the bar to get his phone. At the same time, Robert saw the girl fumbling in the boy's pockets, and she pulled out an insulin pen.

"Hell no!" Robert thought to himself and sprang into action.

He was on the girl in a matter of seconds and grabbed her arm holding the insulin pen. "Is he a diabetic?"

"Yes, I guess so," she said unreassuringly. "I've seen him shoot himself up with this stuff occasionally, so maybe he needs more?"

"Absolutely not," said Robert. "No way, that will make it even worse. Even kill him."

The girl was shivering with fear. "Have I done something wrong?" she said.

Robert was now taking over, busying himself with two things: Making sure the boy was on his side, to avoid him choking on his own saliva, and looking around for the barman. He managed to say, "No, it's not you. What's your name?"

"Maggie," she replied.

"Well Maggie, it's probably his diabetes that's doing this and he needs sugar, not insulin. But we need it urgently and in liquid form that can be injected."

The barman came back.

"I've called an ambulance," he said.

Robert replied, "Good, that's best, unless you happen to have glucose injections on hand in your pub. He's a diabetic on insulin and this is likely to have done it. Too much insulin, or exercise—probably."

The barman answered, "No, I don't know if we have sugar like that. If we have, no one's ever told me about it."

As ever, it felt like ages, but the ambulance arrived within fifteen minutes and the medics were immediately on hand and knew what to do. A shot of glucagon into an upper thigh and, slowly but surely, the boy came back to life, a little dazed. Robert knew then that all would be well and that he would not have to go to hospital. In fact, he could probably even resume his spot at the bar and continue as if nothing had happened.

"Wow that was close," said Saskia. "What would have happened if she had injected more insulin?"

"His coma like-state is already being caused by too much insulin, so adding even more would just make everything worse. And she would likely not know how much she is injecting. Being where we are, close to medical help, it would probably have been OK."

"You looked to be in control. I'm proud of you," Saskia added to let Robert know she admired what he did.

"Someone had to do it. It could only be me because I know what it's like. It also goes to show that people really don't understand diabetes. I get that, because it is complex. It also sends the message it's probably a good idea that all pubs and cafes keep a glucose syringe onsite, just in case."

"Why can't you just give them a glass of water with sugar?" asked Saskia.

"That's a bit difficult when you're unconscious. And you need to get the sugar to the right places as quick as possible."

Saskia looked over her shoulder at the scene behind her. The medics were still there, but the boy, and Maggie, were now on regular chairs. The colour was coming back to his face. All was now well, thought Robert.

"OK, that's me done for the evening. Enough excitement," said Saskia, but not until after the couple they had helped came over and thanked them.

The hotel was only five minutes away, and they already had their respective access keys for their rooms. No need to stop at the reception desk. But they did.

There was a young girl behind the desk now. Robert approached and said, "It looks like we're going to have to stay an extra night tomorrow. Can we arrange that with you?"

Without even looking, the girl responded politely, and knowingly.

"I'm very sorry, Sir, but our reservations department is closed now. We can certainly arrange it for you in the morning."

"OK, no problem," said Robert. "We'll come back in the morning. Goodnight."

"Goodnight."

Robert and Saskia headed up to their rooms. At Robert's door, they looked at each other affectionately, holding each other at a distance on each other's waist. Robert knew he didn't want to be the same overhasty man as in 2019, so he leaned towards Saskia and gave her a kiss on the lips. It was a fleeting kiss, but done with feeling, so Saskia felt it.

Robert said, "I had such a great day. Best if I go right to bed."

"Me too," said Saskia. "Not quite the day I expected but still very enjoyable."

She reached up to Robert and did the same. Gave him a quick kiss and turned to head for her room with a "Slaap lekker." Literally translated, it meant "sleep deliciously," and conveyed more meaning than "sleep well." Saskia hoped her day with Robert meant that they would both sleep deliciously.

Saskia's room was three or four doors down the corridor. As she walked, she felt Robert's eyes following her, so she raised an arm and waved without looking back. Robert smiled and entered his room. Saskia was smiling too.

Once in his room, Robert turned towards his door, which he had just closed, and banged his head a couple of times on the door but not hard. On the one hand, he felt the natural urges common to the male species, but this time he was also proud of himself for not pushing anything. Patience. But he was still excited, and he was momentarily grateful that he had lost a few years of his life—or gained, depending on your perspective.

Saskia too, felt some trepidation, and she started pacing her room. At one point she even had her hand on the door handle as she contemplated going to Robert's room. But she didn't. Instead, she bit her lip.

CHAPTER EIGHT

It was a restless night for both of them, not the 'delicious' one they had hoped for. They had not agreed on anything with regard to breakfast, or even a time. A WhatsApp from Saskia broke Robert's rest.

You awake?

He was awake, and they agreed that Saskia would knock on Robert's door when she was ready, which is what she did. This time, the morning kiss was more of a peck. They both headed downstairs and had breakfast in the hotel.

"OK, we now have a whole day ahead of us, and no plans. Any ideas, burning desires?" asked Robert, and then he added.

"I do have to be at the O2 a little earlier, and definitely for the support act. After all, that's what I'm here for, right?" He continued. "The band is called AlascA. They're four boys from Volendam and they have an infectious sound which is all their own. I think you'll like them."

"I'm sure I will."

"I have to meet up with their manager before the show starts, but I'm sure you can look after yourself for a little while?"

"Count on it," replied Saskia.

Robert continued, "About the rest of the day, I do have a thought. Have you ever heard of Hampton Court? It's not in London, but not far away.

"The name rings a bell. Remind me."

"It was one of the residences of King Henry VIII on the river Thames and it's full of history. There's probably no need for me to tell you who Henry VIII was."

"Our friend with a lot of wives and a tendency to have them killed off."

"That's the one."

"I think that's a great idea," Saskia said. "We have plenty of time. We just need to find out how we get there from here."

She added. "Will we then be going straight from Hampton Court to the concert? It doesn't really matter. As you know, I wasn't planning on two days. My wardrobe is very limited and what you see is what you get. In fact, I'm already wearing tonight's outfit, unless I see something better on the way."

The concert they were going to be at was a rock concert, not an opera. Saskia had chosen something easy going and more in line with the jeans and T-shirt culture expected for Springsteen. No jeans this time but a white T-shirt with some subtle art deco designs, and a belted skirt that ended a few centimeters above the knee. Her shoes were bohemian style wedge sandals, comfortable enough for an entire day. And if that failed, bare feet were also fine.

Robert and Saskia leant close to each other and pored over Robert's phone. It didn't take long for them to find the best route to Hampton, first by tube to Wimbledon and train to Hampton.

"Excuse me," said Robert, getting up to go and give himself a shot of insulin. Then he realised he didn't need to do that and sat back in his chair.

"Excuse you for what?" Saskia asked.

"Oh, I was about to find somewhere private to inject myself but concluded I don't need to do that." He pulled out his vial, put a needle on, pulled up his shirt and injected himself. Saskia leant over to watch more closely and then asked about the needle.

"Let me have a look at that needle. It's so small, minute even. How do they make them so small? I imagined much longer needles."

"It's so easy. It really is. Can you imagine what diabetics used to go through only a few years ago with needles like the end of a javelin?"

"And to think, I was feeling sorry for you. Not anymore!" said Saskia.

Robert got up and, as he was doing so, said, "OK, let's go. But first we need to sort out the rooms."

Saskia nodded, and they headed towards reception where the man that helped them yesterday was at his post.

Robert began, "Hi there. We checked in yesterday with the plan to only stay one night but the concert we were going to has been postponed a day, so we'd like an extra night. Do you still have rooms?"

"Oh, how inconvenient for you. But let me see what I have. I think we're full, but let's look."

After a while of fiddling around with the files on his computer, the receptionist looked up and said, "I'm sorry, we don't have two rooms anymore. I only have one. You're welcome to that if you like, or you could try some other hotels in the area."

Hassles like this were the last thing Robert and Saskia wanted. They looked at each other intently, also affectionately, and Saskia knew she was the one who had to answer.

"I'm OK with that," she said, looking at Robert's face, which was full of anxiety. He didn't want to overstep his mark. As they were still in front of the receptionist, this wasn't an ideal place for a discussion, so Robert simply turned and gave his go ahead.

The receptionist, unperturbed by the sudden merging, replied. "Do you have a preference for the room?"

"Oh, let's take her room." He acceded to the likelihood that it would be easier for him to move than the other way round.

"No problem." The receptionist sorted out the paperwork. "Check out for the other room is 11:00, so it would be good if you could transfer your things before then. And here is a second key."

"We'll do it now, as we want to head out soon."

"Thank you, Sir. And I wish you a good day. It looks like it will be nice weather."

They both turned to head towards their respective rooms, and Robert immediately asked, "Are you sure about this? We can easily find another hotel. Though it might take a chunk out of our day."

Saskia was quick with her response. "Don't be silly. It's alright. I can defend myself," she said with a big smile.

Robert gave Saskia a warm smile back, and they continued to their rooms. "Give me a couple of minutes to get all of my things together and I will bring them to your room," he said.

Once Robert had transferred his bag to Saskia's room—no, their room, they then headed out to the nearest station to make their way to Hampton Court, the last stop on the line. It was a perfect way to spend the day together. The highlight for Saskia wasn't the splendid castle but the maze, the oldest one in the UK. It gave her the opportunity to be like a child again. They spent about 20 minutes going in and out of green cul-de-sacs but eventually found the middle and got back again with no arguments. Occasionally Robert and Saskia bumped into each other as they made sudden and unexpected turns. Neither of them seemed to mind. There were moments when the physical contact was held for more than a few seconds.

After the maze, it was closing in on 4pm, so they started heading back to London. Robert had his meeting planned for about 7pm, but he would call when he was at the O2 arena.

The journey to Hampton Court was reversed, only this time all the way to Waterloo instead of Wimbledon, then they were closer to the O2. It had been a typical date day out, and while they were still getting to know each other better, there were no pregnant moments that made either of them think this was not the right thing to do. Robert was enjoying these new-found moments. The history was the same, but the experience was different, and all new to Saskia.

Waterloo is a main line station. Robert and Saskia made their way from there to North Greenwich on the Jubilee underground line. It was a direct line, so there were no changes and they found themselves at their destination by about 6pm. They were feeling peckish, so had a quick discussion about what to do about eating.

"We ought to eat something a bit more substantial before we go in—and start drinking!" began Robert.

"I would like to say, speak for yourself, but on this count, I'm with you. Food it is. But where?"

Robert started looking around and he could already see crowds of people teeming around the various kiosks. And one thing Robert didn't like about crowds; they meant queuing. He then eyed a sign which pointed in the opposite direction to a golf driving range.

"See that sign," he pointed, "It's a driving range, so they must have food, right?"

"If you can read properly, the sign also says they have a restaurant. I just hope it's not too formal and won't take too long. Let's give it a try."

It was a good decision. The Springsteen crowds had not thought to go there. And they had a great view of the river and the O2, which sat on a sharp bend in the Thames. It was an enormous round structure that looked very much like a tent. It was originally built to celebrate the new millennium in 2000; now it was a very large indoor music and sports venue.

It was now about a quarter to seven, so they paid the bill and retraced their steps back towards the O2 arena. Robert used his phone to call a guy called Justin, who was the manager of AlascA. They agreed to meet by an access door for artists that Justin pointed him to. Robert could not go in, nor did he need to.

By now the crowds really were building up and everyone, as ever, was congregating outside as the doors were not open yet. Robert and Saskia found they had to negotiate some of the crowd as the entrance they needed happened to be on the other side of a few thousand fans.

"Do you want to stay here and I'll come back, or come with me?" Robert asked.

"I'll come with you," said Saskia. "Lead the way."

Saskia didn't hesitate for a moment and grabbed Robert by the arm. He turned, smiled, and squeezed his arm towards his flank, as if to say, 'you're safe with me.'

They ploughed their way through the back end of the crowds, and Robert decided it was a safer bet to hold Saskia's hand, so he grabbed her right hand, a bit too firmly. Still, it was necessary. She smiled to herself, as Robert was busy pushing past people.

Space at last. They eventually broke out of the crowd and Robert could see Justin in the distance. They soon reached him, shook hands, and Robert introduced Saskia to Justin.

"Don't mind me. I'm going to wait over there by the sign that says, "Up at the O2," whatever that is," said Saskia.

"OK, I'll see you over there. Be about 20 minutes, I think?" As Robert looked at Justin.

"To be honest, I don't have much more time than that. The boys are getting ready, and I'll need to get back inside," said Justin.

Robert went for a brief walk with Justin in a quieter area. Saskia, meanwhile, headed off to see what "Up at the O2" meant. When she was closer, she could see photos and then a description. She looked at the enormous arena above her with yellow supports protruding through the roof.

"Wow that would be cool," she thought. "Up at the O2" was a tour that took you up on the tented roof where you got a unique view of London and of course the roof and its construction. The cool part, thought Saskia, was the climb, where you would have to wear safety harnesses. At least helmets weren't required.

There was plenty for Saskia to look at while she waited. She settled into people-watching, which is always fun. The O2 can accommodate some 20,000 people, and Springsteen is a guaranteed full house, so there were a lot of fans shuffling towards the various entrances. People-watching is an art form. You only have a very short period of time to take in the people, what they are doing, where they are going and what they are wearing. For those coming to see a rock pensioner still performing with verve and energy, you would expect to see his older fans. Indeed, they were out in their numbers, but so too were the younger generations. Springsteen is one of those stars who has bridged all age groups.

Saskia became lost in watching. There were lovers closeted close together, not getting quite enough of each other; there were still touts trying to get rid of real, or fake tickets. And in typical Springsteen style, T-shirts were the order of the day. In particular, Saskia liked the one that said, "Some days the supply of curse words is insufficient to meet my demands."

"Having fun?" Saskia was taken aback as Robert appeared from nowhere and touched her gently on the shoulder.

"Just taking in the scene," she answered.

"Shall we go in?" Robert asked.

"I'm ready if you are."

"Yes, all done." Robert put his arm around Saskia and started guiding her towards the entrance that was stated on their tickets. Suddenly there was a yell.

"Mum?"

Saskia turned, as if on a coin, because she recognised the voice immediately, her daughter Lynda. It had not escaped Lynda's attention that a strange man had an arm around her mother.

Saskia broke away from Robert and hugged her daughter, who came out with the most obvious question, "What are you doing here?"

"We are doing the same as you. Springsteen," she said as she waved towards the arena and the mass of people. "But what a surprise! And such a nice way to meet up."

Looking at Robert, Lynda said, "And whom do I have the pleasure?"

"Oh, darling, I'm so sorry. This is Robert, a good friend of mine. He's in the festival business and he invited me along. I could not refuse."

"It's very nice to meet you, Robert." She extended her hand.

"You too. Your mother has spoken of you, and I understand you're studying here in England."

"Yes, and enjoying it a lot," answered Lynda, who realised Robert was likely more than a friend if he knew about her. "I'm here with a whole bunch of friends from Bristol, over there." She indicated a group of about six people. "I won't introduce you as we really should be going in. Mum, let's call at the end of the show and see if we can meet up for a drink."

Saskia could not really say no. It wasn't that often she saw her daughter; but they did talk regularly. They kissed and parted to their respective entrances.

Robert and Saskia had good tickets along one of the flanking sides, with an excellent view of the stage. Once in their seats, Robert was naturally very interested in all that was happening around him. He already knew the business well, but he was always keen to absorb more and pick up on new ideas. The Volendam band AlascA was only due to play for about a half hour. It was strange for Springsteen to have a warmup band, but he would appreciate their style of music, with a combination of harmonies and folk rock.

A Springsteen concert was predictable. You knew you were going to hear some new material, many of his big numbers, and some of his great ballads. Despite his age, Springsteen still had remarkable stamina and would happily go on for more than three hours.

Robert and Saskia were clearly enjoying every moment, a couple more beers helping oil the atmosphere. Once Springsteen got into numbers like *Badlands* and *Dancing in the Dark*, there was no stopping the dancing in and around the seats. Robert also shared his first passionate kiss with Saskia. The moment was just asking for it, and it felt right; for both of them.

Getting out of the O2 with 20,000 other people was the challenge it was always going to be. It was already late, but Robert and Saskia took their time to let the crowds diminish as they wandered slowly towards the tube. Saskia tried calling Lynda but only got voicemail on each occasion. She was not that sorry. She was enjoying her time alone with Robert. With these crowds, there was no way they would bump into each other, so they decided to go back to Kensington, first of all in a very overcrowded Jubilee line train. It did give them the opportunity to cuddle closer. Standing room only.

There was no doubt that the nearer Robert and Saskia got to their hotel, the more comfortable they felt about their togetherness. Saskia held onto Robert's arm most of the time, and occasionally they would hold hands.

Robert presented his key to the door of his room. Once Saskia heard the click, she grabbed Robert gently round the waist and started pushing him inside, as if to say, "I want you." She continued pushing until they were inside, and then reached up and put her arms around his neck. Robert had to bend down slightly to make it easier for Saskia.

"I had such a lovely time. Thank you. You're a nice man. Nicer than the ones I normally fall for." As she stood on tip toes to reach Robert's ready lips. It was now their second genuine kiss, and the message for both of them was one of growing desire. Almost a need. Their kissing became urgent now, and Saskia stayed on the tips of her feet for as long as she could. Robert moved his hands from an embrace to the part of Saskia's body that he loved so much, her firm and perfect bum. His hands stayed there as he maneuvered her towards the bed as Saskia also tried to get rid of her shoes. This was easier said than done when you were still in someone's powerful arms.

The sex was mature and loving. Robert took his time and used his hands, mouth, and tongue to maximum effect. Saskia basked in the attention she was getting and just laid back and let the experience take its course. It had been a long while since she had physically felt this way with someone and as far as she was concerned it could go on all night. Robert, too, was not being ignored, as Saskia explored him with expertise and sensitivity. In Saskia's case, the orgasms were multiple. When they had exhausted themselves, they just lay prostrate on the bed until Saskia broke the silence.

"I have to pee," she said. She got up and went to the bathroom. Robert just lay there, an immovable object. He felt different. This wasn't the same as before. He did not recall ever feeling so much for Saskia as he did now. In his previous life, he remembered, it was more about the sex, now he felt much more closeness. He avoided the word love, but he knew it wasn't the same.

Saskia emerged from the bathroom, still naked but ready for bed. After all, it was already well past 2am. She jumped into bed on the side that was open. Then she asked:

"What side of the bed do you normally sleep on?"

Robert thought that was a bit of a cliché question for middle-aged people having an affair or starting a new relationship. If you were in your teens or twenties, whoever asked that question? Once you are settled, routine sets in, and a chosen side of the bed is one of the fixtures of your life. There were many more, but right now the open question remained.

"Oh, it's not important," Robert lied. "But I normally sleep on this side," he said, firmly staying where he was on the right side of the bed as you look at it from the foot.

"Fine by me," Saskia lied too, as she slid under the duvet. She moved towards Robert, but he was still on top of the duvet, so their bodies did not touch. She leant over, kissing him on the lips.

"Now, I'm tired," she said.

Robert looked towards her and ran the back side of his hand over her face.

"Me too. Time for me to have a pee too. Back in a mo."

By the time Robert got back, Saskia was almost asleep. The lights were still on, so Robert turned them off, got into bed and gave Saskia another goodnight kiss. Not much came back, other than a mumble. They had both had a long day and an exhilarating end.

106

Robert woke up to the gentle sound of steam. Saskia was already up and making coffee, or what passed for coffee in the UK. She was still naked, and Robert could not help but just stare at this vision. Saskia felt the staring.

"I can see you," she said.

"I can't help it. You are a sight to behold, clothed or not," Robert prodded.

"Black or white," she said, following with "Sugar, no sugar." It was all very decisive. "Stay where you are, it's coffee in bed."

"Milk, no sugar… Please."

Saskia returned with two cups, handing Robert one. He was now sitting up, took the coffee and set it on his side table. It was too hot. He sank back down and moved closer to Saskia.

"I missed you," he said.

"Not sure what that means, but me too," Saskia replied with a smile.

"In the middle of the night," said Robert, looking at Saskia for some form of recognition. "I don't know, I just thought we would wake up in the middle of the night and learn more about each other, if you follow me? But I slept the whole night. Sorry, sorry."

"Don't fret about it. I slept too, so we were both in the same boat. Besides, we don't need to check out yet. You once said to me the tongue never tires, remember?"

The hint made Robert forget his coffee and moved closer to Saskia's warm body. His free hand glided over all of her body and the physical contact again ignited the passion of the previous night. Robert again devoted a lot of his hand and tongue time to exploring Saskia's body, at one stage to the point that he got a sudden verbal response.

"Hey fella, I've got two tits, you know. I also have a left one."

Robert stopped what he was doing, looked up at Saskia, and then realised his mistake.

"I like the attention. And I am pretty sensitive there, but you know, you are allowed to give both breasts equal attention."

Robert's problem was that he became lost in paying unequal attention to Saskia's right breast as he was trying, ever so subtly, to hunt down any early sign of the breast cancer that he knew she was going to get. He knew it was the right breast. He was only trying to help, but she obviously didn't know that, and never would. But he had to give Saskia an answer.

"I'm an asymmetric lover."

"Weak answer," she said. "But go on. And be fair to both."

He did. In the hotel room that day, and many times more at Saskia's place on the Herengracht. The months passed by, but Robert was not feeling like the same Robert.

His relationship with Saskia now was on a different level from before. Was it because he was three years older, or at least he thought he was. Was it because it was a second time around in the same boxing ring? Or was it because he felt he had discovered more about Saskia this time than he had before? He didn't know. Saskia was, to him, still mature and beautiful, intelligent, a good listener, but warmer than he remembered. And more empathetic. She didn't suffer fools gladly, but Robert could see past that because it was always short lived, and he didn't think she really meant it anyway. He often felt she was testing him.

All of this was putting him in a quandary because he didn't want to destroy his marriage and his family. He sensed Belinda's own frustrations with him. Saskia was important to him, more so than before. He found himself wondering more about the path he should take.

Robert was cool headed and analytical when he needed to be. Maybe that was a side effect of his unfinished pharmacy studies in Groningen. He certainly felt a genuine affection for Saskia, but he had passed the stage of the stirring cocktail of chemicals that were driving his initial passion. He didn't want attraction love to become attachment love, because that is the slippery path to destroying what you have already built up with someone else. No, it was time for some harsh decisions.

Robert knew in his heart of hearts what he had to do. He was already feeling his own form of guilt, and there was only one way of handling it. Conceptually, it did not differ from the last time, so what difference would it make if he broke off the relationship now? "After all," he thought, "I failed in 2019."

This time it was going to be much harder. The passion, the intimacy, the warmth, had all got to him. Nevertheless, it was the time to go and see Saskia for the last time. He wasn't looking forward to it at all.

It was mid-week, a Wednesday to be precise. The kids were off to school, and Belinda was at an appointment. Robert had already WhatsApped Saskia to tell her he was coming over, but no alarms as to what it was about. For Saskia, it was just another visit.

Robert had a late shower and decided on jeans and a tan-coloured jacket over a white shirt. He didn't want to appear sloppy. He grabbed his wallet and put the old coin he had picked up into his jeans pocket. He had acquired a strange attachment to it, almost as if it was a mascot, and planned one day to make more enquiries about what it was.

He had a couple of things on his agenda first. He had to go to the chemists to pick up some more insulin. He grabbed his backpack, slung it over his shoulder, and wound himself into the car.

Robert picked up packages of some basal insulin and fast acting insulin; basal was a long-acting insulin that provided a foundation for the enzyme in your body; the fast acting was for when you wanted to compensate for an overload of glucose, no matter where it came from.

Robert threw everything into his backpack and returned to the car. His route to Saskia had become a bit of a routine, whether by car or bike. It was a nice day. He drove past the back of the main railway station, then left towards the centre. Once on the canal ring, he turned onto the Brouwersgracht canal and his phone started ringing. He stopped, because he could, and started fumbling around in his backpack for his phone, at the same time throwing the new insulin packages onto the front passenger seat. A couple of cars suddenly appeared behind him, so he thought better of answering the phone and quickly put his backpack on his lap. He turned left at the old West Indisch House, went over the bridge of the same name; and blacked out.

PART III

The Massacre

CHAPTER NINE

Another jolt, a momentary blackout, and he was looking ahead at a totally different Herengracht, and a totally different Amsterdam.

"Holy shit," he exclaimed. "Now what?"

He was just too stunned to take it all in, but he had no choice. His hands were on the steering wheel of a totally alien vehicle, and he came to a stop. It was a thin Bakelite wheel, so his large hands sat on the wheel like a snake coiled around a branch. He knew enough to see he was probably in a Jeep of some sort. It was typical camouflage green, very filthy and highly uncomfortable. There was no sign of a roof anywhere; it was open to all the elements. He felt extremely uncomfortable, to the extent that he could feel the welling up of an urgent need to have a crap, and the crowds around him made him even more anxious.

Robert stared ahead of him, still in shock, his hands frozen to the steering wheel. He recognised the Herengracht, but now it was teeming with people all dressed in drab clothes with drab colours, almost the same as his Jeep. There were trees, but not nearly so many. There was barely a car in sight, and when he could see one, he couldn't recognize it. He did see what looked like a Beetle. Whenever he could make out a car, they were all black.

The people walking by were all beaming, jabbering to each other and clearly having a good time. If anyone had a bike, they weren't riding it. It was like a street party. No one seemed to have a destination. Robert had never really seen people seem so happy en masse. He stayed rooted to the same spot in his Jeep for what seemed like an eternity. He wasn't holding anyone up. He allowed himself to relax and let any thought of fear dissipate.

People were staring at him as they passed by. Some intensely. He was in a Jeep, but he wasn't exactly dressed in keeping with all the surrounding people. He realised now he was in a different time period. Again. He didn't need a newspaper to tell him that. A newspaper might help for the date, but that would come later. In the meantime, he had to figure out what he was going to do; more and more people were taking notice of his strange and very healthy-looking appearance. Not only was he dressed smartly—and differently—he was a picture of good health compared to everyone around him. Robert was suddenly in the company of a population that had clearly been suffering. Not an overweight person in sight.

One of these passersby stopped right beside Robert. He leant over and looked into the Jeep, and in particular at Robert in his jeans and jacket. Fortunately, it was a tan jacket, so he felt that he fitted in a little, but clearly close fit denim was unknown to these people.

"Hey, I speak English," the local said to Robert.

Robert smiled and said, also in English, "Yes, I can hear that." He then continued, "I also speak Dutch. In fact, I am Dutch."

"Really," said the man, "You're not Canadian?"

Robert suddenly made the connection. He had travelled to 1945, and this was clearly the end of the Second World War in Amsterdam. He knew enough history to know that if he was being asked if he was a Canadian, then it meant he had arrived at a time of extreme relief and joy for the inhabitants. They were now rid of their German persecutors. No wonder they were out and about celebrating. It didn't change the immediate challenges facing their daily life, but all that was forgotten in the moment's celebration.

Robert eventually answered, "No, I'm helping the Canadians." He purposely left it very vague, hoping he would not suddenly have to answer more awkward questions.

"Well, any friend of a Canadian is a friend of mine," the man said as he presented his hand. "But where did you get those clothes from? I have never seen anything like that. And they look so new."

"That's true. I'm working with the Canadians, and they brought this style with them. The style isn't new, but I agree, you don't see them here. The trousers are very strong, so maybe they will catch on sometime," answered Robert, thinking he could get away with this. He also knew that this question was going to be like a broken record for as long as he was dressed like this. Right now, he didn't have any alternative, and he also didn't want to abandon his clothes for what he was seeing around him.

Robert had to move from where he was. He was still on the apex of the bridge and people were passing him on either side, offering their hand and generally wishing him and everyone else a healthy future. It was a huge street party.

With some difficulty and crunching of gears, he managed to get the jeep into the first gear position, but he needed to consult the diagram on the dashboard that told him the first gear was backwards and not forwards, unlike modern cars. He gently drove a hundred metres or so down the Herengracht. He had no intention of trying to drive any further and selected the best possible place to stop on the side of the canal. There were no other cars, so choosing a spot was easy. Unlike 2019, it was parallel parking with the canal, and there were none of those kind metal barriers to stop you from rolling into the canal.

"Oh, fuck," Robert said to himself, "How do I turn this off?" He looked around everywhere and it was clearly unfamiliar territory. He was technical enough, but all he could see were knobs. Fortunately, they were labeled. He had lights, choke, and then an unmarked switch. He tried that. It worked. It was a power cut off, just like he was used to.

Robert stopped and got out. He still had his backpack with him, so he put that over his shoulder and sat on the bonnet of "his" Jeep. He was purposely looking away from the people on his side of the canal because he wanted to avoid any awkward questions. He also leant back to look in the car and specifically at the passenger seat. Nothing.

No sign of the insulin and they weren't in his backpack either, but he already knew that. A shiver of fear went through him as he realised he was in an unknown time and place without the medicine he needed to stay alive. All he had was what was in his pocket.

As critical as it was, he would have to address that later. Now was time to take in more of the surroundings. The Herengracht looked bare. It was spring and the trees were in leaf, but they just looked so sad. He knew from history that these were extremely hard times for the population, and wood had become one of the most precious commodities for warmth and cooking. Robert looked to his left, at the Brouwersgracht where he had just come from. It too lacked the number of trees he was used to. Robert was shocked to see his city in such a sorry state.

Robert was on the northern side of the canal, looking back over to the other side where he could see number 85. From the outside, the house looked the same as he remembered it, perhaps a little tired. As on his side of the canal, there were people going back and forth and in and out of their houses. Robert could see that right outside the house there was a gathering of people, presumably from the houses there. They were congregated around a couple of tables and a chest. The tables and chest were being used to dispense cold drinks, and presumably other delights that they could manage to produce or acquire in these harsh times. It was all part of the partying scene that was unfolding around Robert.

Robert looked at his watch. It said ten past one, but he had no idea if that was correct. It felt about right, and the sun was in the right place. What he didn't know was the date. He knew it was 1945, and he knew it would be May, but the exact date wasn't so important at the moment. He decided to come out from his self-imposed cocoon of thoughts at the front of the Jeep and head over to the house he knew so well. He could not retrace his steps backwards over the West Indisch Bridge because the small pedestrian bridge on the other side was blocked, and not even in use. Instead, he had to go the long way around, continue down the side he was on until he reached the next bridge. He had to run the gauntlet of people staring at him as if he was an alien. He marched on, occasionally smiling, and wishing people well as he went. He was still in his own shock bubble, wondering how he got to be here and how he was going to extricate himself, if he even could.

He crossed the next bridge and turned left to walk back along the other side of the canal, admiring all the flags hanging from the houses. As he approached numbers 85 and 87, he could see more clearly that there was a small crowd of people hovering around the houses. He stopped and stood back by the canal edge, staring at what he saw in front of him—Saskia. Or was it Saskia? She looked exactly like his "Saskia," same face, same colour hair, same build. In short, all the pieces in the right place, but dressed very differently and with a different composure; and thinner, like everyone here.

There was a small bench close to him, and he had to sit down. He was now in shock for the second time in a matter of minutes. He kept looking in the direction of the woman, who was busy chatting with her neighbours and random passersby. He also looked more intently at the wooden chest out on the road being used to support the food and drink. Again, it looked very familiar.

Robert sat there for a while and took it all in. He was lost in one of those paralysed stares when "Saskia" approached and suddenly greeted him.

"Hello there," she started. "Isn't today the best day ever?"

"Unquestionably. I'm taking it all in," answered Robert.

"You look lost, even out of place," said "Saskia." "It doesn't look like you are from around here. I've never seen clothes like that, and they all fit differently. I should know, I work for a fashion magazine." She was looking in particular at his jeans.

Robert could see that and answered, "Yes, I know. These are denim trousers, called jeans."

"Jeans?"

Robert realised he was on tricky ground. "I've heard some people call them jeans, but they aren't new. They come from America."

"But look at how they are stitched. We don't do that. And your legs," she said, as if asking a question. "The trousers follow the shape of your legs. Look around you; trousers should just hang from the waist."

Robert had already noticed. While some of the women were wearing a bit of colour, the men were as drab as could be. They were almost all in worn-down suits, various shades of brown being the predominant colour. And "Saskia" was right, there was no shape. All the men looked as if their trousers were hanging only by either their belts or braces, and the jackets were only staying in place because they sat on a pair of thin shoulders. It didn't help that everyone looked so pale and unhealthy. One look at their belts told the story. Not only were they very old and worn, you could see they had been pulled in a number of times, equating to the constant loss of weight.

The women were different. They had made more of an effort, using whatever they could, even the nylon from the parachutes. They wore either dresses or skirts and blouses, in many cases with a cloth belt with the colours of the Dutch flag, or orange—the colour most associated with Holland. Their dresses or skirts generally ended just around the knee, and most women wore short socks and sandals or shoes. "Saskia" was different. She stood out from the others because her skirt was a patchwork of colours, was a touch above the knee, and she did not have socks on. Just sandals with a bit of a heel. "Yes," thought Robert, "she knows what she is doing, more of a free spirit, and probably does work for a fashion magazine." Maybe she was similar to the same character he knew in 2019. He wondered what her name might be.

"I'm Saskia," she said as she held out her hand to introduce herself. "You look lost, so why don't you join our little party." Saskia waved her arms around and said, "And these are all my neighbours. All passersby are welcome. It's a day to be remembered."

"Hi," said Robert, and then changed and made it more formal. "Hello, I'm Robert, Robert Dekker. It's nice to meet you. Really nice," he added and meant it. "You look ready for a party," said Robert, trying to pay a compliment.

"You like my skirt?" asked Saskia, rhetorically. She answered her own question. "I made it a few weeks ago when we started hearing that the Allies were getting close to Amsterdam. It's about all the cloth I had left over, but it makes for a colourful skirt, don't you think?"

Robert admired what she had done and looked at her again, now paying more attention to her face and hair. This Saskia was not the same Saskia he knew before. Her hair was still black, but now no highlights, and occasionally a little sign of grey hair. It was shoulder length, and she had clearly washed it and put in curls for the occasion. Her hair was pushed up at the front; in the back she had tied a ribbon of bright orange, also for the occasion.

"I really like it," Robert said. 'It makes you stand out." Which was probably the intention, he thought.

"Come, stranger," said Saskia, as she held out her hand to Robert, who was still sitting on the bench. "Come and get a drink. We have mainly soft drinks, but we also have some beer. And cakes. Freshly made from what we could scrounge."

Robert grabbed his backpack, flung it over his shoulder and stepped towards the familiar chest and tables where all the drinks and food were. He was getting hungry, so he also took the liberty of grabbing a couple of cakes, but he stayed clear of the beer.

Robert had to field yet more questions from the neighbours as Saskia introduced him, so he found himself in a repetitive mode of trying to explain his jeans, his jacket and now his backpack. It was a simple backpack, but what attracted their attention was the big red star and the modern Heineken logo. Heineken was also a big beer brand in those days, but their logo was very different, more in keeping with the look and feel of the times.

"Your bag, it says Heineken, but is it another Heineken?" said one of the neighbours.

"No," said Robert. "The same beer as you have over there," realising yet again he had got himself into a hole.

"Heineken has a number of different logos, and some are still experimental. I know them well. See, the star on your bottle, it's the same, just larger and in colour."

It was more of a conversation starter from the neighbour than an interrogation, so Robert didn't need to dwell on it any further. He continued chatting with the neighbour as best he could without talking himself into another corner. The conversation revealed that these people living on the Herengracht were definitely more privileged than others. While their clothes were tired and well used, they probably had more to start with than the average Amsterdammer. And they had the ability and the facilities to be more creative and do more with it. Saskia was clearly a good example, especially with her fashion background.

Saskia turned to go up the short flight of stairs to her house and Robert could not help but notice her legs. Yes, they were as beautiful as his Saskia's. He knew they were bare because he had been studying her with more than passing interest, but running down the entire length of her legs was a painted line. This represented the seam of what would normally have been tights. Robert knew that women in those days loved stockings or nylons as they were called, but he knew they were extremely hard to come by during the war. What struck

Robert more, and perhaps the reason why he noticed, was that part of her "seam" had parted on one of her legs. So he thought he should point it out to her. He followed her up the stairs and gently grabbed her by the arm.

Saskia turned and said sharply, "Mr Dekker, is there something wrong?"

Robert was immediately struck by the terse response and the use of his surname. "No, but I hope you don't mind me being very blunt— I am trying to be of help."

"Please, I get a little nervous when someone comes up behind me like that. What help?"

"Well, you see, I noticed that you have seams drawn on your legs. That's very creative. But on one of your legs, they have partly been erased."

Saskia immediately twisted her torso to have a look and said, "Oh my gosh, you're right. That's awful."

She immediately leant on the bar at the top of her steps and yelled to attract the attention of her friend. "Hey, Dinie, can you come? I need your help."

Robert realised then that this was a job for two people, and without thinking started saying, "If you like, I can be ..." And then he stopped as his sentence died away without Saskia noticing. As much as he would like to help Saskia, in 1945 it was not the role of a man to do something so intimate as paint a seam line on an unknown woman's legs.

Saskia turned to Robert and said, "Thank you for telling me. Fake seams are just something we do, especially on joyful days like today. But you have to be careful. Sitting down is not a good idea." And then she grabbed Dinie's hand as she came up the stairs and led her inside.

Not long after, they both came back, and Saskia briefly and discretely showed off her new legs to Robert. Restored lines. She made the automatic assumption that Robert understood. Everyone in her circle of friends did this, use eyeliner to draw a line the full length of the leg that was in view. Nylons were almost impossible to buy anymore, so this was the next best thing. In 1945, they even had a liquid browning lotion to make your legs more tanned, which also highlighted the seam down the leg and made the woman feel more put together. Even in times of hardship, fashion still ruled.

Saskia came down the steps with a new packet of cigarettes, yelling to everyone in earshot, "More cigarettes." She first offered Robert a cigarette.

"Mr Dekker, cigarette? They're good for you."

"Oh, no thanks, I don't smoke. And, please, call me Robert," he answered, making no attempt to try to explain the perils of smoking.

"Oh, I'm not sure I can do that. I really don't know you," said Saskia, as she lit up on her own cigarette.

"I think you'll be surprised," Robert answered, but he left it at that.

Robert then saw almost everyone accept a cigarette, either from Saskia or taking them from their own supply. Literally, almost everyone. It was like a plague, and it wasn't just confined to Saskia's little group. The Herengracht was busy, and many of them were smoking. The Canadians, who were primarily responsible for liberating the city, were handing them out like confetti at a wedding.

Robert retreated to the bench where he had been sitting and continued to take in what was around him. The houses on the Herengracht looked tired from years of little maintenance, and the same could be said for the road. The gloominess was more than compensated for by the street-wide carnival going on around him.

Someone then yelled, "Hey, everyone. It's time we were going."

Suddenly there was a hive of activity as people looked at their watches, nodded and started tidying up. The chest and tables went into number 87, the house next to Saskia, and what remained of the drink and food went into Saskia's house.

Robert was puzzled as to what was happening, so asked the nearest person to him, "Excuse me. Where is everyone going?"

"Don't you know?" came the answer. "The Canadians are due in the city, so we are all going to the Dam Square. The party continues there." He pulled the *Het Parool* newspaper from his inside pocket. "See, the parade is due at three o'clock."

CHAPTER TEN

Robert was in serious need of a quick history lesson, but he could hardly ask his hosts. He was still more concerned about his predicament. He was now back in a year far removed from either 2019, or even 2016. He had no money, no way of earning money, he was dressed like an alien, and he looked far too healthy. This really was unfamiliar territory. He knew the war ended in 1945 and that the Canadians came to liberate the city, but that was about it.

As he watched the remaining cakes go back into the house, his thoughts returned to his diabetic predicament. He had some insulin and a few needles with him, but that would only last him a short while. What then? He had no idea when insulin was invented. And even if insulin was invented where—or when—he now was, how would he even be able to come by some? If he could not get any, then he would die, eventually. And it would not be a pleasant death. He knew that much. Just the thought prompted more nervous bowel movements.

Saskia shut her door and came down the stairs, herding her friends to head for the Dam. Robert interrupted her, saying, "I apologise, but before we go, can I borrow your toilet?"

"You can use it, not borrow it," she said, as she turned and went back up the stairs. Robert followed as she put the key in the door and pushed it open. Robert was already halfway in the corridor with his hand on the door on the left as Saskia said:

"It's there on the… left." Robert had already disappeared into the toilet before she could even get her last word out. "Oh, I guess you know where it is," she said, somewhat bemused. It was still in the same place.

The group had already started walking, but Saskia had to wait for Robert so she could lock her door. She didn't mind, because she felt mildly attracted to Robert. He was different, very different, and that appealed to her. And he was tall.

Robert reappeared, and they started walking a few paces behind the main group. Saskia started the conversation and Robert knew something like this was coming.

"I don't understand. I have lived here all my life and I have never seen you. And this is a small city."

"No, no. I am not from here. I come from Groningen," Robert attempted, knowing that if he got questions about Groningen, he could probably bluff his way through.

"But then, what are you doing here, how did you get here? And, where do you get those clothes from?"

Robert was thinking on his feet but had also partly prepared an answer. "I have been working for the Canadians. That's my Jeep over there." He pointed to his vehicle on the other side of the canal. "If you like, I am an advance party doing reconnaissance and I've been

123

feeding information to the Canadians as and when I can. And I speak English fluently."

"So, you are a spy? But on the right side?"

"I wouldn't go that far," replied Robert.

"I'm going to call you a spy," said Saskia sarcastically. "But, how can you be a spy wearing clothes like that? They are far too conspicuous. You stand out like a sore thumb."

"Ah, those. Well, it's like this. These denim trousers are very common in Canada, and they are used on farms and other places of work. Not like here. And the Canadians also help me with clothes."

"But come on. Those trousers are very tight. Look at everyone else."

"I know, it's because I'm so tall. It's not easy to just come by the right size in a war, but I like it. It will be the fashion of the future. Mark my words."

"You still look too smart," Saskia said.

"Part of the desired image," responded Robert, hoping that would be the end of it.

Fortunately for him, they had already turned the corner and were heading toward the Dam Square and the crowds were getting denser. People were starting spontaneous conversations with each other, hugging and kissing in the ecstasy of the moment.

Suddenly Robert was on the receiving end of one of these physical moments. A man in uniform took his hand and shook it vigorously, at the same time looking up at Robert.

"I am so pleased for all of you. My name is Harry ... Harry Potter. Royal Engineers."

Robert immediately looked at his breast pocket, and the inscription indeed said Harry Potter. He looked like him too.

"Of course," said Robert, as he rolled his eyes. "Nice name. You have a big future." He moved on, as Harry went on to say the same thing to more people.

It was the interruption Robert needed, because they now walked on, exchanging congratulations with anyone and everyone. Not unsurprisingly, Robert was still the subject of many stares, but people were too wrapped up in their celebrations to make a big deal of it. Robert was acutely aware of his imposing presence. He gave a brief thought to how it would have been if he had travelled from 1945 to 2019. Going the other way, probably no one would take much notice of someone dressed in drab wartime clothes. Robert could be on his way to a costume party, or a reenactment of part of 1945. Or people would think he just liked the style.

The ribbon of people snaked its way towards the Dam Square. Robert naturally knew the way, but he followed and constantly looked up around him at the houses, the roads, the canals, the means of transport. Everywhere, there were signs of wood having been taken to feed the need for energy, even parts of the supports in the tram lines.

They crossed from the large Post Office and into the Dam Square, or Dam as it was colloquially known. This was a different Dam from the one Robert knew. It was still the same size, had the same buildings surrounding it, but there was green around one of the sides, a bit park-like—still pretty dull as far as city squares go. Even today, the Dam was still a somewhat boring square of grey paving stones, normally home to thousands of tourists mingling with street artists and occasionally used for large congregations of people—whether that be for a strike, a fair, a memorial, or a music event.

Nothing was happening yet, and there was no sign of the Canadian parade. As they walked towards the middle of the square, Robert looked around. All familiar buildings. The palace on the northern side; the New Church on the west side; and various well-known shops that exist to this day.

Robert stopped suddenly, while Saskia walked on. The image of everything around him seemed eerily familiar from photographs. Suddenly, he was scared, not just for himself, but for everyone around him. If he was right, the stage was being set for the massacre on Dam Square. All Robert had was an image, but he knew many people lost their lives on what should have been a day of celebration. He was convinced he knew what was about to unfold.

He moved forward and grabbed Saskia by the arm which took her by surprise. It was a firm grip.

"Hey, that hurts," she said.

"We've got to go," Robert said. "The Germans are here."

"Are you mad?" Saskia shot back as she pulled her arm away. "What are you doing?"

"Bear with me a second, but let's please walk over there," Robert said as he tried to take her by the hand. Robert was not sure where the firing would come from, but he recalled it was machine gun fire. He also remembered seeing images of people huddled behind a street organ, so that was his plan for cover if needed. The problem was that Saskia was still resisting.

"We are safe here," said Saskia. "There are soldiers everywhere and the Germans are all gone. No, I am not going. I'm staying with my friends. You can stay with us, or not. Your choice."

Robert had no idea how he was going to convince her. They were still about twenty metres away from the organ and he was getting more and more nervous. Nothing happened. Robert hovered close to Saskia, looking up to see if he could see any activity. If he knew which building it was, that would help, but he didn't. That was in the history books. He certainly wasn't planning to be a victim himself.

Robert tried again. "Listen, I have to tell you something," Robert said. "Yes, there are Germans here and they are about to open fire on us. I promise you; I know this. If you come with me, I'll tell you, but we need to at least get behind the organ—or away from here."

"Don't be ridiculous."

"Please, come with me."

At that point, Robert heard the first crack of a gun, but he was ready. Without looking up to see where, he grabbed Saskia by the upper arm, this time very hard. With some stumbling, he pulled her quickly the 20 metres or so to the back side of the organ. Now there were bullets flying everywhere, and Saskia had woken up to the danger of the situation as she saw others fall in agony. She and Robert reached the organ quickly, but not quickly enough. Saskia screamed as she was hit in the leg, just as they crept behind the organ. In no time there were about twenty people huddled up behind them, all seeking cover.

The firing continued, and the screaming got worse as more and more people were hit. Robert looked around and could see victims who clearly had not made it, and many more who were wounded. Robert and Saskia had sought cover behind the organ, but there was very little other safe cover, short of trying to reach the edges of the square and hide in the lee of a building. Not far from the organ was a lantern; there were people using the lantern to protect themselves. It was a strange sight. The lantern itself was barely as wide as a person, people were cowering behind it in one single line.

Robert had his arm around Saskia and looked at the wound in her left leg. "Are you OK?" he said.

Her face said it all. She was in pain, but she managed. "No."

Their fire cover was reasonably good, but Robert wanted to turn and see if he could stop the bleeding to make Saskia more comfortable. The problem was that there were too many other people trying to save themselves, and they were partially on top of Saskia. Robert decided to become more aggressive. Without pushing any of the other people into the line of danger, he managed to reverse himself and get access to Saskia's leg. She had been shot in the calf and it was bleeding profusely. He took matters into his own hands and pulled the loose cloth belt from her waist. First, he rubbed away the blood and was relieved to see that it did not appear as if the bullet had hit any bone. The bullet was lodged in the muscle. Robert wrapped the same belt around the wound and bound it tightly. The belt was nothing more than the colours of the Dutch flag made from different pieces of cloth, but it suddenly proved more useful than as decoration.

Robert reversed himself yet again, so he was face to face with Saskia.

He asked again, "Is that better?"

Saskai nodded but said nothing. She was still in shock. Robert added, as reassurance, "It looks OK. You've got a clean wound, and it's now covered, but we need to get you home, or to a hospital."

"Thank you," said Saskia, looking gratefully at Robert, who added, "But you need to know you have lost the seam on your leg."

Saskia wasn't amused. "How about my friends? Where are they? Have you seen them?"

"No," replied Robert. "I was paying more attention to you, and you were all becoming a little dispersed. Hold on, let me look around. If I can."

The Germans were still firing, but not as much as the initial rounds. Although it felt like ages that they had been behind the organ, it was in fact only a matter of minutes. Robert looked behind them first, because that was easier, but could see no one. He then edged towards the side. He didn't know all of Saskia's friends, so worked to recognize them. He saw one behind the lantern, and a couple more over by the church away from harm.

He was then absolutely horrified by the scene that unfolded in front of him. The square was now empty of people, but there was a small boy, maybe three to four years old, who was walking into the middle, firmly holding his ice cream, and calling for his mother. He was very much in harm's way, but no amount of shouting at him could convince him of the danger. All he was interested in was his mama. Then, out of the corner of his eye, Robert saw a man bravely head after the boy, picking him up and running back to safety. The Germans did not fire on him, but he was not to know they wouldn't. The man and boy disappeared into the crowds. Hopefully the mother was found.

Robert turned to Saskia, back to the subject at hand. "I can only see three people that I know, but I don't know their names. They're safe. But I can't see any of the others. That doesn't mean they're not safe. I just can't see them, and I'm not going out there... not just yet."

Robert and Saskia had to stay squashed up against the organ with the other twenty or so people. They weren't going anywhere either, so after a while there was the surreal scene of people politely introducing themselves to each other while lying on the ground, even shaking hands. It probably took a half hour before there was any sign of counteraction and the Germans eventually stopped firing. Robert did not know, or could not see, what caused them to stop, but it wasn't the result of a firefight. It didn't matter, eventually there were Dutch and British soldiers, no Canadians yet, who indicated it was safe to move.

Robert looked around to see if there was any help from an ambulance or other vehicle. The simple answer was no, and the help that there was, was being given to people in much worse condition. There was one ambulance, but that disappeared quickly with victims. The rest were being loaded onto hand carts and then to hospital.

The group behind the street organ slowly got up and walked from behind their protection. Robert helped Saskia to her feet and supported her all the time. He was constantly looking at her to see how she was managing. His look alone asked the question, "are you still OK?" He maneuvered her in such a way that she was next to his right shoulder, so he could support her while walking. Robert took Saskia's left arm and slung it over his shoulder and round his neck, though he had to crouch in order to do this. He felt confident enough to say.

"If you can trust me, I suggest we take you home. I can take you to a hospital, but I don't know how much attention you'll get and I think we can treat you at home. If you trust me?" he repeated.

"But you're not a doctor," said Saskia, "and I have a bullet in my leg."

"Yes, I know. This is also a quick 'get to know Robert,' exercise, which you probably didn't ask for. But I once studied pharmacy, and I know enough to get you through this."

Robert looked at Saskia to see what type of response he would get, but she simply nodded. It was a 'Yes, OK' nod. A war hospital did not appeal to her.

"What about my friends?" said Saskia.

"My major concern is to get you home. Let's assume they are all OK, and you will see them again. First, you," Robert said firmly.

CHAPTER ELEVEN

They retraced their steps to the Herengracht. It was not that far, but it was slow progress while Robert half dragged Saskia as she limped along, hanging onto him. Towards the end, as they turned the corner onto the Herengracht, Robert lifted Saskia and grasped her in his arms for the last one hundred metres. It took the weight, and the pain, off her leg, which was becoming more inflamed.

"Where's your key?" Robert asked.

Saskia fumbled in one of the pockets on her patchwork skirt and found the key. Robert opened the door and took Saskia to the back of the house where he laid her down on a brown sofa close to the windows which opened onto the garden.

"The most important thing right now is water and making sure we clean you up properly."

Robert removed the temporary bandage and continued to apply pressure on the bleeding, which had still not stopped. He asked Saskia to apply the pressure while he got some warm water. This was the first opportunity that Saskia had had to look down at her injuries. It was indeed a clean entry, but it hurt. And now it was hurting more.

"The bullet is still in there," she said.

"I know," said Robert. "It's not big and I suggest we leave it there. If we try and remove it, it will probably bleed even more and we may be inviting infection. There are countless people walking around with bullets still lodged in their bodies. I suggest you join them," Robert said, trying to make light of the situation.

"Are you sure?" Saskia asked.

Robert wasn't, but he wasn't going to give her an option.

"I think this will be better. Let's clean you up, really carefully. Stem the bleeding, put antibiotics on it, if you have some?" Robert applied more pressure. He held on for much longer. He really had to stop the bleeding, otherwise he would have to take Saskia to hospital.

Saskia knew about antibiotics, but didn't have any, "Sorry, that's a luxury I don't have."

"That's OK," Robert answered. "I didn't expect so, but we'll figure something out if we can. It's not essential." he said reassuringly again, knowing that he would prefer something topical.

"Now, do you have any bandage in the house?"

"That I do have," said Saskia, almost triumphantly. "If you go to the kitchen, you will find a tin in the drawer on the right of the sink."

"Found them!" he said after he had fumbled around in the drawer.

Robert now spent time making sure the wound was spotless. Fortunately, it had been a clean shot and there was no additional debris in the wound, so he felt confident he was doing the right thing. He was taking a little liberty with his pharmacy background. This was more like mini surgery. Still, he thought he could get away without even having to do stitches. The wound looked good, and the bleeding was beginning to die down. There were bandages of sorts in the house, and they looked clean and new, but no topical antibiotics. That was a pity, but he also didn't really know if they had them in 1945. They had penicillin but he would need to go out and see if he could come by some. In the meantime, he put a compress on the wound and neatly bandaged it. He was happy with the result.

"There you go. How does that feel?" Robert asked.

"Are you sure it's alright?" said Saskia.

"It's certainly good enough for now, but we will need to keep an eye on it and keep it clean. So long as there is no infection, it's probably best to keep it like this. The bullet will become encapsulated in tissue and you won't feel it. If we try and extract it, we may run more risk of infection."

"Maybe I should go to the hospital?"

"I can take you if you like, but I really have no idea how much more they can help."

"No, we'll wait. You've done a great job. Thank you... but it still hurts like hell."

"That's to be expected. And you mustn't put any weight on it for a while," Robert added, as he pushed her leg further up on the sofa. At the same time, he got a cloth with cold water and cleaned off what was left of Saskia's fake seam.

"I don't think you'll be wanting that anymore. Your legs are just as nice without," said Robert in his first real attempt at flirtation.

"That's very forward, Mr Dekker. Er, I mean Robert."

"I know, but it's true," Robert said, and Saskia just smiled in response. She winced as she felt the throbbing get worse.

They put the radio on to see if there was any news. Nothing yet. News didn't travel as fast in 1945. If this was 2019, there would be hundreds of video feeds on social media and live news reporting. The Dam shooting was to become a major event at the end of the war and put a real damper on the celebrations. It never became exactly clear how many people died, but the hospitals would be busy.

Robert was already concluding that this Saskia was just as nice as the previous Saskia, but he was also being very calculating. He had arrived with nothing more than his clothes and his backpack. Well, and a Jeep. He had no home, no friends, no money, and no place to sleep. He was now in a house he knew well, but it looked so different. The corridor towards the back of the house was the same, but now there were separate rooms instead of the more open plan schemes of modern 2019, and it was one house, not two apartments. The rooms were dark, and each had a function. A living room, a dining room, and a kitchen. The furniture was all very functional, simple rack back chairs, a sofa, and a couple of matching seats. Saskia's sofa did at least have a bit of life in it, insofar as it was a floral pattern on a light brown textile. The rest of the house was dark: dark walls of paneled wood and wallpaper, dark eastern rugs on the floor, and a meagre, very black mantelpiece and fireplace.

Taking into account the social conventions of the time, Robert had now set his eyes on this being his temporary home until he got out of his dilemma. Although a tragedy had just occurred, Robert now saw an opportunity as Saskia's saviour. He needed to tread carefully.

Saskia suddenly said, "Do you mind making me some tea? And I'm hungry."

"That's a good sign," said Robert. "Of course." As he got up to start learning his way around the kitchen. He also retrieved his backpack and pulled out a Mars bar.

"Here. Try this for starters."

"What is this? It's so neatly packaged," Saskia said as she studied the strange object in her hand. The name Mars was totally alien to her.

"It's a chocolate bar," Robert said. "Canadian." He decided that everything he couldn't explain was Canadian.

"Go on. Try it. I assure you, you'll like it. Millions do," he added.

Saskia unwrapped the package and took a bite. "Mm. It really is good. Very sweet." She followed with a strange question for Robert.

"Where do they get so much sugar for a product like this? There is no sugar."

Robert knew what Saskia was getting at but couldn't help but say, "There's plenty of sugar in Canada."

"That's no good to us. Do you know what we've just been through here in Amsterdam? I have never known such a hard time. The winter was the worst we have ever had, little to no food, no heat, no power. Just darkness and fear. But this is wonderful, the best thing I have eaten in years. Literally, years."

The smile on her face was unmistakable. Robert wanted to know more and make good use of this time, because he was still at a loss as to exactly how bad things had been, and still were. He had not walked far, just from the Herengracht to the Dam Square and back. Just a pinprick on the map of Amsterdam, but in that short walk he had seen enough to know that it must have been hell. The most telling thing of all was how the clothes hung on people, especially the men with their way-too-baggy suits. They were like walking skeletons. Saskia, too, looked a shadow of her 2019 self.

His goal now was to secure some form of shelter on the Herengracht, and this was his only real chance of a temporary home. So, he asked, "I have obviously been too far removed from what you have been suffering. I have read about it," he lied, "but, can you tell me how you have got through."

"Really?" Saskia answered.

"Yes, I'm really interested," he said truthfully. "I mean, you're not going anywhere, are you? And I still need to get you your tea."

"Well, that will be your first challenge," said Saskia, assuming that Robert would realise what he was up against for such a simple thing as a cup of tea."

He went into the kitchen. Electric kettle, thought Robert, but he quickly dismissed that because he knew there was no power. He did find a regular kettle that goes on a stove, and he proceeded to fill that and was on automatic pilot to put it on the stove. Then he realised that wasn't going to work either; there was no gas. He took the kettle in his hand and walked into the living room, proudly holding up the kettle.

"Got stuck, did you?" said Saskia. "On top of the heater is a round burner. Use that. You'll find enough stuff to burn in the basket on the floor. There are also some matches on a shelf, or maybe you have matches."

"No. Remember, I don't smoke," Robert answered, trying to make light of the situation.

He returned to the kitchen, hoping that what Saskia had instructed made sense. He still didn't know what he was doing, but how difficult could it be to make a cup of tea? He found a round canister where she said it would be, on top of the kitchen furnace, with its flue going all the way to the roof. He was glad Saskia was in a separate room so she could not see how clumsy he was. Putting two and two together, he found that he needed to put a mix of paper and other fire-worthy wood into the burner. Once he had got it started—not without difficulty—he then put the kettle on the burner. He knew it would take a while, so briefly went back to Saskia to let her know that all was well.

It was the hardest cup of tea he had ever made. Once the water had boiled, he still had to go down the well-trodden route of sieving tea and letting it settle. It was a triumph of sorts. He was pleased with himself and presented Saskia with her cup of tea on her throne. He also poured himself one.

"Thank you. And well done," said Saskia. "Few men do that!"

"You're welcome. I'm ready."

"For what?" said Saskia.

"Oh, I had asked about how it has been here in Amsterdam. What you have had to go through."

"I'm injured! I'd forgotten. But sure. I suppose if you come from far away it's like being in a different country?" Saskia asked rhetorically. She added, "And newspapers have been almost non-existent, eh?"

Saskia went on. "Remember, I told you I worked for a women's magazine, called Libelle. Have you heard of it?

"Absolutely," said Robert. "It still exists," he added unintentionally.

"No, it doesn't. It had to close down because there was no more ink. Or paper. It was a superb job, and I had the fortune to have access to more fabrics than other people during the war. That's why this place looks a bit like a textile workshop." She pointed to her sewing machine and other attributes for making clothes.

"Yes, I had noticed. That's a very rare sight when you hear about all the shortages you must have been experiencing."

"Indeed. Well, that was my enormous advantage, and I could use it, especially this last year, to stave off the hunger everyone has been suffering. I used the cloth to trade on the black market for food. You know, the Jordaan area is our black market, so I don't have to go very far. Some women have had to resort to dangerous trips on foot—for example, with a pram, to the fields and farms in the north—just to get food. It has been absolutely awful and too many people have died unnecessarily. I have managed to live off a mixture of potatoes, cabbage and beet, and meat or cheese if you can come by it. Look at me, I used to weigh about 55 kilos, now I'm down at 47 kilos. I can't go much lower."

Robert was listening with very obvious interest. Saskia looked at him, but he simply said, "Go on."

"Well, it's not only the food shortages, but just living. There's no power, no coal, no gas, no light, nothing. And there was a curfew. You couldn't go outside and even if you did, you would be groping in the dark. Do you know it was not unusual for people to simply walk into the canal because they didn't know it was there? The newspapers were full of it at the beginning of the war, and especially the Germans who were not used to living in a city with canals. And they were often drunk. Serves them right. Did you have that in Groningen?"

Robert had to bluff. "Nothing like you. No, it was relatively peaceful. And we don't have as many canals." He didn't know if it was peaceful, but he was on solid ground saying the city had fewer canals.

"Did you see all the tram lines? The trams stopped running here a while ago, but now the only thing that keeps us going is scraps of wood, whether that's from trees, destroyed houses, or even the blocks of wood from tramlines. I hate to see my city like this. And I'm just as guilty. I too need to get wood to feed my stove."

"And the black market?" asked Robert. "What do you get from there? Do you have enough food to keep you going?" This was going to affect him as well.

"I'm alright at the moment. I have some basic food in the house, but it's not much. And, if I can't go out, then I have a bigger problem."

Robert saw his chance. "I can help you. If you'll let me."

"What can you do?" Saskia asked.

"Well, assume your role on the black market, if you point me in the right direction."

Robert didn't wait for an answer but got up to go back into the kitchen and said, on the way, "Do you mind if I take a look to see what you've got?"

Now Robert was no scout or backpack adventurer, but he thought he could at least explore to see what he could find. He was already getting genuinely hungry. He went back into the kitchen and found what was left of some potatoes and vegetables but very little cheese or meat. It was very meagre. In a cupboard, he found a big cardboard box which said "Eggs" on the outside. He opened it to see an unopened bag full of powder, which he assumed to be egg powder. He returned to Saskia, with the bag in hand.

"And this?"

"Oh, I got that from the black market. It was dropped by the English or Americans and, as always, came into the hands of someone on the black market. He sold it to me as eggs, because that's what it says, but I was obviously naïve, and in need. I don't understand what to do with it. I also got a parachute, but I know what to do with that," said Saskia, knowing that she could easily make clothes out of almost anything.

It was already past 6pm and Robert said. "Are you hungry?" And after a small pause. "Don't answer that, you need to eat. I'll make you something, from this. You still have some bread, I see."

"What are you going to do?" Saskia was not used to men cooking, but she was modern enough to think this would not be a bad idea.

"Wait and see."

Robert turned and went back to the kitchen. He had in his hands egg powder, commonly used in hotels in 2019 for the scrambled eggs at the breakfast buffet. All he had to do was mix the powder with water or milk in a pan, and he had scrambled eggs. It didn't take long. In the absence of a functioning toaster, he found a separate pan to toast the bread. The result was on the table, so to speak, in no more than ten minutes. There was a dining room table in a separate room, but Robert didn't want Saskia going anywhere so he presented it to her on a tray. He had also made a plate for himself.

"Oh my God, this is delicious! It tastes just like egg. I haven't had eggs in over six months," said Saskia.

"It's simply dried eggs in powder form. I agree, the packaging is confusing, it should say egg powder. But you can't drop eggs from a bomber and hope that they'll survive the fall," Robert said.

"I know, I know. Stupid of me."

"That is not a small package you have, so you are set for a while with something to eat. And maybe we can find some other ingredients to add for an omelet," suggested Robert as he thought of salmon, paprika, bacon, tomatoes—all things he could probably never find.

Saskia was taken aback. "What do you mean by 'we?'"

"Oh, nothing dramatic intended. But now you ask the question, I do have one for you. This wound you have is not going to go away in a day and you really have to watch it closely. I would feel guilty if you ended up with an infection and a fever. That's why I'd like to see if I can find you some penicillin—the antibiotic—to prevent the likelihood of infection. I know I know very little about you, but is there anyone here who can take care of you?"

"I'm not like many women. I like my independence."

"Yes, I know," muttered Robert under his breath without Saskia hearing.

"I live here alone now. Until last week, I had a renter who was living in my second bedroom. I wasn't particularly fond of the idea, but I needed the money, and in these days you cannot deny people a roof over their head. Because the allies were closing in on the city, he could now get out and go back to his home in the south."

"So, you've got no one to help you?" asked Robert.

"Well, I've got good neighbours. But I can look after this myself. Or are you suggesting something else?"

"Yes and no. I don't want to impose, but I also need a room and it would kill two birds with one stone if I could also maybe help you at the same time."

"What about the Canadians? Don't they look after you?"

"Yes, they can," Robert lied, "but, it's just dormitory or barrack-like accommodation and you can imagine how that is. And I don't even know where it is. Now that they are moving so fast, so too are all their moving parts."

Saskia didn't answer, because she started squealing with pain as the heavy throbbing set in. Robert looked at her, sympathy in his eyes, but couldn't do much for her. He was looking intently at her. Her profile was the same Saskia he remembered, but her look lacked the same fiery instincts. Maybe that was expressed by her hair style, which was much more static. Robert didn't really like the curls on the forehead and at the back, but most of the women he had seen today had the same style.

He moved a little closer and sat at the end of the sofa. "You alright? You've lost quite a bit of blood, so you will feel weak for a while, but we'll get you back," he said, with confidence in his voice.

"So, so. You make it difficult for me to say no to your request, eh?" said Saskia, with a smile she could just manage through the pain that was coming and going.

"Thank you. I can also check on your bandaging and clean the wound every day. And cook," he added.

"I may also have to ask you for money," she said, "but that can come later. The guest bedroom is up the stairs and on the left. I won't be able to help you, but you'll find sheets and blankets in the wardrobe in the room."

Robert didn't answer. He immediately felt uncomfortable. How was he going to pay? Tucked away in his jacket and backpack, he still had all the accoutrements of twenty-first century living, a smartphone, bank and credit cards and euros, plus miscellaneous items like a bottle of water, and energy bars—none of which would do him much good in 1945.

Robert changed tack. "Listen," he said, "I'm going to go out and see what I can do about getting some painkillers and maybe some antibiotics. Penicillin."

"Where will you go?"

"If you point me in the direction of the nearest hospital, I'll see what I can do. I'm not hopeful, but you never know."

Most Amsterdammers know where the hospitals are, but Saskia helped by saying, "Try the Prinsengracht hospital, near the Leidsestraat. Same side of the canal as I am here."

"Right," said Robert as he got up immediately to head out.

"So, you know where the Leidsestraat is?" questioned Saskia suddenly.

"Uh, no," he lied again. "I'm being too enthusiastic."

"Turn left out the door and then follow the Herengracht round until you get to the Leidsestraat. Then turn right, down to the Prinsengracht and ask someone. You'll see the hospital when you get to the Prinsengracht."

"No sweat," he answered.

"You say the strangest things sometimes."

Robert was given a key and departed. He knew exactly where he was going, so it didn't take too long. It was getting dark, and he started zig zagging his way to the Prinsengracht instead of following Saskia's instructions. It took him over a couple of canals until he got close to where he needed to be. He was passing by a small alleyway when he heard muffled screams coming from nearby. It was dark, so he could not see much, but after a while he saw the silhouette of two people scuffling. It was a man and a woman, and he ignored it, assuming it was just another part of the celebrations. He walked on, but then retraced his steps after he heard a more distinct scream, one that said,

"Help!" more than it did elation. In the poor light he also got a glimpse of a rifle slung over the man's shoulder. It wasn't being used, but it was clear that this soldier was not friendly.

Robert said to himself, "I don't need this shit." But he could not ignore it. Even if this was not war anymore, he still had a role to play.

Robert moved closer. He still couldn't see who he was going to be up against. Whoever it was was definitely smaller than him, though. Once he was within a few metres, he pounced, because he wanted to keep the element of surprise. This guy was not expecting an attack. It was easier than he thought. The soldier started to fight back, but he was no physical match for Robert.

"You're fucking German?" he said, as he took in the uniform. "What are you doing here?" He knew he wouldn't get an answer because he had started choking him. The girl he was attacking broke free and joined in the attack. She was fierce too.

Robert's anger started getting the better of him, and one heavy punch soon floored the soldier. Then, in a language the soldier clearly wouldn't understand, Robert said, "The war's ended, can't you just go home. You've done your damage."

The girl then leant towards him and said, "Mister, thank you, thank you. I'm not a prostitute, if that's what you think." She tried to explain why she might be out at such a dangerous time, "I wasn't expecting any Germans." She ran off, leaving Robert towering over the German who tried forcefully to extricate himself.

"Don't you know the war is over?" Robert said sharply as he gave him another hard punch that knocked him back to the ground, this time unconscious. Robert bent down to see how bad it was, and then kicked his rifle far away, just in case. He started checking the soldier for his possessions as he suddenly realised he might be able to find money that he could use. In the interests of haste, he decided to take everything he could see, including the contents of a leather bag

143

hanging on his belt. He had no further use for the soldier, so he left him to wake up on his own. Robert picked up the rifle and threw it with some pleasure into the canal once he had exited the alleyway.

The light was getting bad, and he wasn't sure what he had, but he walked on to the hospital. He still needed to get the medicines, if he could. Unsurprisingly, when he arrived at the hospital, the scene was like a zoo. There were just too many people, patients from the shooting waiting to be helped, and worried family members hovering around. This was going to be a battle, and Robert was not sure what his next steps would be. So, now he had a bit of light from outside the hospital, he decided to take a look and see what he had acquired from the German soldier. Wrapped in a handkerchief there was some money. "Good," he thought, old-fashioned guilders in a form he was unfamiliar with, but at least he had something. There was also a bonus in the form of some jewellery, but he didn't pay much attention to that. In the bag, he also found what appeared to be a medicine. The small package had a label that said meperidine. Robert thought he knew what it was from his time studying pharmacy but wasn't sure. And Mr Google was not around to help either.

As there were doctors milling around everywhere, he latched onto one to see if he could help. He was busy with a patient but strangely also taking a smoke break. Robert diplomatically said all he needed was help to identify the medicine. With yet another stare from the doctor at his strange clothes, he got confirmation that meperidine was a painkiller commonly carried by German soldiers, so that was a start. The penicillin would have to wait, and Robert hoped it would not even be needed, especially if he took proper care of the wound.

Robert went back the same way he came, passing the alleyway where he had left the German soldier. He could not see him anymore, so assumed he had managed to find his way home. Good he thought.

Once back on the Herengracht, and after glancing over at the other side of the canal to see the Jeep was still there, Robert let himself in through the front door and walked to the back, where Saskia was still lying, listening to the radio. There was now news about the liberation by the Canadians, and, of course, the attack on the Dam square.

"How's the patient doing?" he said.

"It's still throbbing and now I have a headache."

"I think that's to be expected, but it's a good sign, your body is fighting back. I'm going to have to wait to go back at a quieter time to see if I can find penicillin, but I do have something for your pain." Robert omitted how he came by it. He decided on a dose of two of the pills, which Saskia gratefully took.

"Tell me," Saskia started, "something I don't understand. When we were on the square you shouted, even insisted, that the Germans were there. You were right. How did you know? It's spooky."

"Have you ever heard of people who have premonitions? Not the evil types, just those that have a feeling that something is going to happen. Well, I have that sometimes. And this is not the first time." Robert was not really lying. "I became nervous, and it's only natural to get protective. But you ignored me anyway."

"I know, it just sounded so stupid. Why hadn't the Germans gone? They knew the war was over."

"I don't know. Maybe they were drunk," said Robert, recalling that might have been one of the reasons they gave for their behaviour.

"Well, I wouldn't be lying on this sofa like this if I had listened to you. But, sorry, being a bit of a nonconformist is one of my undesirable traits."

"If it's any comfort, from now on I only see good things happening. Now that the war is over, things really are going to get back to normal quite quickly. Coal, electricity, transport. And food, of course."

"That's comforting, I hope that's a premonition that will be correct. It's certainly an easier one to predict than Germans shooting."

Robert went to make some more tea for Saskia. He would kill for a beer, but the beers he saw in the morning went into the neighbour's house. When he returned, he handed her the tea and asked:

"How long have you lived here?"

"Oh, that's not really a long story. I've been in this house my whole life. I was born here and lived with my parents. That is, until they died."

"They are both dead? What happened?" Robert asked before adding, "It sounds like it was probably an accident if they are both dead."

"Yes, car crash. Before the war," said Saskia, as Robert was stunned by the déjà vu of the whole situation. History repeating itself.

"I'm sorry," he said.

"It has been a while now, but it was naturally tragic at the time. We were all very close. I was married, but my husband and I then moved here because I inherited the house. The war started and my husband went off to London as part of the Dutch resistance. I haven't heard from him since, but the British believe he died on one of their clandestine missions back to Holland. No letters, nothing, so that's what I assume happened."

"God, tragedy on top of tragedy. That's awful," said Robert, realising this was a constant in Saskia's life, no matter which time period she lived in. Robert started wondering what forces of nature might be at work to present him with someone identical to a woman from his own time.

"If we don't quickly get back to some form of normality or I cannot get a job, I can always sell the house. It's far too big for just

146

me. My parents bought it for about 17,000 guilders, so I'm sure I can get that if I had to."

Robert was silent. He was doing a quick mental calculation to work out how much the house would now be worth, and he came to something close to nearly five million guilders, or about half that in euros. If only she knew. He went on.

"Please tell me if I am asking too much, but do you have children?" asked Robert, trying to complete the circle.

"Yes, we did, one daughter. We were living elsewhere in Amsterdam then, and she was going to go to university when the war started. Now she's a nurse, somewhere in the south of Holland, in Zeeland, I think. As you can imagine, since the Canadians and British started their offensive in the country I've had no letters, so I just hope she is still alright."

"I am sure she will be, especially now that everything is coming to a happy conclusion. One day soon she will probably just appear on your doorstep," said Robert reassuringly.

"And then she can become my nurse. Instead of you."

"Don't say it that way."

"Oh, I'm so sorry. I didn't mean to be unkind. You've been very helpful. And a good nurse. But nurses aren't men, are they?"

"Oh, I think you'll be surprised. And why not, we can also be good at it."

"Yes, but you can't have men looking after women."

"And why not?" asked Robert, knowing this was going to be another dead-end conversation. He could have fun with it, but he decided against it. He was not so sure if the 1945 Saskia had the same sense of humour as the one in 2019. And the male and female roles were so set in stone that any reasonable conversation would never get off the ground. So he ended by saying, "Women treat men, so I don't see why there should be any discrimination against the man. I acknowledge, women have much more empathy, but hopefully I can show you the other side of the coin."

"That's very nice of you."

They chatted for a bit but not much later it was apparent that the strains of the day were taking their toll on Saskia, and she was ready for bed. She needed help, at least to first get to the bathroom and then to the bedroom. That meant putting weight on her leg. The bedroom was upstairs, unlike in Robert's time. The house would be split into two apartments much later.

Robert approached her and moved her torso forward so he could support her around the arms. His arm went around her waist and now that she no longer had a jacket on, he could feel her ribs. She really was severely underweight. Robert said nothing, he just handled her very carefully. He maneuvered her up the stairs, taking almost all of her weight, which was easy. Saskia pointed the way to her bedroom, which was on the right. It was a very simple bedroom with all the functional pieces in place. A double wrought iron bed, a brown mahogany wardrobe for hanging clothes, a dressing table with a fixed mirror, and a brown oak chest with three drawers. It looked remarkably familiar, as if it were the same as the one he had seen on the street, but that one went into the house next door.

Robert sat Saskia down on the bed's edge. "It's nice to have such a large bed, isn't it?" Saskia commented, not expecting the answer that came back.

"Well, it's a little too cosy for my liking. I would prefer something a lot bigger."

"Don't be stupid, they don't exist. This is what every married couple has. It's fine... But you are very tall, so you may have a point."

Robert didn't pursue it any further. He guessed the bed was an old standard, 1.4 metres in width and not very long. He was used to 1.8, if not more. Not that he was planning anything, but he knew he would never fit the length of the bed, because the wrought iron at the foot would be in the way.

"Robert. Thanks very much for your help. I can manage from here. I'm doing well."

"Understood. I'll just go and get you some water and some more of the meperidine, in case you need it in the night."

"See, you are a good nurse," Saskia said as Robert closed the door and disappeared downstairs. On returning, he neatly knocked on Saskia's door, and when he entered she was already nearly ready. She had a long nightgown, but still had her skirt on underneath. Robert set the water and pills down and wished her a good night.

"Don't forget. I am next door. If you are in need of any help, just shout. Loud! And, there's a wonderful moon out there, which you may just be able to see from your bed"

"I did see it, it's beautiful. I wonder what someone would see and think if they could be on the moon. We'll never know."

"Don't count on that. One day," said Robert, and he could not resist, "One small step for man, one giant leap for mankind."

"Eh, what's that?" said Saskia.

"Just imagining what someone might say if man ever stepped foot on the moon." Followed by "Goodnight."

The night was uneventful. Robert slept well and didn't hear from Saskia at all. A good sign.

CHAPTER TWELVE

Morning follows night, and both Robert and Saskia were up early. Well, Robert was. Saskia felt well, but putting weight on her leg was still painful and she needed continued help. In the absence of the ability to bathe properly, Saskia gave herself a bird bath and then managed to dress in the same clothes as she had on yesterday. She seemed optimistic that she would be able to go out again in her festive clothes to enjoy the day of celebrations. Everyone was expecting today to be the day that the Canadians would really arrive in Amsterdam.

Robert, on the other hand, took one look at his twentieth century clothes and decided he needed to dress down a bit. But how?

He found a wardrobe in his room which was full of a man's clothing—mainly suits and separate trousers and jackets. There were also some shirts. All white. He pulled a few of them out and not to his surprise realised he would be hard pushed to fit into any of them. But since he was visiting a time when no one was the least interested in men's fashion, he figured he could force himself into something just so he didn't stand out like a mannequin in a shop window. Since it was a warmish day, Robert had compromised and gone for a white shirt and a short-sleeved pullover with a motif in the middle. The pullover neatly hid the tight shirt. It was short and came to just above his waist, but then so too did the pullovers of most other men he had seen the previous day. He had to wear the same jeans because he would never fit into any of the trousers. The result was not appealing, and Saskia laughed when she saw the result for the first time.

"Why did you do that? I like your unusual clothes," she asked.

"I wanted to blend in more. But, I agree, it won't last long as they are a really tight fit. I hope you don't mind. I assume they were your husband's?"

"Yes, and no. Umm… yes they are my husband's, and no, I don't mind. As you can see, he was a bit smaller than you."

Robert was pleased to see that Saskia was in a good mood and clearly on the mend.

Although they were at the back of the house, with the windows open, they could hear the growing crescendo of sound coming from people moving out of their houses and onto the streets. There was more expectation in the air. And it was only 7.30am.

"Why don't you go and see what's going on?" offered Saskia, who was rooted to a chair in the kitchen.

Without replying, Robert headed down the corridor to the front door. He was also curious. As he exited the door onto the top porch, he could see that this was not a normal morning. There were so many people on the canal heading towards the central station which was not far away. Clearly, like the early part of yesterday, everyone was in high spirits and looking forward to what the day would bring.

Robert leant over the railing and asked the first passerby where the action was. No one knew exactly, but the man he asked produced a copy of *Het Parool* newspaper and showed him the headline. It read something like this: "They are coming today. According to reliable sources, we can expect the allied forces to arrive at the Holland fortifications." Whether or not it was right didn't matter. There was clearly momentum in the city and Robert wanted to be a part of it. Momentarily, he was putting his own personal dilemma aside; he wanted to be a part of history.

He returned to Saskia and explained what he saw. The glint in her eye told the same story. She did not want to be left out. But how? The challenge was obvious. She could not walk easily and certainly not for a long period of time.

"I am coming," Saskia said abruptly.

"We'll see. I'm not so sure that is a good idea. You are going to aggravate the injury even more if you put weight on it. And this is not a walk in the park. You cannot stay on your feet all day long."

"I know. But first, give me a couple more of your pills to start with. And I have an idea."

"Yes, madame," Robert shot back as he gave her a couple more meripidine.

"If you go into the garden, there is a shed at the back. In there, you'll find an old wheelbarrow. I plan to be today's luggage."

"And who, pray, is the luggage boy. The one who is going to be doing the pushing?"

"I'm sorry, I should be more grateful and less demanding. I already owe you a lot and now I'm asking you to push me around for what will be the best part of a day."

"That's OK. I don't want to miss it either. And it would also be nice for me for you to be a part of it," Robert added. He sensed he was getting closer to the new Saskia.

They first had some breakfast, again scrambled eggs and bread, reinforced by tea. No coffee in sight. That would see them through a large part of the day, but they also prepared some sandwiches from old bread with a berry jam for later in the day.

Robert then went down the rickety wooden steps from the kitchen into the back garden, one of the hidden treasures to be found behind houses on the Herengracht. They were never visible from the front, but almost every house had a large garden, by city standards; Saskia's house was no exception. The garden itself was scruffy and untidy, but that was to be expected in a time of war. Robert headed towards the shed at the end and opened the door. Pushing old spider webs aside, he entered a decidedly unused part of the property, but he could see a wheelbarrow. His eyes rolled as he took in a large, clunky, wooden wheelbarrow with remarkably heavy looking sides, thick arms, and a wooden wheel at the front. The sum total of everything he saw was enough to make him moan. Why didn't they invent aluminium earlier? He instantly knew this was going to be heavy work.

Robert maneuvered the barrow back to the house, up the stairs and out to the front of the house. Once there, he gave it a good clean with a brush, because it had clearly not been used in a while. After a time, they were ready for the day, one which would prove to be very special for everyone in Amsterdam.

Robert took his time to help Saskia from her kitchen chair to the front, down the stairs, and gently into the wheelbarrow. The last part looked like a piece of a pantomime as Robert first loaded Saskia into the barrow, at which point she yelled.

"Cushions!"

Robert went into the house and grabbed what he could that would make Saskia more comfortable in her wooden cockpit. Cushions were thin on the ground, so he also took some of her ex-husband's clothes and turned them into comfortable rolls. Passersby were also amused by the whole scene, and Saskia took the opportunity to show off her wounds and explain what had happened the previous day.

"Time to roll," said Robert as soon as all was ready.

He lifted the wheelbarrow, which now included the weight of the barrow itself and Saskia. While Saskia was certainly not heavy, after five metres he already said to himself, "Jesus. This is heavy going." He was probably also going to need gloves to avoid splinters, even if it was warm.

The pantomime continued as he returned to the house on the hunt for gloves. The ones he found were on the small side.

While Robert was doing all of this, he surveyed the growing number of people on the canal and suddenly had a thought. He still had his mobile with him in his backpack. It was naturally absolutely useless in 1945 as a telephone or smartphone, but it still had a camera. He had turned his mobile off, but now he had the urge to use the camera to record whatever might happen today. He saw that he still had some juice; if he managed the battery well, he could make some use of it. He even thought he might be able to rig something to make his charger work from the power socket, but that would be for later. Discretely he put his mobile in his pocket; he knew he would also have to use the camera discretely.

Robert resumed his duties and started pushing a smiling Saskia in the direction of the city centre. He looked more the part today, but his low hanging and tight jeans were in stark contrast to the mass of baggy khaki and grey woolen trousers with high waist bands. To a certain extent, his pullover covered that, but he still stood out. It didn't help that he was so much taller than almost everyone else.

"Where are we going?" asked Robert. "Just following everyone else?"

"I am not going back to the Dam square," said Saskia. "The memories are too fresh. Why don't we head to the Post Office? That will be much more of a vantage point, as the troops are likely to go that way at some point. Apart from the bars, the Post Office is the beating heart of a city."

"Post Office. That's almost a relic of the past." thought Robert to himself. He had never really known a dedicated Post Office, at least not in recent years.

"You point the way you want to go," said Robert, surreptitiously trying to get advice on where exactly the Post Office was. In fact, it was in what is now called Magna Plaza, a magnificent neo gothic building which had since been turned into an exclusive boutique shopping centre. The building was just as magnificent in 1945, but served as a Post Office. The interior smelled of bureaucracy, with the many counters serving customers wanting to send letters, packages, and more. All Robert needed was confirmation that Magna Plaza was the place to go, but Saskia would have no idea what that name meant.

"To the Nieuwezijds Voorburgwal," said Saskia.

That was enough for Robert. He knew where that was. Street names don't change that often, unless you are an out of favour dictator.

As they progressed over the canals and streets, the crowds just grew and grew. Everyone was in a party mood, dressed in their best—lots of orange—waving flags, music, all in anticipation of the arrival of the Canadians, and some British troops. As they walked down the Spuistraat, Robert could see people stopping and staring. But at what? As they got closer, he could make out two girls being forced to sit up against a wall in full view of the partying masses walking by. They had had their heads shaved, and they were tarred. Their shame was clear to see. They were now victims of the locals, who had no respect for girls fraternising with Germans. They were paying a heavy price. Robert wondered how something like that would go down in contemporary life.

They moved on, finally reaching the Post Office area close to the Dam square. It was busy, really busy. Everyone was happy. There was an oversupply of hugs and kisses. As Robert wheeled Saskia along, she was very animated, holding both hands out to passersby and occasionally accepting a kiss. Robert was also tempted to give her a kiss, but resisted. He confined his admiration to looking at her for long periods of time. Something which Saskia noticed.

Robert couldn't help but see that some people around him were on crutches. Perhaps not surprising if there has been a war going on. All he was thinking was, "That's what I need, for Saskia. Then I wouldn't have to push this dead weight around." He knew that was an inappropriate and passing thought.

Saskia was relatively comfortable, but the very nature of a wheelbarrow is that the front is steeper than the back, so she had to sit facing Robert instead of towards where all the action was. She didn't mind, because he was worth looking at too. Still, this was a day in history to be remembered, and she wanted to see it all. Robert used his "patient" as an excuse to push through the crowds to the front. He was surprised how accommodating they all were; he didn't see that happening so easily in 2019. There were so many people, yet the discipline was remarkable, and the crowds still left room for a clear passage for the troop convoys. Occasionally, waves of people moved back and forth to get a good glimpse, a bit like a Mexican wave at a football match.

"Excuse me," said Saskia. "I am still facing backwards."

Robert had maneuvered Saskia to the front, but she was still facing him. So he had to do a full 180-degree turn with the barrow to get her to where she wanted to be. That meant more pushing, but the immediate neighbours realised what he was doing and were very accommodating.

"This is not the best place to be. Down here," said Saskia, but I am so pleased we are here. And I have a bullet in me to prove that I'm part of the war too."

In the distance they could hear elevated cheering. Something was happening, and it was coming their way. But it was all painfully slow. Now Saskia was facing away from Robert, he pulled out his mobile so he could at least take some pictures. He mostly did this from waist level, so it didn't raise questions, and he occasionally managed a few using the view finder. No one said anything, but he did get a couple of strange looks. He already had an answer ready, just in case he was asked. A mirror, of sorts, since his mobile had a silver back cover.

Slowly but surely, the first of the trucks, Jeeps and armour started to come into view, but no soldiers. At least that's what it looked like. The vehicles were simply overloaded with Amsterdammers who had climbed onto them in their excitement to be a part of the parade. When they came, some soldiers, for their part, were walking, and that gave them the opportunity to shake hands, kiss, and hug anyone and everyone as they passed by. Saskia could do little more than wave from her wheelbarrow, but she wasn't at a loss for attention from some of the soldiers. A hug here and a kiss there; and there were plenty of cigarettes and chocolates being handed out by the troops. A real scarcity in those days.

Robert admired the attention she received from a distance and then decided that he, too, wanted to be part of the action. He leant down and gave Saskia—at least this Saskia—her first kiss. It was on the lips, and brief. Saskia smiled as Robert simply said, "I am not going to be left out of the action."

It had been a long wait for the heart of the parade, but no one minded, and the day was still young. It would go on for hours yet, but after a while Saskia started feeling the pain in her leg getting worse as the painkillers wore off.

"Robert... Did we bring the painkillers with us?"

Robert liked the "we" part of the question, but his answer was not reassuring.

"Oh shit. No, I forgot to do that. Is the pain getting bad?"

"Yes, I can feel it getting worse. Maybe it's the way I'm sitting, if you can call this sitting."

Robert bent down to take a look under her bandage, He could see no sign of any growing infection. He also felt to see if she was showing any signs of a fever. Also no.

"I think I've seen enough, don't you?" he said. "Let's go home and find some more of the meperidine. It wouldn't surprise me if you are also feeling tired."

Robert pushed his way back out of the crowds and was relieved to get away. As he did so, a woman touched him on the arm and asked.

"Do you have a light?'

"What's a lig…" Robert began, and then realised what was being asked. The woman was holding a cigarette in her hand, but not holding it up to her face, so Robert didn't immediately make the connection. This was such a common question for then, but Robert couldn't remember a time in his life when he had been asked that question. It went to show how things can change.

Robert replied, "I'm very sorry. No, I don't have one."

"Every man carries a light!" the woman replied and turned her attention to other men in the crowd.

Even though it was warm, Robert put his gloves back on for the return journey. They retraced their steps, eventually getting onto the Herengracht canal. As ever, it was uneven, and the wheelbarrow bounced and wobbled with each sudden movement. Suddenly there was a little squeal from Saskia.

"Ouch… Ouch, ouch." She shifted her body a little to reduce the identifiable pain.

"Your leg?" said Robert.

"No. Splinter."

"We're nearly there. Look at that in a minute," responded Robert.

As they reached the house Robert helped Saskia up the stairs and along the corridor to the back of the house. He then went back for the wheelbarrow, cursing heavily that it probably weighed more than Saskia and was considerably less attractive.

"OK, what's first, meperidine or the splinter?"

"Splinter first. But I think I can do it. No, I know I should do it. It's on my bottom. I need to go to the toilet, anyway. If you can just help me."

Robert supported her to the toilet and left her. After a while, she shouted that she was ready.

"Not much luck with the splinter. I can still feel it. I can't even see where it is, so getting it out is difficult."

Robert then took control, which took Saskia by surprise, but she had little choice. She was standing up, supporting herself against the door.

"Just bear with me. It'll be out in a minute."

It wasn't. Robert lifted Saskia's skirt, revealing more expansive underwear than he was used to. He could not really see the splinter because the light was so bad. He took her to the windows by the back and tried again. This time it was better, as he could now pinpoint the telltale sign of wood in skin. The only problem was that it was embedded, so he had to grab a needle and break the skin in order to get to it. Like anyone winning the battle with a splinter, the result was always the same—with some pride, showing the patient the results of their endeavours.

"There you go." Robert showed Saskia a small sliver of wood on the end of his finger.

"I owe you another thank you... but you got to see more of me than I would have liked."

"Oh. I think we are both old enough to be able to handle that, don't you think?" Robert was fishing but got no response. More importantly, he had just had the perfect opportunity to have a good look at the left cheek of Saskia's beautiful bum. There was the small birthmark that he was looking for. But how could that be? He didn't have an answer.

Robert then gave Saskia more of the pills for the pain and they settled down to take in the rest of the day, and to enjoy each other's company. They had found a bit of a rhythm together in the short period of time they had met. This came as no surprise to Robert because he thought he was back in familiar territory. But this Saskia had all the hallmarks of the attitudes and culture of the times, so he had to tread carefully. Very carefully.

More importantly, Robert wanted to get back to his real life. But he still didn't know how. Apart from the obvious cultural mismatch between the decades, Robert's major concern was his insulin supply. He had his backpack, but all of the new supply of insulin was now left behind in his old car. He had two pens containing long and short working insulin. That was all he had to keep him alive.

Put simply, Robert worked out that if things went on like this, his life would be in serious peril after just a few weeks. He remembered now that insulin existed in 1945, but this was war time, and he did not know where or how he could even come by some. Then there was the needle. Robert had become used to injecting himself with insulin by way of the so-called insulin pen with its miniscule needle. He thought of it as a nano-needle, since you barely notice it when injecting yourself, and it made managing diabetes very tolerable. If Robert even managed to get hold of insulin now, in 1945, he would not have the same choice of insulin, and he certainly wouldn't have the same needles. It would be an old-fashioned syringe with a monster of a needle. He actually feared for his life, but he had no one to talk to about it.

When evening rolled around, Robert made a dinner from what he could find in the fridge: again, the egg powder, and what was left of the bread and cheese. Just before they sat down, Saskia surprised him and said that there was a bottle of sherry at the back of one of the kitchen cabinets.

"Sherry," thought Robert. "Who drinks that?

"Now you tell me!" he said.

He grabbed the sherry and poured two glasses. He felt more relaxed, and this time dinner was uninterrupted, as Saskia was feeling fine and clearly on the mend. This allowed them to explore more about each other, but for Robert it was still a tame conversation. He was hoping Saskia would be a bit more open about herself. The conventions of 1945 had other ideas.

"Your Jeep is still on the other side of the canal. Don't you need to be doing something with it? After all, it's not yours, and I assume the Canadians need it," Saskia began, as she started to probe a little further into this mysterious man who was now in her life.

"I'll move it tomorrow," he answered, without knowing exactly what he was going to do. "The Canadians won't be missing it, because they gave it to us for our own activities, so I'm not beholden to them on that count."

"So, where do you think you're going to go when things settle down? What are you going to do now? I mean, you're not staying here forever, and you have a home to go to, somewhere!"

Robert had to think on his feet. He wanted to exit 1945, but he also knew that this Saskia was his best protection for now.

"You're absolutely right. At some point I will have to get back."

Saskia interrupted quickly, "Get back to what?"

"Well, I told you that Groningen was my home. Before the war I was busy with pharmacy and that's what I would get back to. But there's no rush. Everything has come to a standstill, but there will come a time that I need to see how I can help there. Right now, I don't have a schedule, so I'd like to help you get better. After all, you need someone to support you. I mean, literally. There are no crutches to be had anywhere! It's me and the wheelbarrow."

161

"That's nice of you. But I don't know you. You just turned up off the street and no one introduced you. That makes me uncomfortable—though, as I said, you have been very kind, so far."

"I guess in a time of war, there has to be more trust. Nothing is the way it was, and you run the risk of people like me just turning up in your life."

"You are sarcastic."

"I know, it's the nature of the beast."

"I've never heard that expression before."

"It's from… It's something I picked up and means that you are what you are. You and I are both what we are, the nature of our own beast, and we cannot really change what we are. Yes, bit and pieces here and there, but the core of it resides in our DNA and how we were brought up."

"DNA?"

"Deoxyribonucleic acid… Oh, forget that. It's a pharmacy thing, a bit complicated to understand," said Robert as he yet again had to unwind himself from something so common to our thinking now. DNA hadn't been discovered for a while yet, and even when it had been, half the world didn't understand it.

Saskia resumed her interrogation. "Still, how do I explain you to my friends? I cannot have another man in my house, especially as I am single. At least, I think I am."

"A lodger?" suggested Robert, "Especially in a time of war."

"That can work for a while, but you are going to have to leave soon."

Robert looked intently at Saskia as she said that. His disappointment was obvious.

"That doesn't mean I don't like you, and that I'm not grateful. I am. I just don't know how to explain this."

"Why do you have to?"

"Isn't it obvious to you? You don't just move into someone's house and live with them after a couple of days!"

"Oh, you'd be surprised."

"What's that supposed to mean?"

"Nothing. I just think that there's more that goes on behind closed doors than you might think."

"This is becoming uncomfortable for me. To anyone else, let's just agree that you are a lodger. But only until I get better and can do everything again for myself. I've managed for the last few years, so I don't see why I cannot do it again. Right now, I'm a little hindered!"

"Indeed, and that reminds me, we need to change your dressings before bed. And tomorrow, since I have a vehicle, I am going to take the Jeep outside town on a hunt for something healthier to eat than bread and eggs."

Saskia changed tack completely:

"Today is such a momentous day, so let's at least toast that." Robert did the right thing and looked into Saskia's eyes as they toasted, and Saskia continued, "And what do you think is going to happen now we are at peace, or at least we will be when the Germans are completely defeated? It will take forever for us to get back on our feet. There has just been too much suffering and almost total destruction."

"Oh, I think you'll... well, be surprised. We are a resilient folk and very industrious," Robert said, but he was struggling to keep track of the right context and verb tense, because he had to put himself in the now. Nevertheless, he could not resist making a few very certain predictions, if only to see what the response might be.

"Don't forget, we are not alone. The allies will come to our aid, especially financially, and it will be much easier to build up an economy if you have already been in hell. There is only one way: up. The growth will come, both industrial and social, but it will take time. Houses will be built, factories will be built, and cars will become the norm for most families. Roads will take you from city to city in no time at all. For example, why not Amsterdam to Rotterdam in less than an hour?"

"Are you mad?"

"No. I am perhaps a little more optimistic than you. I would go so far as to say that one day you could fly between Amsterdam and New York in less than four hours. Why not? You never know. And… Why not a man on the moon?"

"Why not a woman, since you are already being crazy?"

"Why not indeed?"

"And I suppose you are going to tell me that we find cures for every type of disease."

Robert decided he would back off a bit, so answered, "It wouldn't surprise me that we make huge strides, but not everything can be cured. We will all start getting much older, so we will be going to meet our maker a bit later."

"You are a real optimist, aren't you? And you always seem to know a lot, but it won't wash with me. I guess some of your ideas will become reality, but really!"

"Let's see," Robert replied. He was seriously contemplating telling Saskia that he was from the future and didn't belong here. It would make him feel better, but he was afraid that would scare her even more. He kept quiet.

164

They poured more sherry and continued chatting into the evening. Robert started noticing that Saskia was becoming quieter and less animated, so he broke the impending silence and said, "Let's see about that dressing of yours."

She remained in her seat and Robert put her leg onto a stool. He then removed the old dressing. It all still looked pretty good, but there were signs of some redness on the edges of the wound. But he didn't worry about it. He cleaned it up again and put some fresh bandage on the wound.

"How do you feel?" Robert asked.

"Pretty good. I can feel it, there's no question about that. It throbs constantly."

"OK. Let's give you another pill for the pain and maybe you should go to bed."

Robert and Saskia repeated the same process as the night before and they went their separate ways after Robert had helped Saskia to bed. Robert slept peacefully, and so did Saskia. At least to begin with. During the night, or rather the early morning, she was starting to sweat and showed signs of a fever. As best she could, she called through the doors and walls for Robert's help. He responded almost immediately and went into Saskia's bedroom to see her looking very different from the night before; she was pale, sweating, and feeling bad. He immediately knew what that meant. Infection.

He pulled back the covers and inspected the wound under the bandages. It was turning nasty, but all he could do at this stage was help keep it clean, provide more pain killers and keep her hydrated.

"I'm afraid it's started turning on you and there is a bit of an infection. It doesn't look too bad… I know that's no comfort to you, but we need to keep a close eye on it."

Saskia managed some humour and a bit of a smile as she said, "I guess you did this. So you could stay longer."

Robert smiled back with sympathy in his eyes and gently ran the outside of his fingers against her cheek and forehead.

'Mmm… that's nice. It's cool."

Robert then started gently massaging Saskia's eyelids, something that his "real" Saskia loved.

"Even better," said Saskia, as she warmed to the attention she was getting.

"Alright. Change of plan," announced Robert, authoritatively. "First, I'll get you a tea and something to eat. And then, I'll go in hunt of some penicillin."

Robert did exactly that. He was going to go on a hunt round hospitals to see if he could somehow get hold of penicillin without having to take Saskia to a doctor. He didn't really know, but that would be his starting point.

He went back to his bedroom, got dressed into what could only be described as a hybrid of clothes. He had to wear his tan jacket, because he simply couldn't fit into anything else, as well as his jeans. He put all the money he had, including his faithful old coin, into a side pocket of his backpack and in saying goodbye to Saskia, said, "May I?"

The "May I" was said as he very obviously leant in her direction to give her a kiss.

"I suppose, if you feel it is necessary," she said sarcastically.

"See, you can be sarcastic too," replied Robert as he gave her a quick peck on the lips, and left.

Robert walked down the Herengracht and crossed the first bridge and then back to his Jeep. It had clearly been used as a rubbish bin because it was full of the remnants of empty cigarette boxes and chocolate wrappings. He thought to himself, "I guess nothing changes."

Robert jumped into the Jeep, almost as if he was used to it. He switched the power button back on and heard the faint sound of a battery coming to life. He then tried to move the switch further, naturally thinking that this would start the Jeep. There was no "further."

"Shit," he thought. "Now what."

He looked around in the cockpit for something obvious, but nothing stood out. He pulled on the choke lever, which controlled the richness of the fuel, but that was obviously not right. He was flailing now, concentrating on the dashboard, the only real reference point for a starter. After what seemed like ages, he moved his attention to the sides of his seat and the middle of the vehicle. Still nothing. He then moved his head lower so he could see under the dashboard and found a foot button to the right of the throttle, but still a little hidden. That must be it. It was, but he had never come across a vehicle that you start with your foot.

After a few attempts, Robert got some life into the engine and then proceeded to give himself a quick hands-on lesson in driving something alien to him. In short, he had to just drive it. All the pedals were in the right place, as was the gear stick, but it was a monster to handle as he went through the gears. He decided not to go to the same hospital he tried last time, but he knew of one in the East of the city near the Tropical Museum. At least, in 2019 it was the Tropical Museum. He didn't know what it was now.

With some stuttering, he managed to negotiate his way to the Lineausstraat, where he had set his sights on the old Burger Hospital, which he thought might be easier. He parked the Jeep prominently in the front so they could see the Canadian markings and made his way to the hospital pharmacy. It turned out to be much easier than he thought. It was war, so he sold them on the idea that he was a doctor in need of antibiotics for a gunshot wound. Robert was used to antibiotics as a regimen of different bacterial treatments, but in 1945 the name penicillin was the gold standard. And really the only one. Matters were helped by the fact that the pharmacy told Robert they had a surplus of penicillin because the Canadians had come marching in with stocks to help them. Robert was surprised and elated and left before they could change their minds.

He put the penicillin in his backpack, climbed into his metal horse, and drove back the way he came. He would leave the hunt for food until later. First, he needed to get the treatment back to Saskia.

Robert was once again on the Brouwersgracht and heading towards the Herengracht. This time he would park outside Saskia's house, but he still had to cross the bridge to get onto the Herengracht. Without a single thought to the bridge and little to no traffic, he sped over the top in second gear, when suddenly he felt another jolt and a temporary blackout.

When he came to, he found himself staring at the back of a horse's head, holding a pair of reins in his hands from the front seat of a carriage. The horse was not moving, so they were motionless at the bottom of bridge.

Robert put his head in his hands. "What the fuck now!" he cried out to himself. "This is not happening to me. Not again. It can't be."

PART IV

The Eel Riots

CHAPTER THIRTEEN

Robert knew immediately he was in yet another time period. But what, when? "Who is picking on me like this?" he thought. "It's not fair."

Robert tried to calm himself. He faced the immediate problem of negotiating a horse and carriage away from the bridge and, hopefully, not into the canal. He was uncomfortable around horses, but at least he was not on one. He looked around. There were people in the distance, but no one in the vicinity. He quickly took in the immediate surroundings of the inside of his new form of transportation. He had seen plenty of pictures of carriages. This one was functional, with four equal sized wheels, an olive-green wooden body frame and a simple bench seat covered in black leather. It was open to the elements, much like the Jeep.

Now he looked at his horse. He, or she, looked friendly enough and was showing signs of restlessness, so he figured he should probably see if it would move forward. Robert was only planning to go a short way and then stop and take better stock of the situation. Déjà vu, as it were.

The reins were already fairly loose, so he waved them a bit and made a noise that came as close as possible to what a cowboy might make when he wanted to get his horse to go. Robert had seen a few westerns. It worked, and the horse moved forward, faster than Robert would have liked. It didn't take much time for him to start feeling uncomfortable again. He pulled on the reins, just a bit, but there was little reaction from the horse, so he pulled some more, and more, until he came to a stop.

Robert had no intention of staying in the carriage. He jumped out, holding the reins as he walked in front of the horse. He wanted to make it clear to his four-footed acquaintance that they were taking a break and going nowhere. As they were still in the middle of the canal street, he led the horse and carriage a little to the side. He wondered if it was really necessary, since there was so much room. Now, he could take things in.

Robert slumped against the carriage. He was in the same spot as he had been with the Jeep, on the Herengracht canal, and opposite Saskia's house. He could see it from where he was, and it looked more or less the same. There weren't as many trees, but for some reason they looked friendlier, as if to say "There is no war here." They were also younger, which made sense. This was clearly a different time, not a car in sight.

One thing was certain. Robert now felt the guilt welling up inside him as he realised he had abandoned the 1945 Saskia, albeit unintentionally. To his surprise he found himself wondering if he could get back to help her. If there was to be any time travel, his priority would be getting back to 2019. "If I could make a stop on the way in 1945 that would also be OK," he thought.

Robert was deep in thought about his new predicament. He looked back at where he came from and stared intently at the bridge. "Could it be?" he thought.

It occurred to him that this was now the third time he had crossed that bridge and been thrown back in time. Three times. It had to be something to do with the bridge. "Surely," he thought. He threw his backpack into the carriage and walked back towards the bridge, where he paused before walking up to the apex. He continued over the top, not knowing if that meant anything. Nothing happened. He saw nothing and felt nothing.

Robert became a little nervous, but he chose to walk back over the bridge again and head towards his horse and carriage. Again, nothing happened. Once he had arrived, he gave his horse of unknown sex a gentle pat on the head. Now what?

He sat for a while on the side of the canal. He glanced around to take in a little more, but now he was paying more attention to the people—not that there were many. It was relatively early in the morning. He was still clothed in what he had put on in the morning to go to the hospital, and it was already clear that this made him stand out in whatever time period this was. He knew he was on the Herengracht, so it was perhaps inevitable that the residents were well to do and well dressed, which was what he could see.

Robert had no choice but to stop the first person who passed by.

"Excuse me. Am I on the Herengracht?" he asked, wanting to get a bit of a conversation going.

"Yes, this is the Herengracht. What are you looking for?" said a gentleman who was walking by. He was extremely well-dressed in a smart black jacket and contrasting dark grey trousers. The jacket was well cut and came down to a level between his knee and hip. He wore a black hat and carried a narrow cane, not exactly a walking stick.

Robert answered, "Well, I was looking for number 85, but now I see some numbers here, I think I am in more or less the right place."

"Indeed, Sir. You will need to be on the other side. This side is even numbers only, so you are not far away."

"Thank you," said Robert, and he continued. "I am visiting, so I will walk my carriage over there and see where I can leave it."

"Why don't you drive it? And there are plenty of coach houses in the area if you are looking for one."

Robert had not yet got as far as thinking about coach houses, but it made sense. How do you "park" a horse and cart, especially when you know nothing about horses? He would indeed have to consider that, but first he had to answer this kind gentleman.

"Oh, I think my horse is tired enough and the walk will be good," Robert replied, as he was not going to risk riding a form of transport he had no affinity with.

Robert still didn't know if he was actually going to go to the house, but he was tempted. There was no sign of life. But again, there was very little sign of life anywhere. He decided on one thing. He did not need or want the horse and carriage, at least not now. He was tempted to just leave his new friend on the side of the canal. He was sure someone would look after it. But he might need transport in the future, and he figured he had better keep what he already had. Time to see what he could arrange.

Robert started walking down the Herengracht towards the next bridge. As he reached it, he was naturally looking all around at signs that might tell him more about when he had landed. He still didn't see cars, just a few horses, and horses and carriages. It was still relatively early. He was about to turn over the bridge when he looked right into the small cross street. It was full of what looked to Robert like garage doors, but they were all open. There was a hive of activity involving horses and carriages. Stable boys were busy with cleaning out the "garages" and polishing the carriages, presumably for their owners on the Herengracht. "Bingo," he thought. "Maybe I can get help here."

He changed his plan and turned into the small street. He struck up a conversation at the very first coach house, where they immediately asked him if he was looking to stall his horse and carriage. Robert didn't even need to enquire. They did not ask for any money, at least not now. This was the gentleman's quarter, and these men were good for their money, even if Robert still looked odd in his mix of clothes. He was grateful for that, because he didn't know if the money from the German he had in his backpack was any good now. He doubted it, but he would cross that bridge when he came to it.

Unlike the other gentlemen, Robert had no hat to tip, so he lowered his head as he departed, replacing the tip with a mimic's version of the same.

Now he was free of his horse and carriage and could recover it if necessary, Robert crossed the bridge and headed over the Herengracht canal. He looked towards the house he knew so well.

He did think about going to the house, but changed his mind. First, he wanted to know where he was, in time that is. He knew exactly where he was geographically, but now was the time for exploration and discovery. He decided to head towards the centre of the city, heading back to the Dam square where he was just a couple of days ago, in his universe that is. There should be more going on there. He was not wrong.

As he arrived at the Post Office, the roads started opening up in front of him and suddenly it was busier on the streets. In his terms, it wasn't all that crowded, but there were enough people going about their business. The Post Office building looked majestic and stood out far more than it did in 2019, because there was nothing in the way of clutter impeding access.

Men, women, and children were milling around. A clear image was now emerging of the difference between the well-dressed and others. The smarter men all had hats and were similarly dressed in long jackets. Others wore shorter jackets and worker caps. There were not many women. The ones that were there wore dresses or skirts pushed up at the back in a bustle. They also wore hats, but naturally with more flair and colour.

Still no cars, so Robert guessed that he had arrived in the nineteenth century. From where he stood, the main form of transport was the same as he had arrived in, horse and carriage, at least in this part of the city. There were also bikes, but they were very different for a city known for its bikes. Some were traditional in shape, with two equal sized wheels, but he also saw a couple of Penny Farthings; the type of bike where the front wheel was about four times bigger than the tiny rear wheel, and it was like mounting a horse in order to ride it.

There were also plenty of two-wheeled vendor carts which were used like very large wheelbarrows and transported anything from fruit, vegetables, meat, textiles, you name it. He even saw one that looked like a hearse. There was no need to look either way to cross the large road because there was no traffic, but Robert did this out of habit. He then passed on into the Dam square, a place he knew well. It was a different world.

Now there were trams, running east to west over the square, all drawn by horse, or rather two horses, if the trams were of the heavy variety. Robert just stood there and took in and admired what he saw. This was presumably sometime during the industrial revolution, when everything in Amsterdam was turning a big corner, and industry was giving people a new lease of life. It wasn't war-torn 1945. At least that was how it looked, but Robert knew he was in the heart of the city, not the suburbs, where it may well be very different. He looked intently at the trams, which had roofs but were open to the elements on the sides. The ones he was looking at could accommodate maybe 20 people and looked very heavy. He wondered how just two horses could pull such a weight.

He recognised the general layout of the Dam square, but it still looked very different. The royal palace was there, and the church, but what stood out was the monumental building where, in 2019, a well-known department store stood. Robert stared. It was the type of building that did not belong in Amsterdam. This looked more like Rome. It was a grand building with steps leading up to it and four monumental pillars gracing the entrance. On either side of the pillars were thick walls for the building and not a window in sight. Robert thought he ought to know what this was, but he didn't. He would clearly have to start asking questions again. He needed to anyway because he also wanted to know the date.

There was more bustle on the square now, with everyone looking very smart. He approached a small group, probably a family, and asked them.

"Good morning," he started. "I am visiting Amsterdam and wondered if you could help me."

"And a good morning to you as well," came the reply, but everyone was looking at the way Robert was dressed.

"My name is Robert, and I am from Groningen. What an impressive building you have there." Robert pointed to the Romanesque structure. "I didn't know Amsterdam had anything like that, and we certainly don't have anything like that in Groningen."

"Well, Mr Robert. You didn't give us your surname. Don't you have one?"

Robert was taken aback, but then understood that it was just something you didn't do in this time. Your full name was expected.

"Oh, I am sorry, Robert Dekker."

"Well, Mr Dekker, the building there is called the Exchange, and it is the place where traders and dealers meet to arrange deals and transactions. It is very unattractive, don't you think?"

"No, actually, I think it gives the Dam Square a regal presence, as if this were the place to be in the city."

"Well, my friend, you are in a minority, because it will be pulled down one day soon. You see, the space behind it, that's where they will build the new one."

Robert saw his chance, and asked, "Oh, when will that be ready?"

"Not for a while yet. And please excuse us, we really have to move on, as we need to get to church," came the reply.

That was not what he wanted. He was looking for a date. The group he had chosen were not in the mood for a conversation. What he did see was a kiosk right in the middle of the square. It was small and round, actually in the form of a hexagon. Robert walked towards

176

it and could see they sold newspapers. That would give him the answer he needed, even if he couldn't buy one.

Once he reached the kiosk, he picked up a copy of the *Algemeen Dagblad*, which, loosely, meant General Daily. He immediately focused on the date at the top and found it. It was very small, but said 24 July, 1886.

"Is that today's paper?" Robert asked.

"No, yesterday's. Today is Sunday. And that will be 5 cents sir," said the stall holder, as he also stared at what Robert was wearing.

"No, oh… I'm sorry," said Robert. "I was just looking at the headline and I don't have any money with me right now. I'll be back," he lied.

Robert turned and decided he wanted to see more of "his" city. He started to worry again about how he was going to navigate yet another time, in the clothes he was wearing, with money from 1945. And he really was a lot taller than anyone else now. History has shown that the Dutch are perhaps the tallest people in the world, but Robert was knocked back to the reality of life in the 1880s where he was at least a full head taller than the tallest person. At least from what he could see.

He headed towards the main canals again, but his intention was to walk towards the Leidseplein, the square at the end of the main canals. He was curious to see something more than just the centre of the city, so his plan was to go as far as the Rijksmuseum, where he and Saskia—the original, present day, Saskia—had got to know each other better. He wanted to get a feel for the rest of the city. His route took him into much more confined spaces as the roads and canals started getting smaller and narrower. Despite this, it was clear that there was a lot of activity which played out on the water, since everywhere there were barges vital for the supply of goods. The streets were also becoming busier with more people milling around, dogs and cats running uncontrolled, more horses, and more horse-drawn carts. There were fewer carriages in this part of town. Robert was not taking a direct route but passed along the edges of the Jordaan, the heart of where the workers lived in the nineteenth century. Robert stayed on the edge, but the cluttered nature of the dwellings was clear to see. In 2019, the Jordaan was the cool place to be, but not in 1886.

"Shit!" yelled Robert, speaking literally and figuratively as he stepped in a pile of horseshit. The streets here were decidedly less well cared for, and the stink was also becoming more apparent. It was coming from the abundance of horseshit and the less sanitary housing in the vicinity. There were signs of people trying to clean the streets of the horseshit, but it didn't help the smell. The combination of urine and faeces was enough to give the area a distinctive, very unpleasant fragrance. Even the canals were full of it, because that was where they dumped it.

Robert moved on, scraping his shoes along the road as he tried to dislodge the horseshit, but he would need to find some water somewhere to clean off the rest. This still looked and felt like the Amsterdam he knew, albeit more chaotic. Amsterdam is one of those cities that has managed to hold on to its original authenticity over the centuries, and it looked and felt the same with its gabled houses and canals—even if it did not smell the same. He reached the small square he was looking for, but moved straight on across the bridge on the other side because he really didn't quite understand what he was seeing.

He could now see the Rijksmuseum to the left, and ahead of him the largest park in Amsterdam, the Vondel Park. But what struck Robert was that it was already the end of the city. There was little more. There were some ribbon developments in the polder fields, but where was the rest? Given the date, he did not really know what to expect. Ahead of him should be the start of the big and bustling Amsterdam West. But there was barely anything. He was stunned, maybe because he had expected more. In front of him was a postcard landscape of the country he knew from history books; windmills, windmills and more windmills. This was literally what The Netherlands was founded on. Windmills were in use for centuries for industrial purposes, like milling grain, but now they were reclaiming land by pumping water from one level to another. "See, that's what makes The Netherlands the leader in water management," thought Robert. He was impressed; he was seeing the birth of an industry the country was famous for.

Robert sat for a while on an empty hand cart that was parked on the side of the outer ring canal. His thoughts now turned to the realities of the time he was in. His first thought, yet again, was that there was no insulin in 1886. If he could not get back, then his life would be cut short, and it would not be pleasant. He knew enough to know that his organs would start failing relatively rapidly and, in this era, even the treatment might kill him. He didn't know for sure, but he had images of terminal patients whose only palliative care was a priest standing over their beds to ensure that their soul was in the right place before they departed. Robert shivered at the thought. Suicide was a better option.

No, he was determined to find a way out of this mess. First, he needed money. He started fiddling around with his backpack, which he still had, and reached towards the bottom, feeling for the handkerchief he had retrieved from the German soldier. Everything was safe and as he had originally found it, a couple of gold rings, a delicate bracelet, and a necklace. This had to be his passport to at least get some money to help him through. It was time for action. He had given up on any idea of trying to use the coins he had, which were in a side pocket.

Robert walked back, heading towards the centre, but this time he veered off to the left towards the Jordaan part of the city where he hoped to find someone who would trade with him. The more he walked towards the Jordaan, the busier it got, but also the more depressing. This part of town was home to a different class of people, who lived in run-down buildings in run-down streets. The washing hung from everywhere. There was a hustle and bustle of people on the street, and everything was open. Even on a Sunday. "Jesus, these people must work long hours," thought Robert.

Robert knew the streets well, but this was different. For a start, he had to look at where he was going, because the stone cobblestones were all loose and there were only a few streets that were still intact. Some kids were even playing their own form of boules with the stones. Groups of men, women and children were often huddled around. Unlike the other part of town, their uniform was definitely working class—breeches and tunics for the men, and long skirts and white aprons for the women.

Robert decided to backtrack a bit. This wasn't the place to find what he needed. Things were better by the main canals, and he started making enquiries as he went, to see if there was a gold trader in the vicinity. It seemed everyone would be a trader if the terms were right, so it wasn't long until Robert found a jeweler who could help him. He had no idea of the value of what he had on him, but he was happy to accept whatever was on offer. Not for everything; he held onto the necklace as insurance, just in case he needed it. Robert did balk a little at the first price he was offered, just to show that it wasn't enough. He ended up with a collection of coins and notes, and the jeweler added, "You should be very happy sir, you've got a ten guilder coin there, in gold. It's new and not French, all Dutch."

Robert just mumbled a sincere thank you but did not understand what the jeweler was talking about. The jeweler could see the doubt on Robert's face, so went on, "Don't you know sir, the French influence is over, and we now produce our own coins."

"Oh, indeed, I had heard about that, but I hadn't been paying much attention," Robert lied, for the umpteenth time. He fumbled around with the coins he had been given and put them in his pocket. It had been a while since he had carried so many coins; he was so used to paying by card.

He exited the shop and headed back to the Jordaan, this time along the Prinsengracht canal, the outer ring of the main central canals. His eyes were always drawn by the hive of activity in the Jordaan streets, which were off to his left. As he progressed further round the canal, almost to the end, he reached a canal called the Lindengracht. Then, in 1886, it was a canal, but Robert knew it as one of the few wide paved streets in the Jordaan. Now he could see how it was before they filled it in. As he stood at the end of the canal, all he could see was masses of people, all gathered around the side of the canal and on bridges that crossed it. What was going on? He had to investigate.

Whatever it was, it looked like a party of sorts, a lot of cheering and clearly a lot of alcohol being enjoyed. Robert edged closer until he was at the back of the crowd. Robert being Robert, he again towered over everyone else and could see the spectacle before him. He had no idea what it was. Between the two bridges there was a rope that spanned the canal, and which was attached to a house on either side. Hanging from the middle of the rope was what looked like a snake; it was very much alive, wriggling vigorously from the rope in an attempt to free itself, but to no avail.

The crowd lining the canal was about three deep, and Robert was standing behind a group of women all wearing white aprons that looked as if they needed a good wash. Robert gently tapped the shoulder of the nearest woman to him and waited for her to turn towards him. She did. For a brief second, he was horrified by what he saw and took a step back. The woman with an unfortunate face was looking up at Robert with a big smile and sense of awe, as if he was someone from a different planet. In turn, Robert was looking down at a woman who had clearly seen better days. She was not old, but life had taken its toll on her. Her big smile was completely wrecked by a mouth only half full of teeth. She had a deflated face, as if she was pushed up against a pane of glass. Her hair was unwashed.

Robert recovered his composure and asked, "I'm not from here, so I was wondering what all of this is about. What's going on?"

"This is one of our popular pastimes," answered the woman, who added, "You look cute... but very tall. How is that possible?"

"Too much milk and cheese," replied Robert politely. He tried to steer the conversation back to what was going on. "And...?"

"See that rope. In the middle, hanging from it, there is an eel, one of those very slippery things."

"Ah ha," said Robert. "Now I see."

The woman continued, "Nothing is happening right now, but in a moment you will see a boat come by; each boat represents a café from here in the area. There is a man standing up." She stopped briefly as a cheer went up and a rowing boat came into sight with a man standing on the back step of the boat.

Between turning her head towards the action and pointing, the woman said "Now he's got to try and grab the eel and get it down from the rope. It looks easy, but those eels are not only slippery, they move around a lot... Watch."

Sure enough, the man reached up towards the eel, only managing to finally get hold of it as the boat moved further forward. He was already losing his balance, but if he expected to get any support from the poor eel, he was out of luck. It was so slippery that he could not get a good hold and the dual perils of a moving boat and an oily eel meant that he soon found himself in the water. This was what it was all about, and the crowds erupted in joy at the spectacle, all helped by the evident alcohol. Robert didn't even want to think about the perils of falling into the very unsanitary water.

"That's how it's not done," said the woman, as she turned to Robert extending a hand of introduction. "My name's Mariska," she said hopefully, cleaning her hand on her apron before finally giving it to Robert.

"I didn't know such a game, maybe I should say sport, existed," said Robert.

"Well, we still play it, but actually it's now been banned because the idiots at the council think it's cruel. We eat them anyway, so they're going to die one way or another. Stupid, don't you think?"

Robert knew exactly how such a pastime would go down in 2019. A party like the 'Animal Party' would have a field day with it. The Dutch were probably the only country in the world to have a political party that looked after the interests of animals, and they actually won seats in parliament. This "sport" would be a no brainer for them, but it sounded like the local council had beaten them to it.

Robert thanked Mariska, who was disappointed that he decided to move on. He headed towards one of the bridges as the next boat came through, amid a lot more cheering. On the bridge he paused and again took in the view below and the crowds along the other side of the canal, and more people hanging out of windows. All of a sudden, his eye caught a familiar face, one he knew so well, Saskia. Or was it her?

He was now really concentrating on the woman, who was no more than twenty metres away from him, on the other side of the canal. He no longer had any interest in what was happening on the water. The face was the same, as was her figure, but that was now more difficult to tell. She was dressed in much smarter finery than the local population, so she didn't really fit in. It didn't look like it bothered her. The only thing that he could not determine was her gait, that familiar swing of the hips he liked so much. He had to investigate more. This was becoming another dramatic turn of events.

Robert crossed the bridge and stood no more than a couple of metres from "Saskia." He was now guilty of staring as he took in what he was looking at. Impulse got the better of him and he leant over and asked, "Are you Saskia?"

"Who is asking?" came the response. This was clearly a different woman than he had just encountered on the other side of the canal, much more sophisticated, and educated. He only needed to hear three words to determine that.

"My name is Robert…"—and after some hesitation—"Robert Dekker. I know it sounds like a strange question, but if you are Saskia, then we have met before, in a previous life, as it were."

Robert knew this was provocative and he would have to think on his feet for an answer to the inevitable response.

"Yes, I am Saskia, but I don't know you. I would remember someone who was so tall and wearing a mish mash of clothes that probably belongs in a circus."

Robert looked at his clothes and again saw nothing wrong with them, other than they were out of place in this time period. Saskia's response made Robert's reply even more difficult.

"It is true that I am taller than many people, but I was probably sitting when we met. To be honest, I just cannot recall when it was. It was a long time ago at a friend's house, I think on the Herengracht," Robert said hopefully.

"It is customary for a man to stand up when he is introduced to a woman, so if you were sitting, then that was an inauspicious start. Don't you think?"

Robert thought that was a smart response, but he was distracted by more cheering as another boat went through. Saskia continued, "I do live on the Herengracht, so I guess it is possible, but I do not remember. What can I do for you, Mr Dekker?"

"Oh, no. Nothing. I was sure I recognised you and this spectacle is new to me."

"It's something they have been doing in the Jordaan for a long time, but I believe they have outlawed it now. Frankly, I don't know, because they are still continuing with it. Obviously." Saskia waved her arms at the scene in front of her.

As if on cue, there was some commotion stirring in the ranks of the spectators on the sides. Robert then got a glimpse of a few policemen who were now in one of the houses and about to cut the rope across the canal. There was outrage directed at the policemen, but they were in no mood to back down and, once cut, the rope fell towards the ground and the crowd, swiping a small boy on the way. He started crying, and this prompted more active resistance by the inhabitants, who started pushing the two agents around and becoming more physical.

More police joined the two agents. They were accompanying a demonstration of socialists who now took it upon themselves to join in the fray, sowing the seeds of even more chaos, which led to more fighting. The immediate weapon of choice was stones from the streets, and anything else that came to hand.

Robert, with his new acquaintance, was once again on the receiving end of projectiles headed in their direction. Saskia was already trying to move away and now Robert pulled at her to help her navigate the obstacles on the street. It didn't work. She fell hard as a brick hit her on the head.

Robert didn't wait to see how she was. He grabbed her under the armpits and dragged her to safety some metres away and down a side street. It wasn't far, but just enough to keep both him and her safe. There was still screaming and shouting coming from the canal, but now there was some shooting as well. Robert peeked around from his hiding place to see more people lying on the ground. He didn't know if the injuries were inflicted by bullets. He turned his attention to Saskia.

He gently cradled her head. She looked dazed but not in any major trouble. There was blood coming from the side of her head, so Robert took it upon himself to rip off the sash she was wearing over her shoulder and used that as a swab to stave off the blood. He would need to pay more attention to the wound once he was in a better place with access to water—clean water.

Robert looked at Saskia and asked, "How are you feeling? Can you stand?"

"I think so."

"I will help you get home, so let's get you up."

Robert supported Saskia once again and helped her up. Once standing, Saskia started to wobble but quickly regained her balance. "I do feel a little dizzy," she said.

"Let's give it a try," said Robert as he took her by the top of the arm, but he also had his other hand pressing on the wound on her head. They moved off, this time not heading back towards the chaos.

Saskia then prompted, "Turn left at the end of this street."

"Yes, I figured. To the Herengracht, right?"

"Yes... Now I'm getting a headache."

"Well, that probably comes as no surprise," he said sarcastically, but he meant it as a comfort.

CHAPTER FOURTEEN

The part of the Herengracht where Saskia lived was not far, so it would only take them ten minutes or so, provided Saskia didn't hold them back. He was absolutely sure that he would be going back to number 85 on the canal, so he didn't bother asking questions about directions. Saskia could see he was going in the right direction and didn't prompt him any further, at least not yet.

Once they were on the Herengracht, Robert led Saskia onto her side of the canal and toward her house.

"You seem to know where you are going," she said.

"I told you, I've been there before."

"Not my house, you haven't."

"Oh, I think you'll be surprised. Up a small flight of stairs, black and white paved stones in a long hallway?"

"Wrong. Yes to the steps, but I have wooden floorboards, painted red."

Robert was about to change tack, but they were already there, so he helped her up the stairs.

"I guess you do know," she said.

"Keys?"

"You mean key."

No one had just one key, thought Robert, but these were different times. "Yes, I mean key."

Saskia gave Robert a monster of a key that allowed him to get into the house. They entered, and sure enough, there were now floorboards instead of tiles. It looked a lot more dated, but with some luxury trimmings, rugs and curtains, and dark walls with heavy wallpaper, even with doors embedded or hidden within the wallpaper. There were also fireplaces everywhere, to keep the house warm. The Herengracht was still one of the most desirable canals to live on, even if this was the "poor" end of it.

"Listen, Mr Dekker," Saskia began, "I do thank you for bringing me back home, and it seems you obviously knew where I lived. So I suppose we have might have met before, but I don't remember any introduction. Now I think you ought to leave, because I live here alone, and you can imagine what my neighbours will think if I am seen alone with an unknown man in the house. Unlike many others, I am an emancipated woman, but you know as well as I, I have to be careful. And how do I explain someone like you in your circus clothes, and no hat? It's just not the right etiquette, even if I have moved on from the days of needing a chaperone."

Robert was stunned. He really had to adjust to a totally different way of thinking. He knew he was in the company of someone who could afford where she lived and had a status to protect, but he did not really know how he was going to navigate social conventions that were totally alien to him. Puzzled, he answered:

"I appreciate your concerns, but let me assure you, we have been introduced. Please, let me tell you more about that later. Right now, though, I am concerned about the wound on your head, and I cannot allow you to ignore it. It's in a place which is difficult for you to see or do anything about. I assure you, I have done this before, even for you." He mumbled the last part, so she didn't hear it.

"Water first," said Robert authoritatively, so that Saskia could not push back easily.

She led Robert to the back where the kitchen was. Although it was well apportioned, the layout was more like organised chaos. The kitchen was full—dark wallpaper on the walls, a table in the middle, chests and vitrines against the sides, and shelves with hanging utensils. Saskia pointed to one of the cans on the chests which contained water. Robert made her sit down and started to study the wound.

"Ow, ow ow!" was Saskia's starting point, as Robert pushed her bloodied hair out of the way and investigated.

"It's a clean cut, but quite deep, and still bleeding. I'll just clean it off and then we need to find a way of closing it so that it stays that way. I don't think you need stitches."

"Stitches? What are you talking about?"

"Sutures," tried Robert.

"Oh, catgut. No, let's do without that if we can."

By this time, Robert had grabbed a cloth and was dabbing at the wound. At his request, Saskia gave him a clean white handkerchief, which he cut into small pieces.

"The remaining pieces are for when you need to change the dressing," he said. He continued after finding a long enough piece of thin linen, which he used to tie around her head, forming as best as he could what looked like a headband that could pass as if it were intentional. He knew there would be no antibiotics, but he kept quiet about the fact that he had some penicillin because Saskia would not know what this was. It would be a remedy of last resort and he didn't need it now. The injury would just have to heal on its own.

"Thank you for doing this. My housekeeper will be here soon for the early evening help, so I think you should be gone before she arrives."

"Housekeeper?"

"Of course. All respectable people need help in the house to collect and heat water, wash clothes, cook, and much more. Frankly, I would much prefer to be doing a lot of this myself, but it is just not done for a woman of my standing to be seen doing such work. And this is not a small house. That's why I sympathise, to a certain extent, with the socialists we saw today. They are being undermined by our unequal society, and part of that is an equal role for women. Surely you also believe in giving women the vote?"

Once again, Robert was boxed into a corner. The least he could do was give Saskia some kind of hope that things would change, but he didn't know when women won the right to vote in Holland. At least he could see the same feisty attitude as all the Saskias he had now met.

"That's a good sign. You must be feeling a lot better. Absolutely, I think women have just as much right to vote as men, and that will definitely happen. But back to your housekeeper. If you are so concerned, I will leave when she comes and find a hotel for the night."

"You are not from Amsterdam?"

"No, from Groningen." Robert continued with the same story.

"That's really a long way from here."

"Oh, it's not that bad." Saying it was only about two hours would not go down well, so Robert just left it at this.

"I am sure I would have remembered meeting someone from Groningen. As you can hear, I am still having trouble accepting that you have met me before, though fortunately for you I am not one of those women who stands on too much protocol. In fact, I hate it... But it's the way our society is, and I have to accept it. Behind closed doors, I can live the life I want to live. I'm a widow, and now this house is all mine to look after, so you can see I live comfortably. I am not young anymore, but there are still people who keep an eye out for me, even now that I am fast approaching the end of my life.

"What do you mean, end of your life? You are still very young."

"Thank you Mr Dekker, but I am realistic, and well read. We don't live very long you know, but I take comfort in the fact that I have already got this far. True, I'm healthy, apart from this hole in my head, so I have high hopes. But, you'll see, the smallest of diseases can kill you."

"That's tragic. One day we will all be living to over 100," Robert said, injecting his own optimism and his own reality.

"Don't be absurd, Mr. Dekker."

Robert just smiled and, as on many occasions, chose not to go down this path. It would only lead nowhere. He changed tack.

"I don't want to make you any more uncomfortable than you already are but let me tell you more about the time we met. I hope it will convince you. It was a day when there was a bit of alcohol flowing and in perhaps a weak moment you said you had a birthmark on one of your cheeks."

Robert left the wording purposely vague. Saskia touched the cheeks on her face. "I don't, you can see that."

"I didn't mean those cheeks." Robert tapped himself on his own bum in order to convey what he meant. He had concluded that being very direct was not something you did in this century and this time period. Especially with women of a certain standing.

"Mr Dekker! You cannot be serious. That is very inappropriate. And I am definitely not going to answer that." Privately, Saskia smiled inside as she accepted Robert must know more than she wanted to give him credit for. It made her more comfortable in his presence. It was still not done, but nor was telling him in the first place. Did she really do that?

"Please, call me Robert."

"Mr Dekker, I repeat. We don't do that, and we have not been introduced, even if you think we have."

191

"Well, maybe we can just agree that I come from a different time period," Robert said with a smile, "and we are more used to using first names. But that's alright, please use what you feel comfortable with."

"Right now, I don't feel comfortable. But that is obviously for other reasons. Look at me, with this ridiculous head covering. I cannot be seen like this. And I have a headache."

"I don't think you should be going out anyway. But I do have something for your headache."

"What do you mean, you have something? I have nothing here, but we generally use morphine or something similar, if you can get it."

"Wow, morphine. That's dangerous."

"You know?"

"Indeed, it is one of the most powerful and addictive pain drugs and should be used only for really bad pain."

"Maybe in your world. We use it regularly. But I don't know your word addictive."

"You don't?" said Robert, who was somewhat surprised. "It's not mine. Addictive means that once you start taking a substance—like morphine—your body starts wanting more. In other words, you become too dependent on it. Tobacco is another good example."

"I regard myself as well educated, so why haven't I heard of this word? And now you're also telling me that tobacco is dangerous?"

"Indeed. And, I would strongly advise you to be careful and keep clear of morphine; but I'm glad you don't have any."

"Well, what do you have that will help me and why do you carry it around?

"It's called meperidine and is in the same family as morphine. It is an opioid—from opium—but not as habit-forming. Let me fetch it for you."

Robert grabbed his backpack from the floor where he had left it and reached for the sachet of pills. He gave one to Saskia.

"We don't see pills often. But thank you. Are you sure it works? I have never heard of it."

"Please, just try. I assure you, it is safe." Saskia took the pill.

The housekeeper never came, which was highly unusual. She was not a resident in-house housekeeper but chose to live with her family in the Jordaan. It was customary for people of some wealth to have live-in servants, but Saskia had abandoned that after the death of her husband. He was more status-oriented and observed the convention of having staff in the house. They had plenty of space in the basement to accommodate them, with some natural light, but they only got a bit of that from the front and back windows.

"This has never happened before," said Saskia. "I wonder if she was caught in the riots in the Jordaan."

"Is there anything I can do?

"Can you cook?"

"Of course."

"No, you cannot. No man can cook."

Robert knew a staccato conversation like this could go on forever, so he took over and said, "Test me, let me have a go."

"Mr Dekker. I don't have much choice, but I will be interested to see if you can do what you boast."

They were still in the chaotic kitchen and Robert looked around for what he needed: food, utensils, and something to cook on. Saskia smiled as she could see he didn't know where to start.

"You already look lost. And you said you could cook."

"Patience. I'm orienting myself," Robert answered, knowing full well that this was indeed foreign terrain for him. But as he was taking it in, he could see that the pans he needed hung on the wall, as did many utensils. Water was in the cans, and there was a cast iron furnace built into a huge brick fireplace. Robert was getting more nervous about how he might master this monster, but he did know it was permanently hot. So it was just a question of using the right parts. There was no sign of any food.

"Do you have any food in the house, or should I go out?"

"The food is where it normally is, in the cellar."

"Of course, stupid of me." Robert headed for the cellar.

"You know where the cellar is?"

"I am assuming," Robert answered as he headed to the cellar. He knew where the stairs were, but now there was a door leading down, while he was used to everything being open.

He headed down the rickety, open wooden stairs into the cellar. It was cold, really cold compared with the warmth upstairs. He understood why. This was the only way to keep the food as fresh as possible. There were only simple ingredients, but he found what he needed for what would pass as a meal. A big chicken that looked and smelt acceptable, potatoes, and carrots. He also selected some green beans, so that there was some contrasting colour to what he would cook, even if the idea of colour combinations in cooking would be totally foreign to Saskia.

He returned upstairs to find that Saskia had chanelled the heat that he would need and he was glad she spared him that task. Robert set about chopping the legs off the chicken as he would not cook a whole chicken for just the two of them. The large legs would suffice.

Saskia sat back and admired from a distance. Here was a man who seemed to know what he was doing, though he was clumsy with some of the implements. She watched Robert trying to peel potatoes. Had he never done that before with a knife, she asked herself.

Robert did his best to add what spices he could find and then served it up. He would have been perfectly happy to eat at the kitchen table, but no, there was a dining room. That too was heavily decorated with a fireplace, a huge mirror, and a big Persian style rug. Very opulent for this end of the Herengracht, thought Robert.

Dinner was a more formal affair than he was used to. Saskia had not changed, but she had added a choker around her neck, which added to the formality. She sat bolt upright, but that was probably a result of the corset she wore, which showed off her comportment. They sat opposite each other, and the conversation allowed Robert to learn more about this Saskia; how she had lost her husband in a horse-riding accident; how she inherited the house and some assets; and that she had a daughter studying in Paris. Déjà vu, of sorts.

At the end, Saskia said, "Mr Dekker, I owe you an apology. I am not used to men being able to cook, and this is highly unusual. But it was very good. You clearly have some hidden talents that other men can learn from, even if you are strangely dressed."

"The dress is experimental. One day maybe this will be popular."

"I have my doubts. Men need to be smart."

After a while, Robert suggested that he should be going as he needed to find a hotel before it was too late. Although he could tell that Saskia was warming to him, he did not expect the following.

"Mr Dekker. As you know, I remain uncomfortable with you being in my house, but I have enough space, and a bed, in the attic if you

195

wish to use it. But I do ask you to leave tomorrow, as soon as possible."

Robert accepted gracefully, and he followed Saskia up three flights of stairs to the attic. The attic was very large, and empty except for a couple of single beds. It would do, thought Robert and he accepted the sheets and blankets, which he would put on later. The two of them retreated downstairs. On the way down, Robert came to an abrupt stop on one of the landings as he stood in front of an oak chest he thought he knew so well. It had the same carved twirl on the side and seemed in use as storage for things like towels and sheets. He was now waking up to the fact that this looked exactly like the one he had bought for his son, Daniel, but he had bought it from the neighbour's house, not this one. Small world, he thought. This chest has had a long life.

At the bottom of the stairs Robert made yet another strange sounding offer to Saskia, at least from her perspective.

"Shouldn't we do something about cleaning the dishes?"

"That's not our job. I am sure the housekeeper will be here in the morning. She will do it."

Robert did not make a big issue out of this. He had already seen how difficult the pans would be to clean, and he had to accept the roles of the times, even if it made him feel uncomfortable.

There was no question of any further help for Saskia, and Robert knew his position by now. They went their separate ways for the night. Robert did take some water upstairs as he was fed up with wearing the same pair of underpants for four days. As best he could, he gave them a wash with what he had and laid them on a windowsill to dry in the warm weather.

The following morning Robert would have loved a shower, but showers would not be around for many more decades. Saskia had a bath, but not a bathroom, so Robert settled on a bird bath in a basin, using heated water which he had to warm up from the in-house supplies. Unfortunately, his underwear was still a little wet, so there was no way he could wear them and he put them into his backpack and decided to go commando, as it was colloquially called, at least in his time period; or liberating, depending on your choice. He also gave himself another shot of long-term insulin, turning the injection pen carefully to see how much of the precious medicine he still had left. It wasn't much.

By his reckoning, he had only been away for about four days, but that was long enough to start depleting his stock. If it went on like this, he would be in trouble within a matter of weeks. He had to take his predicament more seriously. It was more than curious that his travelling in time constantly brought him to a different Saskia, but ultimately his survival would have to take priority. He had to find a way back and he had to start now. But what if the "Saskia" constant was also a key to his return? He didn't know.

Once he was clean and back in the same clothes he had been wearing for far too long, he went to check on Saskia's wound. He cleaned and replaced the bandaging and said:

"Your wound looks good. I will be on my way now, before your housekeeper arrives. I hope she arrives."

Saskia got up and said, "Once again, Mr Dekker, thank you for your help. It was interesting meeting you and if you ever stay in Amsterdam again, maybe our paths will cross under different circumstances," and she added, "After you have been to a good tailor!"

Robert headed to the door, picking up his backpack as he went, but not without checking that he still had all his money and what was left of his jewelry. That was his safety valve. Saskia grabbed a formal looking black hat from a hat stand by the front door. "Wouldn't you like a hat? I don't need it anymore."

"No thanks. It wouldn't suit my 'circus clothes.'" Robert replied with a smile, but, as he departed, he turned and mimed a tipped hat as if he did have one. He was secretly beginning to enjoy the learning curve with a new Saskia each time. Still, he had to get serious about his predicament. Not that he had any great ideas. The first step would be to recover his carriage. It was the only form of transport he had, even if he was not at all comfortable with horses.

Robert turned left and headed towards the bridge across to the street where he had left his carriage. Before he even had a chance to reach the stables, he was met by the young boy who had accepted his transport the previous day.

"Hey, Mister. I thought you were coming back yesterday."

"Did I say that?" said Robert.

"It doesn't matter now. It's just going to cost you more, because your horse is now fed and rested."

"How much do I owe you?"

"It's not cents anymore. That will be one guilder, sir."

"Happy to oblige," Robert said as he reached for his money, fumbling a bit. He still had to learn what each coin was. This was unfamiliar territory.

Robert braced himself to confront his horse, approaching him gingerly. He assumed it was a "him," but bent down and looked to make sure. Yes, a him. He grabbed the bit and looked into his eye, because he wanted to be friends with this powerful beast, even if he was uncomfortable around horses.

"Hi, I'm Robert," he said. "Now I guess we should also give you a name. How about Henry?"

198

His horse gave one of those deep grunts, at the same time fiercely nodding his head up and down. "Well, I guess that settles it. Henry it is. The name of kings."

Robert climbed into his carriage, grabbing the reins and settling into his seat. A small shake of the reins and a mumbled instruction didn't work, but all went well once he became more assertive and louder. They moved off back onto the Herengracht, heading towards the bridge which he now feared. He was going to go over it in the other direction, even if he had no logical reason for his decision. The bridge remained the only common denominator with his time travel, but he had already failed once. Let's see, he thought.

The carriage was not like driving in a Volvo or a Jeep. The road underneath was the same cobbles, but wooden wheels and no suspension already made it very uncomfortable, and he had barely been going for two hundred metres. As he was nearing the bridge, he could hear a crescendo of noise, but he could not see anything. The bridge had a steep incline, so he knew it was probably coming from the other side. He continued and, as he reached the base of the bridge, the noise on the other side became much louder. He still couldn't see much. He heard loud voices and now he heard marching, as if in step. Only when he reached the apex of the bridge, could he see ahead of him. There was an entire legion of soldiers heading his way, up the other side of the bridge and marching directly at him. It did not look like they were going to give way, so he pulled on the reins and came to a stop. It was indeed the army. They were armed with rifles with bayonets slung over their shoulders and accompanied by the police. They were clearly on a mission.

Robert didn't know what to do, so he just sat there and waited for them to part and walk past him. They didn't. A couple of the soldiers in the lead, one presumably an officer, took Henry by the bit and turned him around, as if to say, "no, you are going back where you came from."

Robert yelled out loud, "No, no! Not yet, don't do that!" But it was too late. They were barking instructions, telling Robert not to go near the Jordaan. But before he could do anything Robert was propelled yet again into a momentary blackout and a different time.

PART V

The Plague

CHAPTER FIFTEEN

He knew the drill by now, so it did not come as a shock, but it was always back in time and always a revelation too much. This was no different. He was now at the bottom of the same bridge, back where he started, on the same Herengracht canal. But now on the back of a horse. He was already uncomfortable with a horse and carriage; this was even worse. The horse was moving of its own accord, a slow gentle walk down the last part of the bridge. Robert didn't even try to stop, he just let the horse walk on a little until he was about one hundred metres away from the bridge. His first thought was to stop and dismount. Riding was just not his thing, and the discomfort was compounded by his liberated genitals being bounced up and down.

He slid off the horse, not very elegantly, but he did land on his feet. He grabbed his horse by the bit and looked into his new friend's eyes.

"Henry!" He exclaimed. "You came with me. How did that happen?" For some reason, Robert felt happy about it, even if he had only known Henry for a very short time. It was as if he was now not alone in his time travel. He knew it was Henry, because he had the same whiff of white on his forehead, and the tackle was the same. It also looked like Henry recognised him, but he was probably going overboard in his thinking.

'Now what?' thought Robert. He stood on the side of the canal in his "circus clothes" and looked around. First, he looked back at the bridge he had just crossed. It was no longer the same type of fixed bridge. It was now a cantilever drawbridge, which allowed boats to pass underneath. Everywhere he looked Robert could see such bridges, which meant that he had gone even farther back in time. The number of boats in the canal told him life was spent on the water just as much as it was on land. There were now very few trees along the canals, which were the best form of transport for goods, and waste, and Robert started to pick up the stench of everything around him. He took a closer look over the side of the canal wall and into the Herengracht, where he could see signs of excrement being channeled directly into the canal, and the occasional rat scurrying to feed off it.

Robert turned away and focused his attention on the many people walking by and staring at him and Henry. He smiled and nodded but did not want to say or do anything yet. He stood up against one of the very few trees so he could guardedly get to grips with where he was. It was clear he was in a time when Amsterdam was relatively mature, but "relative" was doing a lot of work. From what he could see, there were two classes of people going about their business. This was the Herengracht after all, so he would expect the more well-to-do inhabitants, as well as the staff that served them, and the labourers in their boats and on the streets. The heavy wooden boats were the white courier vans of today, but at least they didn't hold people up on the canal sides as they delivered their goods.

The wealthier men all wore fine tunics, often with large white collars and their women companions were dressed in the finery that suited their status. At least, that is what Robert assumed. Their staff— they were someone's staff—were dressed in simple dresses or long skirts with white aprons and a strange white hood or cap that came down the side of the face, alongside each jaw. It was almost like a uniform.

It was a nice day, so washing hung out of the windows and occasionally on lines in the street. Unlike the Amsterdam of 2019, everything was happening at street level, because that was where deliveries took place, as well as storage of food, washing, and even living quarters for staff. The basement was the delivery entrance, with large doors open to the street.

Robert moved away from the tree and took Henry for a walk. Most of the other people were toiling with delivery or cleaning chores; or strolling aimlessly, for those that were showing off their status. They gazed intently at Robert, but said nothing. Once again, he was even taller than before, and stood out. Not only did he have "circus clothes" on, now he might even be considered a circus attraction.

He and his horse walked back towards the bridge they had just come over. As they reached it, Robert looked more intently to see why the bridge was the likely culprit for his time travel. This one was now a drawbridge, with large bulkheads on either side to link and support the struts in the canal and ultimately the bridge lifting mechanism. At the moment, the bridge was open to allow boats to pass under, and there were a lot of boats going back and forth. They were a mix of rowing sloops and small sailing vessels, all wood of course. It was the best way of transporting heavy goods like coal, and Robert could also see a lot of barrels for the liquids and sacks for food items such as potatoes. Now Henry had more friends because there were more horses, and many could be seen making themselves useful by pulling a few of the sailing boats up and down the canals. The canal streets were now also a towpath.

Robert walked on in a westerly direction down the Brouwersgracht, the canal heading towards the Jordaan and the Lindengracht, where he last was for the eel pulling. As he got closer, he caught sight of a large barge being pulled along the canal and coming towards him. There was no one on the barge, which he thought was odd. He looked closer as it came alongside, and he could see bodies lined up on deck and wrapped up in shrouds. There were a lot of them. Robert naturally became curious, so he approached one of the men guiding the boat from the canal side.

"Excuse me, are they what I think they are?"

"Bodies, you mean?"

"Yes. I have never seen so many like this."

"Where have you been for the last few years?"

Robert returned to his Groningen roots story, "I'm not from around here. I'm from Groningen."

"I don't know where Groningen is, but I can only assume you are a long way from home. These are today's bodies from the Pest. Just from the Jordaan," came the reply.

"My God. Is that where I am?"

"What do you mean?"

"Oh, nothing, just a figure of speech. I didn't realise it was that bad."

"This is everyday reality, my friend."

"Where are you taking them?" asked Robert.

"Out to the sea, where they will be burned. I am surprised you don't know; this has been going on for a long time. Doesn't news reach you from where you come from?"

"I guess we are too far removed," answered Robert.

"Well, my advice, stay well away from these people," came his last remark.

Robert moved on towards the Jordaan, but now he started thinking back to what he knew about the "Pest," as the plague was known. At university, they covered some aspects of large viral and bacterial infections when he was studying pharmacy, but it was very limited. As most plagues were now managed by vaccines and antibiotics, the history of it didn't play a large role. But what was this one? Viral or bacterial? It would come to him.

He walked to the end of the Brouwersgracht, at least to where the buildings ended. From here he could see the Lindengracht, where he had been for the eel pulling, but now it was only half built. The closely packed houses for the working population weren't there yet, but it was still a very sorry sight. The buildings were mostly built of wood and did not look sturdy, especially on the unstable foundations. He decided to investigate further and walked on to the Lindengracht. As

205

he passed down the canal, some residents started vigorously signing to him to stay away, for their safety and his own. As he walked, he could see rats and mice scurrying in and out of the houses; there were also wild dogs and cats. From the houses he heard the occasional muffled scream. The people crouched on the street were also suffering. This was their plague, manifesting itself for all to see.

Robert remembered that the Pest was not the danger that it was made out to be. Its deadliness was largely down to a lack of knowledge and a large dose of misinformation. He was therefore not as concerned as the residents, as he approached a mother and small boy who were sitting on the wooden steps in front of their rickety dwelling. He was looking at the boy, who was not in any pain. He was wearing a long nightshirt. Saying nothing, as if as a warning to Robert to stay away, the mother lifted the boy's nightshirt to reveal severe boils in the groin area. They were bubbling up on his skin and he was in growing discomfort.

Robert was now less worried about himself. He took a step back and moved on, saying nothing to the mother. There was nothing he was going to be able to do for anyone here. This was bacterial and, given what he had seen from the sanitation and abundance of rodents, it mostly came from them. There was no cure, at least not in this time period.

He backtracked and again headed towards the Brouwersgracht. In the distance, to the north, he could see nothing but a wall of masts and sails from the harbour. It all looked much closer than he was used to. He only had a short walk to the harbour where the quay was lined with warehouses and workshops full of artisans who made products like ropes, barrels, baskets, and much more. He took his time to peek in at what they were doing and admired their handiwork. Ahead of him were flotillas of boats—not hundreds— maybe thousands. He knew the sea was there, but all he could really see was a sea of masts. This had to be the high point of Amsterdam, when they were probably the principal trading nation in the world. It was just incredible.

It was well organised chaos, with managed areas where ships would moor. Across the harbour, Robert tried to see if he could see what would become Amsterdam North, but there was nothing there apart from a sliver of land. This was all sea, open to the real sea, the North Sea. In 2019 it had long been hemmed in by a huge dyke and, over time, become a fresh-water lake. "Amazing," he thought. Now he could see why the Dutch became so accomplished at water and land management.

This was too good an opportunity to miss for a few photos, so he opened his backpack and got out his mobile. He turned it on and saw that he still had a good twenty-five percent charge. When he got back to the main canals, he would also take some more of the whirlwind of activity on the water.

Robert walked with Henry along the harbour road, which was busy on both sides. This was where the main railway station would one day be, on more reclaimed land, with all the lines coming into it from east and west. As Robert ambled along, he was focused on the industrious activity in the premises around him, which clearly supported the shipping business.

Suddenly, someone said, "Robert?" and again, "Robert?"

Robert looked to his right to see a woman sitting on a bench dressed in a dark green dress and a black tunic. He was stunned by the combination of a face he knew so well, and by the recognition of him.

"Saskia? No, it can't be...You know me?"

Saskia jumped up from her bench and ran over, hugged and kissed Robert, but then backed off.

"They don't take so kindly to open shows of affection here. It is you, right? And with your favourite jacket. It has to be." She pulled on his jacket to emphasise her point.

"Holy shit! Am I glad to see you," said Robert as an emotional release started to overwhelm him, something that he had been trying to suppress for the last few days with all the other Saskias. "Wow…wow." He sighed a long sigh of relief. He had a friend.

"I need to sit down," said Robert as he turned to his horse and tied him to a railing, even if he did not know if it was a proper knot.

"Sorry, Henry, we're taking a break."

"Henry?" said Saskia.

"This is my new friend, Henry. Long story. But first you."

"Hello, Henry." Saskia continued, "Robert, this is a living hell!"

Robert interrupted immediately, "But what year are we in? I've only just got here, and I've been walking around. I've already seen the horrors of sickness and dead bodies being shipped out to sea. And then I came across you. Thankfully."

"I've been here longer. We're in 1664 and there's not much of the city you and I know well. You can walk around it in less than an hour. The big problem is the plague, and I understand it's been going on for a couple of years. There is death everywhere."

"Yes, I was in the Jordaan and saw the suffering everywhere. I think it's caused by infection, so probably transmitted by rodents. And they are all over the place. Where are you living?"

"You won't believe it, but…"

"Yes, I will," interrupted Robert; but Saskia continued:

"I'm living in my house on The Herengracht, the same house Robert. It's so strange. What is stranger is that I am the mistress of the house. Now I have the whole thing, not just the downstairs apartment. I have servants to cook meals, clean the house, and do the washing. They treat me like I was a queen. It's not right. As the saying goes, at the end of a game of chess, the queen and the pawn go into the same box. Not here."

"But how did you get here?"

"I don't know. One moment I was in 2019, and the next thing I knew I was in my house, but in 1664. And everyone working in the house recognised me…as the mistress. It was very spooky. Everyone was afraid of me. They still are."

"Do you know exactly how long you've been here?"

"A bit more than a week. That's more than enough for me. I have spent the week trying to make it look as if I know what I'm doing and that I am indeed in charge of the house. Take it from me, that's not easy, especially when you don't even know how to find a toilet in the house. There isn't one. Just buckets."

"I know. Believe me, I've had enough of the stench in the streets. Now, and in the other years I have been visiting."

"What?" said Saskia. "Other years?"

Robert proceeded to tell Saskia about his travels through time, and how, on each occasion, he met her living in the same house, but there was no recognition. It was another Saskia. But still identical. "Even the birthmark on your bum!"

Saskia's mouth was already open in surprise as she took this in.

"And, how pray, did you get to see her bum in such a short amount of time?"

"Experience! No, seriously, the circumstances were all very different." Robert explained more in detail, how he reacquainted himself with his Saskia in 2016, the attacks on the Dam square in 1945, his encounter with the police in 1886, and how he now suspected that the bridge over the Brouwersgracht had something to do with his travel through time.

"Wow, you have been on a trip. Even after travelling back in time, I still find that hard to believe, but I'll take you at your word."

If you were at the eel riots, did you also see people being killed? I read about that once."

"No, it was just a riot and you and I got caught up in it. Nothing more than that."

"Are you sure? It was more than that, I thought. Many people were killed. By the army."

"That explains it," said Robert. "No, I didn't witness that. But, thanks to an army marching towards the Jordaan, I'm now here." Robert told Saskia the story about his last encounter with the bridge and being forced back over it.

"It's nice to know I was with you all the time," Saskia added sarcastically.

Robert then moved onto more pressing matters. "But what are we going to do now? First, I don't have anywhere to stay and second, I don't know anyone… other than you, that is. I'm also on my last units of insulin, so it will only be a matter of weeks before I'm in serious trouble."

"Robert, we will figure something out, but I need to tell you something."

Robert looked at Saskia, now with some concern. Her tone had changed.

"I'm married. Apparently."

"What!" he exclaimed. "Why? Why apparently?"

"Well, I haven't seen him yet. He is a trader and often away, so that pleasure is yet to come!" Saskia then added, "But I plan to be gone by then. Somehow."

"So, being selfish, I assume I can find a way into your house for as long as I'm here?"

"As far as I am concerned, of course, but we will have to come up with a credible explanation about who you are. I have nosey neighbours. And my servants. Saskia put the emphasis on "my," if only to lighten the conversation. It was strange for her to think of having her own household staff.

"And where is the other Saskia? The original Saskia."

"Frankly, I have no idea. Probably in my house in 2019, having a ball."

At that moment, there was a grunt from Henry, who appeared to be getting a little impatient.

"OK, Henry, we're going," said Robert as he got up and attempted to untie the knot he had made. He managed, but only after a few frustrating attempts. "Clearly, I haven't been watching enough spaghetti westerns," he thought. Cowboys always had the knack of just flipping the rope and it comes loose.

Saskia joined him and they headed back into the city, this time by way of the canal that led to the Dam Square, which Robert last saw in 1886.

"Please feel free to ride on Henry if you would prefer," said Saskia.

"No. As much as I'm now becoming fond of Henry, it's not a good idea. I've already tried."

"Not your thing?"

"True, horses and I don't bond well, but I'll tell you more. You know how men love to hear a woman say she's not wearing any underwear? Well, now it's your turn. I'm not wearing any underwear. But it's not for any provocative reason. Last night, I washed the underwear I have had on for four days, hoping they would dry in time. They didn't, so I decided to go without. It's not as comfortable when you're riding a horse… as you can imagine."

Saskia laughed. "No, that news doesn't do much for me. Now I will disappoint you. Under pressure from my housekeeper, who is the guardian of my clothes, I am wearing several layers of very uncomfortable under garments. I can't possibly call it underwear. I'd love to tell you I'm not wearing any underwear, even a simple slip would be welcome."

"Another opportunity missed," Robert joked.

"Yes, but we also need to get you into some other clothes, because what you are wearing really stands out. How did you get away with that in other times?"

"I palmed the whole thing off as experimental, and said I was from far away."

"That is not going to work here. Amsterdammers live such a hierarchical existence, from the Regents down to the poor working class and everything in between. Religions don't get on with each other either, but what's new in that? So, you will need to fit in, at least until we can get out of here."

"I assume you have a plan?"

"My as-yet-unknown husband has plenty of clothes at home."

"But is your husband tall?"

"How would I know?" And they both smiled at the thought.

CHAPTER SIXTEEN

They approached the Dam square from the north. For Robert, this was yet another eye-opener. He had been here twice in the last four or five days, and each time it was so very different. Now there was no huge monolithic Exchange building, quite simply because it had not been built yet. On the other side of the square, he could see a dramatic looking building straddling the canal, something where today there was only a road and trams.

"Do you know what that building is?" Asked Robert.

"As a matter of fact, I do, because I also had to ask. It's called the Exchange and it's used for meeting and trading purposes. I guess the forerunner of what we now have as a stock market."

"Wow, it looks nice. Much nicer than the one I saw in 1886, which was more like a Roman mausoleum."

Robert and Saskia now made their way back to the Herengracht, walking over familiar territory, but it all looked so different. Saskia looked at Robert.

"You don't happen to have something like a Mars bar in your backpack, I suppose? I would die for some junk food," she said.

"Sorry, not anymore, I have very little in fact. Just my phone, a water bottle, some medicine, money and jewelry."

Robert told Saskia about his exploits with the German soldier and how he came by the jewellery, but there was only a necklace left over. The medicine was even more of a story, because he had got it from a hospital and was on his way back to Saskia when he got thrown into 1886. He hoped that his 1945 Saskia had recovered without needing it, but he would never know.

"And what do you plan to do with a phone? It's useless here."

"Not if you preserve as much battery as possible for the camera. I've already taken some photos, but I've had to do it very discretely."

"Wow, can I see them?"

"Of course. When we get back. But I also want to take some photos here."

After taking a few more photos, they rounded the corner towards the house at number 85. Robert was now even more curious how it would look two hundred years earlier. That it was still there was already a testament to how well some Amsterdam houses have stood the ravages of time, and especially on foundations that sink.

"I will need to find a home for Henry."

"Don't worry, there are plenty of stables. We can walk over there." Saskia pointed to the same street where Robert had been before. They approached the first stable and were about to ask for help when the stable boy said:

"Ah, Mrs Lohman. Is Mr Lohman back yet?"

"Uh, no. Why?"

"Well, his horse is still here, and of course in good hands. When are you expecting him?"

Saskia didn't know what to say, so she tried, "He did tell me, and I thought it was soon. Do you know?"

"Not really, but he said he would be away at least a month or two, and it is already close to that. On a VOC ship, right?" Now the stable boy stared intently at Robert's clothes, and his enormous height. He didn't say anything.

"Something like that," answered Saskia. "Well, can you also look after this gentleman's horse as well? His name is Henry."

"When will you want him back?"

Robert spoke. "I don't know exactly, but you'll see me coming." He was trying to make a joke, but it fell flat.

They left Henry behind and headed "home." Robert was looking up as he passed the houses. For the time they were in, they didn't look bad, but there was much more activity on the streets. These were not just houses for the rich. Some were functional warehouses, or even a combination. Cargo sloeps were mooring alongside and emptying their goods, some of which went into the basements, the rest up to the attic via the well-known pulley system ubiquitous to Amsterdam, indeed the whole of Holland. The canal houses were generally not wide and the stairs inside the houses were narrow, often very steep, even winding. Saskia's house was no exception. The pulley allowed you to lift heavy and bulky items up the outside of the building and bring them in through a window or shutters.

They reached the house and were greeted in the kitchen by the main housekeeper, Maria.

"Maria, this is Robert Dekker. He is my cousin from Groningen."

Maria looked puzzled and was looking Robert up and down.

"Groningen, that's in the north. Far away?"

Saskia could see Maria was having difficulty taking it all in. "They are different up there, as you can see. What we will do is give him some of my husband's clothes so he fits in more easily in Amsterdam. Don't you think?"

"But Madam, you never mentioned that we would have visitors. And I don't think the master would like it if someone else wore his clothes."

"I think it is the right thing to do. Maria, can you see if you can find some things that might fit. That will be the difficult part."

"Yes, Madam. Welcome, Mr Dekker."

"Call me Robert," Robert said mistakenly, realising that he would get the inevitable response.

"Oh no, I cannot possibly do that. It is below my station." She turned and headed upstairs.

Robert turned to Saskia. "I know a shower is out of the question, but what about a bath?"

"Dream on. A shower... This is 1664. I am constantly having a battle about the bath with Maria. They think that having a bath is not good and may even give you the plague. Can you imagine they think that way?"

"Really, water gives you the plague?"

"I know, crazy, right? Fragrances are the order of the day. That is what they use to camouflage the smell. And if you go into the poorer parts of town, I'm afraid it's even worse. They don't have the luxury of perfumes. But don't let it prevent you from having a bath. I'll get Maria or Liesbeth to arrange one for you. Liesbeth is the maid here."

"You are rich, aren't you? All these servants," Robert said jokingly.

Saskia sought out her staff and instructed them to pull a bath for Robert, and to find some clothes. It was a long process. Drawing water, heating water, finding some form of soap and filling a metal bucket, though Saskia didn't think of it as a bucket as she knew it. A very big bucket was probably the best way of describing it. Once Robert got in, he found it very upright and not at all comfortable. Nevertheless, it was a welcome change, and he enjoyed the short time he was in there.

After he was dry, he tried his newly acquired, or rather loaned, clothes. They naturally didn't fit properly, but he forced his way into them until it was as respectable as it possibly could be. There was underwear of sorts, but not something he had any thought of wearing.

216

His own underwear was now just about dry, so he put that on. The rest was a longish white gown which protruded out from the tunic as a collar. He looked smart, with a blue tunic, and trousers coming to his knees, knee length socks, and boots to complete the picture. Even if the boots were tight.

"I feel like a new man," Robert said on his return.

"You look like someone out of a Rembrandt painting. Maybe you should be a model," Saskia replied.

"Do I get paid?"

"No. Interestingly, I have discovered that our next-door neighbour is an ex-student of Rembrandt, but I haven't met him yet." And then she said, "Robert, come with me."

"Lead the way. Where are we going?"

They went upstairs, two floors to the bedrooms, or bed chambers. When they were out of earshot of either Maria or Liesbeth, it was the first time Robert had an opportunity to privately get physically closer to Saskia and he took it, albeit briefly. They kissed passionately and Robert fumbled as he explored Saskia's heavy clothing, trying to get a little further than the outer layers. Saskia could see "expectation" in his eyes.

"Robert, as much as I want you, this is not going to work. At least not now. I came up here to show you the sleeping arrangements, because I think this is going to be our next big problem. Sleeping together is definitely out of the question, simply sleeping easily is going to be difficult... for you. You know what a box bed is, right?"

"Of course."

"Well, that's all we've got."

Saskia immediately opened some shutters to the first box bed. "Holy shit," said Robert, as he felt the claustrophobia and took in the size of the box bed. The box bed was essentially a large cupboard containing a mattress, and was completely enclosed, except for the entrance. It might have helped you to stay warm when there was no heating, but the bed was narrow and very short.

"Is that really all you've got?" questioned Robert.

"I'm afraid so. Not exactly designed for people like you, eh?"

"It's less than one and a half metres, so do I just sit?"

"That's what a lot of people do, apparently. They're superstitious about lying completely flat, as it represents death. Can you believe that? Maybe you can sleep in a fetal position? Alone!"

"Yeah, sure. Isn't there an alternative? There is more than one box bed; we could take these uncomfortable looking matrasses out, join them together, and then we could sleep together. On the floor. It is summer."

"It's a nice idea, but I've already witnessed how nosey the staff are and we can't be together. I'm married, don't forget!" Saskia said, with a big smile. "For the time being, I'll sleep in a box bed in another room. But we'll find time alone, don't worry," she said as she sidled up to Robert and gave him an affectionate feel.

Robert felt much more at home now that he had a soul mate in the same time period. After a while, they found ways to explore their sexual urges without attracting the attention of Maria and Liesbeth. It was really quite simple. Almost every day required a trip to the market to buy meat, fish, and vegetables to feed all four of them. The difference now was that Saskia asked Liesbeth to go with Maria, so that she too could learn the art of selecting the food and haggling with the vendors. That gave Robert and Saskia the time to assuage their physical desires and they did so willfully and passionately, even more so than when they were in the twenty-first century. Their common dilemma drew them closer together.

218

All around them, the plague was taking its toll. That became clear from the many times they both went for a walk around the city. For Robert, it was still an eye-opener, as he took in the way of life, the chaos in the canals, the filth of everything. Yet there was a group of people, especially around the richer inner canals, who radiated wealth, class, and superiority over others.

The edge of the city was now only a very short distance from the centre, and Saskia led Robert to a place called the Overtoom. In 2019, the Overtoom was a main thoroughfare in the centre of the city, not far from the Rijksmuseum. Now it was a part of the polders on the outside of town, in the fields which spread out from the city.

"I wanted to show you something," Saskia said as they walked a short way up the Overtoom from the Leidseplein. "See that building there?"

"Yes."

"That's the Pesthuis, or Plague House, whatever you prefer to call it. If you wait long enough, you'll see barges bringing plague patients. This is the place where they are isolated from the rest of the city, quarantine, if you like. Most of them won't make it."

"It's completely moated," said Robert, as he looked to see that there was no way in other than via boat or a small drawbridge. More importantly, there was no way out.

"Did you know that the word quarantine comes from quaranta, which means forty in Italian. They set quarantine at forty days, so we have the Italians to thank for that."

"No, I didn't. But let's move on."

Robert was impressed to see the inventiveness and added, "Maybe you have become used to it, but just look at all those windmills. I saw many more in 1886—wall to wall windmills—but this is how it started, and it's such an impressive sight. Don't you think?"

"I'm sorry, I don't share the same fascination with them as you do, but I agree, they do have a certain magic about them, especially in such numbers. I know they're used for milling our grain, sawing wood, and even making paint. Or, rather, the raw materials for paint."

"Moving water came later, eh? For the land reclamation."

"There have to be some for moving water. But maybe not so much for creating polders, not yet."

"I don't know... Polders are such an interesting phenomenon. I've never understood how we Dutch came to give the word its two meanings. There's the obvious one, polders are reclaimed land surrounded by waterways. We've been doing that, very successfully, for generations—or we will have been doing that...I lose track. And then we have the other 'polder' which has basically turned the word into a verb, 'to polder'. So you naturally think it means to reclaim land. Right?"

"That would be your first thought. But we know better."

"We now use it to mean being pragmatic and finding a common consensus. Such a strange shift in meaning. But I suppose that was true for people who were reclaiming land. You can't do it on your own; you have to work with others, with your neighbours. Unless you're a king and happen to own the whole country!"

"Can couples polder?" asked Saskia. "I mean like you and me."

"Why not? We compromise, don't we?"

"Compromise is something for marriage! You and I are freer to do our own thing, and that's what we do. Right now though, I feel we need each other to get through this. So, yes, let's polder. But at the moment I don't have anything to be pragmatic about. In fact, I am lost for ideas to get us away from here. I'm pretty resilient, but one day I will break."

Robert sensed the fear in Saskia and gave her a hug. They then returned to the Herengracht.

CHAPTER SEVENTEEN

As best as they could, Robert and Saskia put aside any thoughts of the return of Saskia's "husband." They would cross that bridge when they came to it. In the meantime, life was spent watching their servants scrub almost everything clean, from floors to outside pavements, as well as cooking pans. Washing clothes and sheets in huge vats of boiling water also took up a lot of their time, as did the whole process of cooking. It was a struggle for Robert and Saskia not to be more proactive and even help with some chores. They made a couple of attempts to ease the burden on Maria and Liesbeth, but it was not welcomed because they interpreted it as a threat to their income and livelihood. They had been brought up to expect to serve in this fashion, and they were content with their lot. Nevertheless, it strained Robert and Saskia, so the only thing they could do was to compensate them by either giving them more time off, or money.

Church was another dilemma. Neither Robert nor Saskia were drawn to want to be a part of it, or even attend services. Even with Maria and Liesbeth, who were Catholics, the looks on their faces told the full story if Robert and Saskia even mumbled objections about going to church. In those days, Catholics and Protestants didn't really mix, but they tolerated each other and respected their beliefs, probably because they did at least share the same God. With some reluctance, Robert and Saskia went to church, though they had to find out in a very roundabout way which was their church. One time was enough for them to conclude that it was still not something for twenty-first centurists, though it did give Saskia the opportunity to try other, more formal clothes suitable for church. She liked the bright yellow mantle that draped over her shoulders. A bit of colour at last.

221

Robert and Saskia had now been in 1664 for close to a week, and it was getting serious for Robert. His insulin was as good as finished, and he did not fancy the idea of a starvation diet. That would be the only thing he could do to temporarily stave off an untimely death. The inevitable would happen if they could not get back to 2019, or even 2016. Right now, he didn't care, either would do. Robert returned to the bridge on the other side of the canal, since he still suspected that that was the common denominator. But nothing happened as he walked both ways over the bridge. He wondered if the fact that it was now a drawbridge made a difference. He didn't know. And since Saskia had no idea how she got there either, they were both drawing blanks.

Another day rolled around. It was a nice day and Robert and Saskia were sitting in the garden in the back when Maria suddenly came down the rickety steps and announced.

"You mother is here, Madam."

"My mother?"

'Yes Ma'am, I just asked her to wait a bit, and she didn't like that."

"Oh, well, I guess I cannot be a recluse. Show her here," said Saskia to Maria, who didn't really understand what a recluse was. Saskia turned to Robert:

"Woah. I have a mother!"

Saskia's "mother" made a regal entrance at the top of the stairs and came into the garden.

"Saskia, I think we should talk. Alone."

There was no introduction or speaking to Robert. He just sat there staring at her "mother" and immediately concluded that he was going to dislike her. She was dressed with some severity, all in black, and wore a stiff white collar, as if she was either going to—or coming from—a funeral. Saskia followed her "mother" inside to the living room at the front. They didn't sit.

"Who is that man, and what is he doing here? This is no way to treat your mother, or your husband for that matter. It's an embarrassment. People are talking."

Saskia realised she was going to have trouble explaining that Robert was a cousin, so she first went on the attack, even if she had never seen this woman before. She did try tact.

"Mother. You should not concern yourself about your own embarrassment. This is my decision, but I see no reason why I cannot accommodate an acquaintance from a far away place who is in need of help. His name is Robert, by the way."

"You are in no position to be doing this, but it is not my role to punish you. You have a husband for that, and I am sure you will face the consequences when he returns."

"No doubt I will, but that is a matter for the two of us."

"You seem too sure of yourself, young lady. But I cannot call you a young lady anymore. You are old enough to know better."

"Mother, I only have a friend in the house, nothing more. And it horrifies me to know there is such a poisonous grapevine in this city. I have every right to decide what happens in this house."

"You are not listening to me, are you? I hope your husband returns soon. You deserve what's coming to you."

At this point, Saskia's "mother" turned abruptly, exited the living room, and headed for the front door. Saskia followed—she did not know why; she had nothing more to say. She stood staring at the figure disappearing down the canal.

"Oh… hello Saskia, how are you?" came the sudden greeting from the street level. Saskia looked down to see someone at the door of the basement to number 87, her next-door neighbour. She was surprised she was being addressed by her first name.

"Hello, good morning," she replied, immediately trying to absorb what she could about who this might be. If he knew her name, then she had to know him.

"And a good morning to you. How are you?"

"Busy."

At that moment, Robert joined Saskia on the steps, because he had heard that there was no more arguing. As soon as she saw Robert, she changed the drift of the conversation.

"I'd like you to meet Robert Dekker, a cousin of mine from Groningen." She stuck to the same story.

Robert descended the steps to shake hands with the mystery man, who immediately put out his hand and said."

"It's a pleasure. I'm Saskia's neighbour, Cornelis Drost, Cornelis." He immediately added, "An artist, of sorts! At least I try."

"Thank you, Robert," thought Saskia. Now she had a name, and she realised they were on first-name terms.

"Cornelis, good to see you again. You look busy, and a little dusty."

"I'm working on a couple of new chests with Willem, one of my students. I am in need of more storage space, and I have discovered Willem has more talents than just painting."

Robert was less interested in the carpentry, so he pressed on the painting. "Is painting your main occupation? I mean, can you make a living from it?"

Cornelis took a step into the street and looked back at the extent of his house and answered with a big smile, "I have not done badly, eh? But I also had training from the best in the business."

Robert now looked more closely at the house. It was different from Saskia's, insofar as it was a little higher and had much more light coming in from a vast expanse of latticed windows.

"Indeed, it is a nice house. And I assume you get a lot of light through those windows, which helps. What type of painting do you do? Landscapes?"

"No, not at all. My master for my apprenticeship was Rembrandt van Rijn. You may have heard of him. He was, and to a certain extent still is, a successful painter of the wealthy. So, when I was one of his pupils, we had a strict regime of first following the basics and then moved on to copying his paintings. So, my style is formed on his, but that was many years ago. I now pursue my own interests. It has been profitable, as you can see. And Willem now is one of my students."

"So the house doubles as a studio and your living quarters?" Robert asked naively.

"Of course, who doesn't do that? We cannot afford to have both. Why don't you come in and have a look?"

"I'd love to."

They walked up the front steps and into the expanse of a wide hall with reddish floor tiles, a hallway to the back, and a wood panelled stairwell to the higher floors. As they were going to look at Cornelis' work, they had to go upstairs to the second floor, which was where all the action was. The ground and first floors were clearly reserved for the living accommodation.

At the top of the stairs to the second floor—there was also a third floor and an attic—it opened out into a vast expanse, one room extending from the front to the back of the house. The daylight came

225

in from both ends, and Cornelis had set up his studio to take full advantage of the light. It was almost like a combination of an artist's studio, with the commensurate mess, and a theatrical costume archive. Cornelis clearly kept a vast choice of garments and props to adorn or enhance the looks of his subjects. Cornelis, like Rembrandt, was a painter of live subjects, preferably for a pre-agreed fee. Along the walls, there was a mix of paintings hanging and waiting to be bought, while others were leant up against the foot of the wall, presumably also for sale.

"Well. This is my studio. My clients come and sit for me here and I use the light from the windows as it best suits my preferred style, and naturally what the client wants. As you can see, my focus is live portraits. Unlike van Rijn, I have not yet included dead bodies in my repertoire," he said with a smile.

Robert and Saskia looked around some more. It was a big room. There was a section reserved for making the paints from the available raw materials, as well as the new canvases being made ready for the next order. There was even a small part where some etching was done. It was a mini factory and Cornelis was proud of his achievements.

As they moved towards the back of the house, Robert and Saskia could see the work being done on the chests that Cornelis had been talking about.

"These are the chests you are working on?" said Robert.

"Yes, do you like them?"

Robert had a reason for asking. He had been momentarily silenced as he realised he was looking at the chest he had bought in 2019, at least one of them. He could now see there were two of them, ingeniously designed so that when pushed together they formed a symmetrical whole, though asymmetric when separated. Each chest had on one side a twirled post at the front that must have been produced on a wood lathe. One on the left for the left-hand chest and one on the right for the right-hand one. The other sides were left unworked, so when pushed together they became one long chest. There was method here, thought Robert. That way Cornelis could more easily get them in and out through the windows, if needed.

"Very much so. One day, I'd like to own them." Robert could not resist the irony, which naturally fell flat on Cornelis. "You must have put a lot of work into them," he added, "but I see they are not quite finished yet."

"Indeed. We are still working on some of the drawers. They are over there."

Robert moved a little closer and could see that Willem, or Cornelis, had started painting over an old panel which already had a painting on it. It was a portrait of a woman, but half of it was already covered in a brown paint.

"Needs must, as they say," Cornelis said. He could see Robert showing some concern that he was ruining a perfectly good painting. "It's an old panel from van Rijn, and he didn't want it anymore. The painting is of his first wife, Saskia, who died many years ago. He has done so many paintings of her. I have had it lying around for a while, so we are now going to use it as the underside of one of the drawers. Good idea, eh?"

There was an inaudible "Oh my God" from both Robert and Saskia. All that came out was from Saskia. "I am in good company, with my name."

There was a pregnant silence, mainly from Robert, as they took in the magnitude of what they had just seen. Robert had never paid any attention to the chest he had bought for Daniel, other than knowing it was a pastel blue now, but it looked very much like one of the ones he was now staring at. It had the twirl on one end, but frankly he had no idea which chest he had. Looking at what was in front of him was not going to change that, because not all the drawers had been placed yet, and it could be in either one.

"Wow," said Robert. "Just the one painting from van Rijn?" And then he felt a big dig from Saskia's elbow. "I mean, are you using more panels like this?"

"No, just this one from van Rijn. We don't really use panels for painting anymore, just canvases. I have one or two of my own panels from years ago, so I may use those as well."

"Well, I hope they serve you well when you are finished. And, I hope they have a long life."

Robert felt another dig in his side, a message to say that he was overdoing things.

They stayed a short while and chatted with Cornelis, and his student Willem, who was also a lodger and assistant. They learnt more about how the Guilds controlled the different trades in the city, especially how that related to the painters. As Cornelis described it, it was a bit like an education accrediting body but on a much smaller scale; the Guild determined who was entitled to teach apprentices, and they took a fee in the process. Cornelis had once been an apprentice of van Rijn, but was now a Master in his own right, with his own students.

Cornelis walked them to the door. "You don't have far to go! And, Saskia, don't forget, my offer still stands."

Cornelis could see the blank look on her face. "Your portrait. One day?"

"Ah, yes, we'll see. Have a good day, Cornelis."

Just at that moment, Cornelis hesitated and said to Saskia and Robert, "Wait there."

They were poised to enter their house, but stayed on the front door platform awaiting Cornelis' next instructions. They didn't know what was going on.

In the meantime, Cornelis was headed down the canal where he greeted an old man who was walking in their direction. He was stooped and looking at the road more than ahead of him, but Cornelis took him by the upper arm and guided him further. He was wearing a black beret. Underneath it Robert saw ruffled hair.

Robert and Saskia looked at each other. "Are you thinking what I am?" said Robert.

"I'm pretty sure I am. Rembrandt himself?"

As the two men reached the steps, Cornelis looked up and said, "What a coincidence eh? I would like you to meet my former Master, and good friend, Rembrandt van Rijn."

Robert was used to meeting musical stars from all walks of life, but this encounter fell into a different universe. They both descended the short flight of stairs and offered a hand to Rembrandt.

"An absolute honour to meet you," they both said almost in unison.

"Why an honour? I am but a humble, and fallen, painter."

"Oh, I think you do yourself an injustice. Your reputation precedes you."

"That's very nice of you, but how would you know? My paintings are not exactly on public display."

Robert had to backtrack a little but couldn't help saying, "Oh, I think you'll be surprised." And continued immediately with, "But Cornelis told us of course, and we know of your work for many of the city founders."

Now Rembrandt revealed a bit of his belligerent nature, as if it was a test. "Oh, who, for example?

Robert immediately tried, "Jan Six," because he was the only one he knew.

"You know Jan Six?"

"No, unfortunately not."

"That's probably just as well."

They stayed on the front steps a little longer and chatted some more, but both Robert and Saskia had to tread very carefully with their words to avoid falling into a trap of knowing too much. After all, Rembrandt was now more or less public property in Holland, but the one they were talking to was looking at the bottom of a financial barrel and only had a few years of his life left. He didn't know that, though it was hard for Robert not to feel that he did.

Once back in the house, they asked for some drinks from Liesbeth and sat for a while in the living room.

"Can you believe that? Rembrandt. Wow," said Robert. "And I still haven't used my mobile to get any pictures. I wonder if I can find a way of getting a photo of him."

"Leave it. We don't even know if we can get out of here, so what good is it to anyone? Besides, even if they have no idea what a mobile phone looks like, it would be too intrusive, and you'd have to find a way of doing it very discretely. No, leave it."

"Maybe you're right, but if I do get the opportunity, I'll take it."

There then followed a pregnant silence as they both drank their juices. The silence was strange. They had both just been witness to something dramatic that could impact them if and when they got back. Potentially, one of the chests had a hidden Rembrandt, and Robert knew he had one of those chests. He said nothing. Neither did Saskia.

She knew she also had one of those chests, but which one? She didn't know Robert had one, but that was not stopping her from staying silent on the matter.

In the silence, Robert's mind was working overtime. He told Saskia he was going to go and sit at the front on the canal. He had a plan, but he avoided saying anything about it to Saskia. In the house, he picked up a ladder-back chair and took it down the front stairs and planted himself on it in front of their house. There was plenty to watch on the canals and he was not bored.

Robert was patient. An hour or so later, Rembrandt appeared at the top of the stairs to number 87, together with Cornelis. They were saying their goodbyes and Rembrandt gingerly descended the short flight of steps to the road. For his part, Cornelis went back into his house.

Rembrandt was a slow walker, so Robert had no trouble catching up with him.

"Do you mind me walking with you?"

"Not at all. I welcome the company, Mr... Oh, I'm sorry, I know we have just met, but I have forgotten your name."

"Dekker, Robert Dekker."

"Ah, yes. Are you interested in paintings?"

"Yes, but I am an amateur compared to you."

"You know my work?"

Robert knew he had to answer carefully.

"Only a little. But I was given the opportunity to see the *Night Watch* once, a magnificent painting."

"*Night Watch?* That's not one of mine."

"The large one with the civilian militia. I remember it had a dog in it," Robert was now struggling.

"You mean the shooting company of Cocq and his followers? That was a while ago. Why do you call it the *Night Watch*?"

"Oh, that's just a name I heard someone give it. The other one was much too long."

"What do you expect from ego-trippers who want their names spelled out in the title? And some of the subjects in the painting still grumbled because they weren't prominent enough. That was a good time. I was ambitious then; now look at me."

"We're all ambitious, but for some of us it's a question of what do we do while we are waiting," Robert said with a wry smile. "You were blessed with an extraordinary talent." He had meant to say "are," but it worked both ways.

"Yes, I've done well, but I have not exactly been a model of consistency in my life. My home on the Rozengracht is far removed from what I used to have on the Breestraat, near the Nieuwemarkt. That was a house, and all my students came there."

"Yes, I know," Robert said unthinkingly.

"You know?"

"Uhm, yes, I believe I know because someone once pointed it out to me. One day people will pay money to visit it because you lived there.

"Oh, I doubt that. That house was like a painting factory, but that's the past. Fortunately, I still have a little work, but, tragically, my partner Hendrickje passed away last year from the plague. That was hard."

"I can imagine."

232

"But I still have my son Titus, and daughter, Cornelia. That's all I've got. All the others have died, and oh so young."

Robert thought it best to get Rembrandt off this track, and he wanted to know more about "his" painting. In case Rembrandt didn't know what was happening to the panel, he chose not to mention its future intended use. That might be inappropriate.

"Cornelis showed us an old painted panel of yours that you had given him. Of a woman. Who was the model?"

"Oh, that one. I remember. Yes, it was of my wife Saskia. She died a long time ago. I did so many of her. It wasn't one of my best, as I recall."

"I thought it was good," Robert lied. Most of it was painted over so he had not been able to form an opinion.

By now they were turning off the Herengracht onto the Rozengracht. It was not much further to Rembrandt's house, but Robert had to temper his speed to allow Rembrandt to take his time.

"Are you coming with me the whole way?" asked Rembrandt.

"It's not far, is it?"

"No, but you have already been kind enough keeping an old man company."

"It's not a problem."

A short while later, they arrived.

"Behold, my modest accommodation." Rembrandt looked up and down at his house. "As you can see, we have a small business as an art dealer and some secondhand goods, but I can still paint here. That's the most important. You are welcome to come in if you like."

"I'd love that," Robert said as curiosity got the better of him.

The "shop" was not open, so Rembrandt had to unlock it. Once inside, Robert gazed admiringly at a mish mash of art scattered around the walls, and some on the floor, leaning against the same walls.

"They are not all mine," said Rembrandt.

"It's still an impressive collection. How do you manage to combine this business with your painting?"

"Oh, that's relatively easy. There are not that many people who impulsively buy art, so I do have the time. It's no secret that I cannot run this business, so my son Titus looks after it. If I were to own it, I would have my creditors breaking down the door. I'm afraid I still have a lot people I owe money to, so I need to be creative. They can't go after Titus. Clever, eh?"

"Very," was all Robert replied, as the cogs in his brain were trying to take in the fact that even in 1664 people were protecting their personal assets by creating other entities. Robert wondered why in hell he hadn't done that with *Masters in Paint.*

"Come with me, upstairs. Let me show you my small studio where I still paint."

Robert dutifully followed Rembandt up the narrow staircase and to the back of the house where the best light came in. He had a very modest set up which contained all the accoutrements he needed to paint. In one corner there was an easel, but now the room was dominated by a huge canvas that was supported on an angled structure and went all the way down to the floor.

"Wow, that's looks very familiar," were the wrong words but Robert had no time to correct himself as they came out of his mouth.

"Familiar? Mr Dekker, it seems you have a strange affinity with my work."

"No, sorry, my mistake. I thought one of the officials looked very familiar to me. But what an impressive painting."

"Yes, I was happy with it."

"Was?"

"I finished the painting two years ago. It is a portrait of members of the Drapers Guild, the ones who certify textiles. They have had it for two years, but now they want changes. Can you believe that? After two years."

"But why?"

"Egos. There is no other word for it. See the one on the left. He now thinks I have not made him prominent enough, so all I am doing is highlighting his presence a bit more. They are paying, so perhaps I shouldn't grumble."

Robert's thoughts were now drawn to Maria's guide to Rembrandt's paintings when he and Saskia were at the Rijksmuseum. He clearly remembered standing in front of this work of art. He couldn't remember everything that was said about it, but now he had the privilege of his own more intimate look at the master at work. *Masters in Paint* also had it in their portfolio, but no one had ever ordered it.

At that moment, a young girl came down from upstairs and into the studio.

"Hello, my dear, said Rembrandt," and added, "Say hello to Mr Dekker, he is visiting briefly."

"It is nice to meet you, Mr Dekker."

"This is my daughter, Cornelia. She is now ten years old. I call her Cornelia the third, as if she were a queen; which you are, right?" As Rembrandt looked directly into her eyes.

"The third?" said Robert.

"Yes, she's my treasure, and I want it to stay that way. I have had three daughters, all with the name Cornelia. The other two died very young, so she is all I have now. And Titus."

"God, that sounds tragic."

"We live in difficult times, Mr Dekker. If it's not childbirth that kills you, then it's the plague. Like my Hendrickje."

"Papa, I'm hungry," said Cornelia.

Robert picked up on that and immediately indicated that he had better be getting back home.

"I enjoyed our walk and the visit. I am sure your paintings will endure through the centuries," he said. These were his last words to Rembrandt.

CHAPTER EIGHTEEN

He was welcomed home with, "where have you been? I didn't know you were going on a wander."

Robert told the truth, but also a little white lie. "I came across Rembrandt out front as he was leaving Cornelis, so I offered to walk with him. He liked that. I walked him home, and even got to see his house and studio."

"What did you talk about?"

"It was very generic really, nothing specific. But he did tell me about the tragedy of losing all of his partners, and most of his children. And his financial woes. But you and I have the benefit of history books."

"Didn't you talk about any of his paintings?"

"Not really. I got myself into a bit of a hole because I referred to the *Night Watch,* but that wasn't the original title. I don't know who gave it the *Night Watch* name, but it's a lot better than the original essay of a title."

Robert then added, "Rembrandt also showed me the huge painting he did of the Drapers Guild. He was working on some changes. Do you remember we saw it at the Rijksmuseum at the reception? It's really big."

"Oh, I'm sorry. I don't recall. Should I have?"

"No, that's OK. It was just such a privilege to see it in that setting."

Saskia didn't really know why she was concerned about Robert's intimate moments with Rembrandt. She did wonder if he had asked about the painting on the panel. Robert had seen a similar chest in her house, so why should she worry about it. She now knew there were two chests but didn't know where the second one was. Robert had that one already figured out, so he was in pole position.

Another two days passed uneventfully, apart from Robert being more vigilant about what he was eating and trying to stay away from the carbohydrates. He was often to be found in the kitchen, much to the amusement of the staff who were not used to anything like this. It was more out of boredom than anything else and, one day, when he and Saskia were on their own, they found themselves using the kitchen utensils as percussion for their impromptu singing of the Rolling Stones *You Can't Always Get What You Want.* The choice of song summed up their predicament, which is what they had been talking about. Liesbeth and Maria were outside and alarmed when they heard what to them was a ruckus. They rushed to the kitchen to see two people using wooden spoons, banging copper pans and singing words that did not sit well with their Catholic upbringing. Still, they smiled, because they could see their mistress was having

237

fun, something which they were not used to. She had become very different since Robert arrived.

"What would the Master say if he saw this?" Liesbeth said to Maria.

Robert and Saskia now noticed that their staff were standing in the doorway, and Robert bowed, as if to ask what they thought of their theatre.

Saskia had an urge to be alone with Robert, so asked, "Isn't it time for you two to be off to the market?"

Maria got the message but didn't make the romantic connection.

"Yes, Madam, if you could please give us some money for the market."

"Oh, you are so right. Of course, one moment."

Saskia retreated to a room that was more private and where she kept a locked draw of valuables. It really was forbidden territory for any of her staff. When she returned, she gave Maria a few coins, but Saskia was still struggling to know how much each coin represented. They were so unclear.

"Madam, this may not be enough."

Robert was standing right next to her and his backpack was in easy reach. As he wanted to show he too could make a contribution, he reached into the side pocket and pulled out all the coins he had and held them out for Maria to look at.

Maria was stunned that she was even being invited to make a choice, but as she only saw one coin that looked familiar to her, she grabbed it from Robert's open palm. It was the coin that had been travelling with him since 2019.

"That will be more than enough. Thank you, sir."

"Happy hunting," said Robert. But he got a very quizzical look in response as Maria and Liesbeth disappeared.

As soon as Maria had gone, Saskia asked, "Where did you get that coin?"

"Oh, I've had it a while now. I was having a coffee one day at a café, and it had been left on the table. I've had it with me ever since."

"You mean since you were here now? No, that can't be. Where do you get coffee?"

"No, in 2019."

"You got a current coin for this century, just like that, in 2019. No explanation?"

"Yes. I haven't given it a great deal of thought. Although... I vowed to check it out one day. I've grown attached to it because it's just an odd-looking coin."

As soon as the words came out of Robert's mouth, he heard himself thinking that maybe this coin played a role in his time travel, and not just the bridge. He was looking at Saskia and could see that she was also making the same connection.

"There could be more to this coin than I thought," said Robert.

"You betcha."

"But there's no way of knowing."

"Yes, but right now we have a bigger problem. If it is your ticket, then you have just given it away."

"Where's the market? More to the point, what route do Maria and Liesbeth take? We need to catch them, and in a hurry."

"I'm not sure, but I think it's next to the Dam."

Robert gave Saskia an affectionate hug, but it had to be a very quick one. They then rushed out the door and headed in the direction of the Dam square.

"They should only be about two or three minutes ahead of us, but where?"

Robert and Saskia decided to simply take the shortest route they knew to the market and try and head them off there. If they came across them en route, so much the better. They didn't.

They didn't immediately see them at the market either. It wasn't a big market, but they still split up in order to increase their chances. Robert's adrenaline was really flowing now. After a while, he got a glimpse of Maria and Liesbeth at a fish stall. They must have been moving very fast because the stallholder was already handing over some fish. Robert pounced on poor old Maria as she was fumbling for the money, grabbing her by the arm, but not too forcefully.

"Maria. Sorry, please stop what you are doing."

Maria was stunned. Even if this was not her mistress, there was no reason not to stop, so she turned and faced Robert.

"Mr Dekker. What are you doing here?"

Robert didn't want to fumble with explanations, so he simply said, "Maria, we'd like you to use different coins to pay for the fish. Not the ones I gave you. Could you please give me the money? It's important."

"But where's Madam?"

On cue, Saskia appeared behind Maria and confirmed what Robert had asked.

"Yes, please, Maria, give me the money."

"But I need the money for the fish."

"I know. We will get you some other money. We just need these coins for something else."

"Yes, ma'am." And she handed over all of the coins without any more questioning. It was not her position to question her mistress.

"Thank you," said Robert, as he began to pick his way through the coins to see if he could find and identify his coin. He couldn't—at least not immediately.

"I suggest we all head home and we'll sort this out there and we'll find some other coins for you."

Maria looked on in bewilderment, as did Liesbeth, but they acquiesced, and dutifully followed their mistress home. Once there, Saskia retreated to her room and managed to find a bit more money in the loosely arranged drawer. She apologised once more to Maria and Liesbeth for the inconvenience and they both left again for the market. Needless to say, the two of them could not figure out why one set of coins was different from another.

Once they were gone, Saskia and Robert sat down with a drink, this time some wine in a goblet.

"You know, we still don't know if we just did the right thing—if the coin plays a role," said Robert.

"I know, but we have nothing to lose and it's now our only realistic lead. What do we do?"

"Well, for one thing, I'm not sure which one is my coin. I think it's this one, as he held it up, but I am going to play safe and lay claim to all, if I may. Even if it's not all my money," said Robert, as he leaned forward looking into Saskia's eyes. "But my biggest concern is that it only applies to me, and I want you with me. You arrived here on your own, but we still don't know how."

Robert could see tears welling up in Saskia's eyes as she realised that he might now have a passport out of the seventeenth century and, indeed, she didn't want to be left alone. But she knew Robert had to try, no matter what.

Now that the two girls were gone, Saskia got up and went to sit on Robert's lap and submerged her face in his neck. She wanted to be close to him, but all thoughts of some romantic time together had gone out the window. Now was time to address what they could do.

"We have to make an attempt at the bridge, don't you think? I am not optimistic, but we should at least give it a try. And I am totally done here," Saskia said.

"You're right. There's absolutely no point in hanging around. Let's go and at least pick up Henry, just in case he is also part of this strange complot. After all, he came with me, at least on the last leg."

Robert picked up his backpack.

"'Do you really need that?" asked Saskia.

"We don't know what is going to happen and I don't exactly have pockets in this outfit. Nor do you. I am going to take what insulin I have, and let's take some bread and wine with us, in my water bottle, just in case. A picnic. Of sorts."

Robert made sure he had the coins with him, and he and Saskia left the house to take the short walk down the canal and over the bridge to the stables. Henry had been there for a while and had been exercised. Robert wanted to think that Henry would be happy to see him, but there was no feeling of warmth. Robert asked for Henry to be saddled up, and informed the boy looking after Henry that they were going for a ride and would be back later.

Another stable boy recognised Saskia and came over to speak to her.

"Mrs Lohman. It's good to see you again. It has been a while. You must be very happy?"

"Very happy?"

"Yes, your husband."

"What do you mean, my husband?"

"He's back from his trip. I saw him about an hour ago. He came to get his horse."

Saskia didn't say anything, but she could see that Robert was already on his horse—not looking particularly comfortable, but at least he was on it. He looked a picture, in seventeenth century clothes and a twentieth century backpack with a Heineken logo on it. He was not looking at Saskia, so had no idea what was going on in her head. He was talking to Henry as if he was a kid, if only to calm his own nerves.

"Robert."

"I'm still here."

"We have a problem."

"I know that," answered Robert, thinking of his horse.

"Apparently my husband has returned."

"How do you know?"

"The stable boy just told me. He came and picked up his horse and is somewhere in town. That means he will be back soon, and we don't have a plan. No matter what happens, I'm staying with you. Are you clear on that?"

"Absolutely. But let's get away from here. We know where we're going anyway."

"I'm with you." As she went in search of a horse, even if it wasn't her own.

At that moment, an elegantly dressed man on a horse rode up to the stables. He was dressed in black, with boots up to his thighs, a tunic with gold edging and a broad-brimmed hat with a square emblem at the front. He also had a small sword. The expression on his face was enough for Robert. He assumed immediately that this was Saskia's husband and, while he may be elegant, he was short and blushed in the face. Too much wine maybe. Or was it anger?

He dismounted and waited as Saskia came back from the depths of the stables. He stood firmly in front of her, with both hands on his hips, as if to say, "I am the boss around here."

Saskia guessed immediately what she was facing. She put aside any seventeenth century female deference and went on the attack.

"With whom do I have the pleasure?" she said.

Just that one sentence was enough to make her unrecognised husband boil over. He got really close to Saskia, but she stood her ground, looking up at Robert on his horse.

"You, woman, are coming home with me. I have only been back a few hours and you are the talk of the town." And then to Robert. "You, sir, have a lot to answer for, but I will come to you later once we have spoken to the elders."

Robert decided to get involved. "You are already making some big assumptions without even introducing yourself. And you are?"

"Don't be stupid. You are of no standing here and I demand that you stay away from my wife."

Robert stayed put on his horse as it made him feel stronger. His possible opponent was a lot smaller. But he did have a sword.

"Saskia," said Robert in very measured tones, "I suggest we leave this gentleman to his anger and go on our way." She was ruggedly following the strategy of declining to know who he was.

Saskia nodded and moved to some form of protection behind Henry. She still didn't have a horse, but that didn't matter, and they walked away from the stables towards the Herengracht. Saskia's husband was not used to being defied, especially by a woman, so he pursued, on his remounted horse.

As Robert and Saskia turned onto the Herengracht, they both felt the hot breath of pursuit and heard the hooves getting closer. Saskia turned to see that her "husband" had now taken out his sword. He was not after her, because she would be easy prey once he had dealt with Robert. Saskia yelled at Robert.

"He's got his sword out. You go!" And then she added, "But come back for me."

Robert felt his opponent getting very close, yelling and threatening him. Against his better judgement, he gave Henry a whack, but Henry didn't need it. He felt the danger too and bounded off down the Herengracht with Robert clinging on. He bounced in some form of rhythm with his horse, learning quickly. The two horses were matched for speed, but now there was the bridge ahead of them. Robert's bridge. Fortunately, it had not been raised, so was not open. Traders with their goods on donkeys and ponies jumped to one side as they passed.

Robert was at the bridge and wanted to turn left so he could go back for Saskia, but he was going too fast. Henry seemed in no mood for making the turn, and Robert wasn't even sure he could turn at the speed he was going. The incline to the bridge was now steeper than before, but that was no obstacle for Henry. He bounded over the apex. All of a sudden there was silence, a momentary void as Robert's world changed around him.

PART VI

The Discovery

CHAPTER NINETEEN

He was back in his blue Volvo, not the red one, the blue one.

"That means 2019. The present." It was his only thought. He was getting used to the sudden time travel, but now the important thing was he was back. He saw confirmation in the familiar mess of his car. He could see the insulin he had left behind sitting invitingly on the seat next to him. Relief overpowered shock. This was so what he had been hoping for.

Unlike in earlier centuries, the bridge was not a good place to stop the car and take in the sights, and Robert wasn't interested in them. He wanted to find a parking place, so he navigated between the bikes and cars until he found a spot where he could stop. His backpack was still on his back and pressing uncomfortably against him and the car seat.

He exited the car and immediately removed the offending item. He had parked in a spot reserved for electric vehicles, but he didn't care and couldn't keep himself from hugging the charger in front of him, as if it was the sign he needed, telling him he was back in the right century, even the right year. There were not many people around, but those that were started staring at him, very obviously looking him up and down, taking in a strangely dressed man hugging a charging point. He knew the drill—being stared at—but now he was in seventeenth-century attire and everyone around him was in jeans, even shorts.

Although he knew he was back, the first thing he did was retrieve his mobile from his backpack and turn it on. It didn't have much juice left, but enough for him to see that it was working, and by the time the phone connected with a network it showed him the date and time he wanted to see, 2019. He was indeed back in the world of the living, his living.

Robert was about to put his phone away when he suddenly realised that something didn't feel right. He had looked at the date very quickly—all he was really interested in was the year. But now he was looking at the home screen and in particular at the date and time. With what he had just been through, he was expecting it to tell him that he had been away for a couple of weeks or so. But that wasn't the case. The date was the same as when he left. The time as well, he guessed. How could that be, he asked himself. "I know full well I travelled to different centuries, and I also know it was more than a few days." Robert was once more beginning to question his own sanity.

"I have photos. They don't lie," he said to himself.

But they did. He switched quickly to his photo gallery. Nothing was there. Empty. "How could that be, have I really not been anywhere?"

On the face of it, the absence of photos seemed to make logical sense. If he had only been away for nanoseconds, or even not all, there wouldn't be any photos. That appeared to be the situation he was looking at. Maybe he would find out more when he got home, or at Saskia's place, if she was there. Right now, he needed to do something about his clothes.

In order to avoid more stares, he got back in the car and sat for a while. First, he would go and find a shop where he could acquire new clothes, not from 1664. "Surely that's also proof of where I have been," he thought.

His other concern was Saskia. Where was she? He knew it was unlikely she would be travelling with him, but his urge now was to see her and to know she was safe. More so than to go and see his wife. That thought made him feel both uncomfortable and excited, but given what he and Saskia had been through, she was now his priority.

Robert left the car where it was, not too far from Amsterdam's main shopping street. He still had money and cards from when he first left, so he didn't need to worry about paying for anything. He would, however, have to run the gauntlet of more people staring at him, but this was Amsterdam, and Robert often saw the weirdest of outfits anyway.

He walked to the Nieuwendijk, a popular shopping street. He didn't really care about what he bought, so he selected one shop where he could buy everything.

"Nice outfit," said one person as he was entering a department store.

Robert was ready for this. "Yeah, you like it? Just finishing some scenes for a TV ad. Roasted peanuts!"

Robert didn't take long to find what he needed. He wasn't in the mood to be selective. He bought a shirt, jacket and jeans, as well as some new underwear, which was a priority. Shoes would follow later. He paid for the goods, but immediately returned to the changing rooms and removed his 17th century outfit. He didn't throw them away, as this was now his only link with the past, and he wanted to hold onto them.

Once he was outside, he called Saskia. There was no reply, just voicemail. He didn't leave a message; she would see that he had called. As he was not too far away from her house, he decided to walk over to see if she was home. The suspense was killing him. To be on the safe side, he went back to his car first so that he could leave the backpack behind. He was not going to run the risk of crossing any bridges with the coin that he now suspected of being at the root of all his troubles.

He reached Saskia's house and pressed the doorbell. It required several attempts before the door was opened and Robert found himself looking at a much bruised and badly injured Saskia. She was wearing loose pyjamas and a light dressing gown. On seeing Robert, she limply fell towards him as if to say how much she needed him. She was exhausted.

The most important thing for Robert was that there was immediate recognition. This was his Saskia. There was a moment where he thought he might be confronted by a 17th century Saskia, but he now shared his relief with the real Saskia.

"Thank God, it's you." It seemed like a strange thing to say, but Saskia knew what he meant.

Her reply came, "Robert, I'm so glad to see you." She said it with emphasis and emotion as she stayed on the open doorstep in Robert's embrace. "You can see what I have been through. I'm so glad to be back."

They stayed like this for a while and then Robert gently maneuvered Saskia back into the house and closed the door.

"Stupid question, but are you OK? Or do we need to get you to a doctor?"

"No, to the first question. And no to the second," came the reply.

"OK, then let's at least get you comfortable and have a look at your injuries."

Saskia didn't reply and allowed herself to be looked after by Robert. He was free to treat Saskia as a "patient," and he dutifully made sure he could not see anything that required immediate attention. He couldn't. Just a lot of black and blue over her whole body and occasional grazing.

"You have been in the wars, haven't you? What happened?"

"After you were chased down the Herengracht and you disappeared over the bridge."

"You could see I disappeared?"

"Yes, I think so, it all happened so quickly."

"My 'husband' returned in an absolute fury" —Saskia raised both hands with curled fingers pointing upward to highlight air quotes as she put emphasis on her so-called husband and continued— "He had lost you but naturally still felt the need to deal with me. Despite the fact that he was small, I have to say he was quite strong, and he dragged me back home, literally. I was resisting as best as I could and naturally no one on the street helped me. I was the pariah."

"Holy shit. And?"

"By the time we got home, my clothes were already torn, and the bruises were beginning to show. The assault continued behind closed doors without him even making an attempt to ask me for my story. The jury of public opinion had already done its work in our small city."

"So, how did it end?"

"We were in the kitchen. The scuffling became violent and I really felt threatened. I managed to grab one of the pokers in the stove. It wasn't red hot, but it was hot enough to inflict some damage, so my husband will have a scar on his face to remember me by. Unfortunately, that made him even angrier and he maneuvered me to the top of the basement stairs and pushed me down. In the process, I must have been knocked unconscious, and the next thing I knew I was back here, also in the basement, at the bottom of the stairs."

"Well, if there is another Saskia who has gone back to him, he will be utterly perplexed if she has no injuries to show for all his anger."

"Maybe, but I wouldn't like to be in her shoes."

"No need to be. We're back together now and you're safe with me." This was a thought Robert wanted to plant firmly. "Now, what can I do for you right now?"

251

"Nothing really. I'm OK, just a little weak and tired. The bruises will mend, and I'll be back to normal," she said, then asking, "But what happened to you? You're in jeans?"

"As you say, you saw me disappear, and I ended up in my car, as if nothing had happened. So, I immediately went to buy some replacement clothes, naturally not without smart-arse comments from passersby on what I was wearing. And, as far as I can determine, you and I have only been away for nanoseconds. My phone display gives day and time exactly where I left off. And all my photos are gone. Not there."

"So, nothing from any of your time periods. No Rembrandt?"

"Nope. Zilch."

"That's not good." And then Saskia re-thought what she said. "Well maybe it is good. It'll be our secret."

"I like that." At the mention of Rembrandt, the question both had left unsaid in the past returned to them. Did they have a Rembrandt in one of their chests? Again, they both kept quiet.

After a while Robert could see that Saskia was getting tired and he ought to head home. He had wanted to ask more questions, but that would come later. He had a nagging urge to start investigating the chest in Daniel's room, but there was also no rush there. The world around him was turning as before, and there were only two people who knew about the chest.

Robert drove home, charging his phone via the car adapter as he went. He still had his house keys and entered as if it was just another day. Belinda was at home, as she often was.

"What are you doing home so early? I hadn't been expecting you," she said.

"Change of plans," muttered Robert. By now he knew that he would not have been missed, but that still didn't feel right in his own mind, because he had been away for a long time; that's the way it felt.

Belinda caught a glimpse of Robert putting down a shopping bag in the hallway as he came into the open living room area.

"Eh?" said Belinda with some emphasis. "Didn't you leave here this morning with jeans and your tan jacket?"

"Yes. But I had a mishap with some coffee and it went everywhere. And it wasn't just a cup of coffee, it was a full jug. I figured the best way to solve the problem was to buy something new, because I was not about to walk around all day in wet clothes."

"And I dumped them as well," Robert added, since he knew Belinda well enough to know she would eventually wonder where the dirty clothes were.

"Are you crazy? They were perfectly good clothes, and we have a washing machine you know. Or wasn't it coffee?" said Belinda, as if she thought coffee was too convenient as an excuse.

Belinda's frosty response confirmed to Robert that he was back in the reality he wanted but, at the same time, the one he didn't want.

Belinda continued. "You bought more things? What's in the bag?"

"Just some costume clothes we may use in some videos for parts of a festival promotion. He then added, "I'm going to take a shower. To get the stickiness of the coffee off."

"OK. But I definitely can't smell coffee." Belinda edged closer to Robert. He ignored her and headed upstairs.

Once upstairs Robert peeked into Daniel's room. It was absurd to think that the chest was not there, but he still needed to reassure himself that all was unchanged. Indeed it was; the chest was in the same corner, covered in the usual clutter that teenagers have a knack for leaving. He would come back to that after his shower. The urge to investigate was overwhelming.

Robert was back in Daniel's room immediately after his shower, having washed off the remaining grime from 1664. Belinda was busy, so he was unlikely to be disturbed, but he was not about to do anything dramatic. He opened each of the drawers and rummaged around inside so that the bottoms would be exposed. Each one had perfectly normal looking bare wood which had seen the wear and tear of use. There was definitely no painting there. But he wasn't done yet. He also had to look at the underside, which meant emptying every drawer. How to do that without attracting attention from downstairs?

The most sensible thing to do was to wait until everyone was out of the house. Robert knew that, but it's not every day you have the possibility of discovering an unknown Rembrandt. He started at the top and put the first drawer onto Daniel's bed. Not wanting to empty it, he tipped it up so that he could see the underside. "Bingo," he thought, this one was painted over in a solid brown paint and looked pretty old. The paint looked similar in colour to the one he saw in Cornelis' house, but it was cracking and peeling and looked like the cracked mud you would see in deserts. He grabbed a pair of small scissors and, ever so gently, started scraping at the edges which looked like they would peel off relatively easily. Still, this was not the time or place to try and scrape paint from the middle of the drawer.

Robert was not overly excited by what he found, probably because he was working on one of the edges, but he was pretty sure there was something there. He put the chaos of the contents back as more chaos and resumed his day as if it were just any other.

Robert called and WhatsApped Saskia regularly, much more so than before. This was not only because Saskia was poorly, but because he now felt that their lives were merging together through the catalyst of time travel. If things were to take a dramatic turn in their lives and were to bring them ever closer, none of their friends would understand, nor would they ever be able to explain how or why it had happened. Who would believe them?

When he found time, Robert called on Saskia, if only for a brief visit. They had moments together that were close and romantic, but long afternoons of sex like they had had in the past were something for the future. Their relationship was moving to a different level. Saskia was still in some pain and even the simple task of a passionate kiss was difficult for her, as much as she wanted that.

Robert waited until he had his house to himself to take a more rigorous approach to studying the chest, first emptying the contents and then, with a delicate knife, working his way inwards from the edge to see if he could find a sign that there would be something magical in his possession. His methods were not scientific and he knew it, but he could hardly go to a Rembrandt specialist and have them believe his story, at least not yet. He would be shown the door. He needed more; but he had all the time in the world.

The peeling paint made things a little easier. He stayed away from any sections where the two layers of paint appeared to be bonded more tightly. He did find traces of another colour, which was encouraging but did not dare expose too much. He needed help.

He was at a loss to know what his next steps might be. He put everything back as it was, but not before taking pictures of the bottom and measuring it. His plan, eventually, was to replace the drawer bottom, but there seemed little point in rushing—he would then have to explain a large piece of wood in the house which might well get thrown away by mistake. "Good," Robert thought, it seemed he still had his wits about him.

He was still being very secretive about his possible find. He was not a patient man and wanted to explore more, to get to the bottom of his mystery. His conscience was also bearing on him to do the right thing and be honest, if indeed there was something of value there. The problem was what, how, and who with? He felt his relationship with

Belinda slipping away from him, but he had no reason not to be fair to her.

In the meantime, he settled down to a lot of Googling. Apart from the next steps with the painting, he wanted to know more about where in time he had just been. All he had to show for it was some fancy clothes, but he had lost all of his photos and any real evidence that he could use. He had checked again and again on his phone, but it told the same story; there was nothing there.

Today he was searching online for the periods he had visited, first 1945. Not surprisingly, that would be the only period with any photographic record. Sure enough, it was easy to find a collection of both stills, and some film. Robert concentrated on the film, in particular on the scene of the shooting that included the street organ which had been his hiding place for a good thirty minutes. He didn't really know what he was looking for, but he wanted to see how history portrayed what he had been through.

Robert's attention was suddenly drawn to the people bundled together behind the organ. "No, that can't be," he almost yelled to himself, and the screen. A fist hit the dining room table hard. He was now backtracking and freezing the film with each click. The picture was naturally in black and white and extremely poor, but he could make out what he thought was himself, and Saskia, right where he remembered them being. He couldn't believe it. He wanted to share the revelation with someone, preferably Saskia, even if his Saskia was not the one he was with in 1945. She would at least listen to him. Now he knew that he had been there, and he was not going insane.

One success on Google prompted Robert to go for another, so he continued looking beyond 1945. There was naturally nothing in the form of real time visual images for 1886 and 1664, but he did find enough on the history. The key takeaway for him was that everything that happened to him when he was "away" actually happened. The eel riots and the army in 1886, and the plague and Rembrandt in 1664. He had nothing to show for it yet. But he would if there was an actual

Rembrandt in the chest, the portrait of his wife Saskia. Again, that name.

A week went by and Saskia was mending well. She was still tormented by the violence she had experienced but was slowly managing to put that behind her. She felt safe. She was back in more civil times, and she had her Robert. He was now coming to visit more regularly, and Saskia was sensing his growing emotional gravitation towards her. They had experienced a closer emotional bond in 1664, but Saskia felt there was more that had changed Robert, though she had not been a part of it. She was only with Robert in 1664, but she had heard the stories of the other "Saskias."

Nevertheless, it all felt good, and she felt her resistance to a closer union ebbing away. Their lovemaking was more passionate, their talks were deeper, and their time together was measured in many more hours. It wasn't days, because Robert still had a family to go to, but he was fast approaching the point that he was going to have to break cover.

After lunch one day at the weekend when the kids were with friends, Robert took the bull by the horns. He went to the fridge and grabbed a beer, which immediately prompted a snappy remark from Belinda.

"A beer now? It's midday."

"I know, but there's something I want to talk to you about and I need your help." He continued, "Forget the dishes for the time being, and grab a wine for yourself."

"Whenever you say something like that, it sounds ominous. Is it about us? I know we're not in a good place at the moment."

"No. But what I'm about to tell you... well, you may think I'm crazy, even if you don't already."

"Alright, I'm listening."

"Please do me a favour. I'll keep it short, but please let me finish before you say anything. Facial expressions are fine, but I'd like to try and get this out in one go."

"Have you been rehearsing?"

"The basic thread, yes."

Belinda then gave him a slight wave of the hand as if to say, 'go on,' and Robert started.

"In my mind, I once said to you I had the feeling that I felt as if I had been thrown into a time warp, like time travel. I know you won't remember, but that's not the point. Right now, I'm asking to you to assume I have this ability, I was away in time and I learned something that I think could be very significant."

Belinda's face already showed incredulity, but she said nothing. She simply drew the shape of a zip across her lips to say that she had been told to keep quiet.

"The story of my time away is not boring at all, but now is not the time for that, and you won't believe me anyway. The result is that during my travels I came across the chest you and I bought for Daniel—the blue one, upstairs."

"And?"

"Well, I saw the chest being created. In 1664. And I was not in a dream."

There were more signs of incredulity, head shaking and rolling of eyes, as if Belinda was realising that her husband had some serious mental issues. But she said nothing.

"The chest was the creation of one of Rembrandt's former students and he had been gifted a painted panel from Rembrandt himself. Well, he ended up painting over the panel and using it as the underside of one of the drawers. And I think we have that upstairs."

"Can I talk now?" When Robert nodded, she said, "Have you completely lost your marbles? You haven't been anywhere. I've seen you every day, and night. We still share a bed you know!"

"I know what you're thinking and if I were in your shoes I would feel the same. I agree, for you, nothing has changed, only for me." And then Robert continued. "Listen, the only way I can try and resolve just a small amount of this is if we go upstairs and I can show you what I've found so far."

"I'm not even going to go along with this madness. You do what you want to do," answered Belinda sharply. She wanted to distance herself from the stupidity.

"Listen Belinda, I am only asking you for five minutes of your time to have a look. I know it will still be hard for me to convince you, because I can only scratch at the surface of the drawer and I'm not about to start scraping away at something that could be worth millions. Agreed?"

I am not going to agree, because it's all so damned stupid. You're becoming a fucking idiot. And if you think I want to be around you like this, then you have a second thought coming. Absurd. Ridiculous. Even comical."

Robert slammed hard on the kitchen table and released a bunch of coins which he had in his hand.

"I've also got these. Coins from the period. How else do you think I came by them?"

"I don't know. Coin shops? That says nothing."

"Five minutes, please. Come with me."

"If it releases me from this hell, OK. And be quick about it."

Belinda was really barking now. There was a lot of tension in the air. Robert led her upstairs to Daniel's room, where he pulled out the

259

top drawer, turned out the contents, turned it upside down, and placed it on the bed.

"If you take a close look, I have scraped away at the brown paint and at the edges and very carefully in the middle. I don't dare do any more than that. The rest is there to discover. See, there's definitely something underneath."

Belinda went along with what she considered to be a farce and looked more closely. She wasn't convinced.

"And I suppose you can also tell me what the painting is?"

"As it happens, yes. I am pretty sure it's a portrait of Rembrandt's first wife, Saskia."

"You're loopy. My five minutes is up. You do what you like, just leave me out of it." Belinda stormed out of the room, and, shortly after that, out of the house.

Robert had not expected to be believed, but he had hoped for more empathy and understanding. Now he had hit a brick wall with her, he strangely didn't feel uncomfortable about it. Saskia was becoming more important to him, and she would be his support. But he still hadn't spoken to Saskia about the chest either.

CHAPTER TWENTY

The ensuing days were uncomfortable for everyone in Robert's family. There was a distinct chill in the air, and they all felt it. Between work and Saskia, Robert devoted his time to trying to obtain more information about where and how to have "his" painting scanned.

His first port of call, after some Googling, would be someone who was open to accepting his crazy idea of there being a work of art under the paint. Someone who had access to the technology which could reveal it. Remote sensing at a micro level was what was needed, and he discovered it would likely be some form of X-ray radiography. But who had such equipment? Certainly, the museums, but Robert was still wondering what his story of provenance could possibly be.

After some investigation, Robert unearthed options on where to get his drawer looked at in some detail. The most obvious choice was the Rijksmuseum, home to everything Rembrandt, but he elected to go outside the country for help—albeit not very far—he opted for the University of Antwerp. They had a special department with expertise in these techniques and, at this stage, he only needed confirmation that there was a painting below the surface. Hopefully they could also determine it was a portrait. Once he had an answer like that in hand, he would then be armed with the evidence he needed to go to beyond the exploratory non-invasive work.

After several calls, Robert made an appointment with a Professor Merckx in Antwerp. It involved a drive of only an hour and a half. He abandoned any idea of removing the bottom of the drawer, as he had concluded that any surgery on a more than three-hundred-year-old piece of wood would be a dangerous undertaking. "No, play it safe," he thought. And with that in mind he arrived in Antwerp with the complete drawer. He was greeted by Professor Merckx, a man who looked to be in his fifties, with a typical academic appearance and unassuming nature.

"Welcome to our city, and our laboratories," opened Professor Merckx.

"It is nice to meet you. And thank you for seeing me so quickly." Answered Robert as he placed the drawer upside down on a workbench.

261

"I'll be honest. If we get paintings to study, they are normally already in a frame, and we are interested in how the artist has changed the painting as it was being created. You'll be surprised how many well-known paintings began life slightly differently. Your story is very different. Though I still struggle to see why you would think there was something to see. How did your idea come about?"

Robert was still comfortable lying. "Oh, one day I was busy with my son painting the chest blue—as you can see—and the underside of one of the drawers caught my eye as it was very different from the others and covered in a brown paint which has serious cracks."

"Yes, I can see that, but that won't tell you anything."

"You can also see that I have picked at the edges, and a bit in the middle, but only where the paint was already peeling away. I could see signs of other colours underneath."

"Yes, but that's not really enough to conclude that you have anything special."

"I agree, but I'm an optimist," answered Robert with a smile.

"Maybe you know more that you are telling me?"

"Maybe."

"I don't need to know. Let's get to work," the professor said, as he moved the draw to where his equipment was and embarked on an explanation of how the system worked.

"We can make a start now, but you do realise you will need to leave this with me for a while? We can try now to see if there is anything we pick up, but it takes time to build a full picture and then stitch it all together."

"I understand," said Robert. He knew this but was a little uncomfortable about leaving his "baby" behind.

"We are using X-ray radiography, which is harmless to the painting and can pick up on the pigments used. You see, different materials in the paints absorb and return different X-rays when bombarded, so we use that to create a picture of a picture, if you get what I mean."

Robert nodded. "I find it fascinating," said Robert.

"All we are going to do now is reach a point that will hopefully tell you if there is anything under the brown paint layer. Beyond that, there are techniques, such as chemical imaging, that will tell you more about the pigments and techniques used, but that is for much later. First you want to know if there is anything there, right?"

"I can't wait. It's a bit like being in the emergency room waiting to see how bad the bone break is."

Professor Merckx smiled and went about his work.

A proper process of discovery requires discipline and patience. The complete process would take a while. The sections they looked at revealed digital images that didn't make much sense to Robert, but the professor's face lit up more and more as he realised he was looking at something interesting. He had no idea what. He could see the telltale signs of pigments, but naturally there was no discernable image at this stage. It was still enough for him to turn to Robert.

"You have something here, my friend. Don't get your hopes up too much, but I think it is worth me taking my time to discover more. You know the financial consequences?"

"Yes," said Robert, now feeling more comfortable that it would be a worthwhile investment, even if Belinda would have had no sympathy for him.

Before he left, Robert made sure he had paperwork and photos in place that acknowledged what he was leaving behind and that it was in his ownership. He knew enough to know that even gentlemen with kind faces can be turncoats.

Robert only had to take one step into the house before he was attacked from almost all sides, starting with Belinda.

"What have you been up to?"

"Nice to see you as well," Robert said sarcastically. "I assume you are referring to the now missing drawer?"

"Of course."

"You might recall you said it was up to me what happens next, so that is what is happening. If you really want to know, the drawer is now with a specialist who's analysing it."

"Who?" said Belinda, snappily.

"You didn't want to have anything to do with it, so I'll tell you when I'm done. And then you can shout at me some more if and when there is nothing to show for it. OK?" finished Robert, trying to put an end to the conversation, but Daniel intervened.

"Dad, Mum has been saying some strange things about what is going on. And now all my stuff has been dumped out."

"I know. I'm sorry about that, but it won't be too long, and I'll make it up to you. Just bear with me please. It's important, but I'm afraid your Mum doesn't understand."

"She has a point, don't you think?"

"Maybe, but I don't want to get into any more debates about that. It's not good for anyone's health."

"You bet," came the sharp response from Belinda in the kitchen.

Robert brooded for a while on the sofa, separated from all of his family, none of whom seemed interested in talking to him or even being of any comfort. He got up and deliberately made a noise and a fuss about getting ready to go out. He had reached the end of his tether.

Quietly, he said to Belinda, "I think it's best that I leave you alone for a while. The toxic atmosphere here is not helping anyone, and it's a pity it's being spread around. Eh?"

"You think so?"

"I know so."

"As I said before, you do what you need to do."

Robert needed no more incentive than that and left the house before there was any interrogation about where and what he might do. In the past Belinda would have grilled him, but not now. She seemed content with his departure.

Robert normally warned Saskia when he was on his way over, but not this time. He felt his newfound relationship with her made that much easier now, and he was not disappointed. Saskia was at home and pleasantly surprised at Robert's sudden appearance. She gave him a big hug and kiss, immediately making him feel like he was at least a part of someone's life.

"To what do I owe this sudden pleasure?" she asked.

"I'll be honest. I need refuge… and someone who understands me."

"That sounds gloomy."

"It is. Things at home have gone from frosty to freezing. I could probably open the fridge to heat the house."

"Well, my fridge can offer you a beer."

"That would be nice. I need it."

"OK, come and tell me everything," said Saskia with genuine feeling.

They sat at the back in the kitchen, Robert with his beer and Saskia with a red wine. Saskia didn't have to say anything. The questioning in her eyes was already the opening line.

"It's not just things at home and my failing marriage. Our whole experience together in 1664 has changed the dynamic, at least for me. And it's not just how I feel about you."

Saskia didn't say anything, but Robert could see that she was waiting for him to continue.

"I need to tell you something else." A pause followed, but he continued, "When we were in Cornelis' house, you may remember he was building two chests and using an old Rembrandt painting as the underside to one of the drawers. Did you see that?"

"Yes, of course I remember."

"Well, where is it now, the chest, and the painting?"

"Are you fishing for what I think you are?"

"Yes and no. The chest you have is almost certainly one of the chests we saw, and I wondered whether you have given any further thought to it?"

"Robert, you're not stupid. Nor am I. And I love you enough to know that if I found anything of any value, then I would share the information with you. After all, we were in this together, it's our story. So, yes, I was curious about my chest, and I got really excited that I might have a genuine Rembrandt in my possession. But, shit, no. I couldn't find anything. It all looks just like bare wood. You are welcome to also take a look."

"No. I'm not sure I need to."

"I would actually like it if you did, just to make sure that I've looked properly. Presumably, there's another chest, but I don't know where, if it still exists."

"No. No need for me to look. You see, that's one of the things I wanted to talk to you about. The other half of the chest, I have it."

"You what?"

"I have it. Well, my son actually has it, in his bedroom. We bought it on Marktplaats from your neighbour, obviously not knowing what it contained. That's the day we saw you briefly at the front door. You'll be amused to know that it is now a pastel blue."

"Now I am going to get really nosey. What's in the drawers?"

"I was going to tell you."

"Yes…"

"There is something there, but I don't know what… not yet."

"The Rembrandt?" said Saskia. She didn't say "a Rembrandt." In her head it was already "the" Rembrandt she had seen.

"I don't know for sure."

Robert proceeded to tell Saskia more of the details about how he found the underside of the drawer painted over in the same brown they saw at Cornelis', and his visit to Antwerp.

"You really are ahead of the curve, but I sense there's more to this. You're not telling me everything."

"Indeed, I was coming to that. I had to explain to Belinda why I thought we might have something of value in the chest. Probably understandably, she was in no mood to accept my explanation as to how I might know, so she's now concerned about my mental health. You're the only one who will ever know and understand the truth. Even if we go to real specialists for confirmation, we're going to have

267

to spin another story. But that will be easy. I don't think they'll really care, as long as they have a challenging restoration project, and this one would be very newsworthy."

Robert noticed that he was now talking in the first-person plural, and he was fuzzily comfortable about it. He liked saying "we." Surely Saskia was becoming his future? It was a question he kept asking himself.

"Robert, I'm excited, but whose is it? The painting. Obviously not mine, but I feel we were a part of this together, don't you?"

"You won't believe how much I think this is part of you and me. No one else. But I don't know what to do and that's why I'm here."

"There's no rush. You only found out today and the painting is safe in Antwerp."

Robert went to the fridge to get another beer and came back with the bottle of wine for Saskia. He didn't sit down again until he had given her a much more passionate kiss which allowed them to linger a while, knowing that a true partnership was developing. The rest of the conversation was continued in closer proximity to each other, and much more tactile.

Robert had reached the point that he had to make some decisions about his situation, so he said.

"Sweetheart, I think …"

"You never call me sweetheart."

"I do now… With all that's been going on, I've decided that some changes to my marriage are coming. I can't go on like this. It's true, time travel has changed me—it's not Belinda's fault—but you have also changed me. And I want to be with you, more and more. I'm not asking to move in, just to be more a part of your life. I know that's going to get in the way of your independence, so prepare yourself," Robert ended with a smile.

Saskia didn't say a word. She simply leant over and hugged Robert tight around the neck. She felt the same way. He couldn't see the little tear that she released, but he did feel one fall on his neck. He smiled.

Not much more needed to be said. It was already late in the afternoon and Robert was staying put. He was not planning to go home; this was going to be the start of his new life. He knew that, but he didn't know how he was going to unravel all the puzzles ahead of him—his marriage, his relationship with his kids, Saskia, the painting; and of course Emerson Parker, the Brazilian-American painter, and plaintiff.

Robert had purposely turned his phone off for the night. Sure enough, the following day there were missed calls from Belinda, and a bunch of WhatsApps. Robert knew this was likely to happen, but he was now resolved in his course of action. He knew Belinda, in her heart of hearts, was likely to agree that parting was the best course for them to take. Like anyone in the same boat, the bit that would hurt most would be the effect on their kids. How could he best find a new balance in his relationships, and his own internal struggle with the lasting effects of time travel? He knew he would never be able to explain his discovery—he was not even going to try anymore—but there was only one person with whom he could share the impact of all that happened. It would remain their secret and an everlasting glue to their bond.

Robert checked his emails while Saskia was shuffling around the kitchen making coffee and something for breakfast. He saw an incoming email.

"News from Professor Merckx," he said to Saskia. "He doesn't have anything concrete yet, but he is sending more unconnected images and he says that signs of a painting are beginning to emerge, and it looks like a portrait. Just as we hoped, eh?"

"That's wonderful."

"There's still a long way to go. We just have to be patient."

"True. Patience is a virtue. It's just not one of my virtues. But I'm still excited."

"You're right. But why can't we hurry a virtue?"

"Funny—for this time in the morning! But seriously, are we allowed to speculate on what it might be worth and what you are going to do with it?"

"I don't dare think about its value if it really is a Rembrandt. If it's in good condition, it would be in the millions, but I don't know. I am really nervous that the combination of time and a thick coating of paint is going to destroy it. That's why we'll need more help than just Prof Merckx and his team."

"Yes, but who?"

"Once we have something to show in the way of a complete image, I could go to the Rijksmuseum; but I'm not so sure that's a good idea. They will probably pay more attention to an X-ray image created by another respected institution, but I'm more inclined to first seek out a professional restorer with experience to get beyond the paint cover. Surprisingly, there are more than you think in this country. Well, maybe I shouldn't be surprised, after all this is one of the most advanced countries in art restoration."

"And what about your wife? It's hers as well?"

"Yes it is. And I would never deny her that, even if she thinks I no longer have my feet firmly on the ground. I will always be fair. But the painting has become our project and we are the only two who will ever believe in it. I'm not sure Belinda would believe something was there even if she saw the evidence."

"But the reality could be that you would become embroiled in a fierce battle about ownership. You know what they say…

270

"I'm not going to let that happen."

"You're a good man, Robert."

"I know," answered Robert with a smile and added, "I need to be going. The kids will be at school and now is as good a time as any to clear the air at home. It won't be pleasant. As Newton said, for every action there is an equal and opposite reaction. But he wasn't referring to the ferocity of a woman. We'll see."

"I'll see you later then, I assume?"

"Count on it."

Robert returned home with one thing in mind, to confront Belinda about their marital situation. He wasn't expecting a warm welcome, so he had mentally prepared himself for the worst. But it didn't happen.

"I'm glad you've come home. We should talk. Would you like a coffee?

"Please," he said, surprised at the civility of it all.

"You know, Robert, apart from your travels, it has been a long time since we've not slept together," said Belinda, referring to Robert's absence the last night.

"Not for me. Remember, I've been away," said Robert provocatively.

"Don't be stupid. I'm talking about your real travels, for business. But that's OK if you want to believe that. I'm not going to get in the way of your *Back to the Future* fantasies."

"Hover boards!"

"What?"

"Oh, nothing."

"Well, with you being busy and away more, I have actually been enjoying being more on my own. It has been restorative."

"Restorative?" Robert said.

"Yes. Sounds a bit new-age, I know. But it gave me the opportunity to reflect on us, aside from your bizarre antics now. Living life together isn't living without problems, it's about solving them. And the only way I know of solving ours is to move on and go our separate ways. So, I need to be transparent."

"About what?"

"I have been seeing someone. And you started it."

"Eh?"

"You once suggested I meet Mark and, well… that happened… a while ago."

"How?"

"He came to the door one day looking for you, so I naturally invited him in. You were right, he is charming, and he also told me more about how the art copying business worked. I did feel more reassured. That's how it started, I guess."

"With one of my best friends?"

"Yes. I can't deny that. It wasn't intentional—it never is—but between that and the growing ravine between us, I want you to know that I think a separation would be best. That doesn't mean I'm going to suddenly live with Mark. No, that's not the intent. Right now, my priority is to find peace in myself. And the kids are old enough, mature enough and resilient enough to manage it. I think. Don't you?"

Robert didn't answer that question.

"Has Mark said anything to you recently about some challenges at *Masters in Paint*?" he responded.

272

"No, why should he?"

"Oh, nothing that cannot be handled. Now you know him intimately, I'll leave him to explain."

Robert felt a huge weight lifted from his shoulders. He didn't know what he was hearing. His Belinda, embarking on an affair with his friend. Maybe he had just missed the signs. And Mark had not let on about anything either.

"Wow, it's fair to say I wasn't expecting that. But I have to be honest, you beat me to it, because I was about to suggest the same. And I agree, I think the kids will be fine, as long as we don't disrupt their routines and we're civil to each other," said Robert, but purposely leaving out any mention of Saskia, as he was busy thinking what his angle should now be.

"I'm not going anywhere," said Belinda, "I have every intention of staying here in Amsterdam and making more of my life. We'll be fine and you also need to be here. Not for me, but for the kids." Belinda managed to get in a bit of a dig, planting the seed that she wanted to stay in the house.

"Who's we?"

"Oh, I mean all of us, whoever comes into our lives."

"Indeed. Then I will continue to explore the past," Robert started, trying to make light of his time travel. "In fact, I met someone called Saskia when I was travelling, and on more than one occasion." He did not lie this time, but he felt he was at least telling Belinda about Saskia's existence, albeit in a very round about fashion.

"What do you mean, more than one occasion? I thought you only went to the 17th century. Supposedly."

"It's complicated, maybe another time. But yes, there were more periods."

"Of course there were," said Belinda with another shake of her head and more rolling eyes.

The opening salvos of sudden news like this were always difficult, but once they were out of the way Robert and Belinda moved onto discussing more practical issues, one of which was what happened to Daniel's drawer. Apart from it being irritating, it was a tiny issue for Belinda, but Robert explained what he had been doing with the University of Antwerp and, in the interests of peace and understanding between them, he asked Belinda to be bear with him. She was surprised he was still continuing with his outlandish story, but she dropped the subject, at least for now. She knew she didn't want to live with someone who had flights of fantasy. More to the point, he showed less and less interest in her.

Robert and Belinda purposely acted as if everything was normal when the kids arrived home and waited until after dinner to tell them their news. That way it would not disrupt a meal, and they could, if they wanted, find their own space to think about it. As it turned out, the news seemed to have a calming effect. Both kids were in tune with parents in strife.

"It's the new norm," observed Daniel. And half our school have separated or divorced parents."

They went on to have a civilised and fruitful discussion and Daniel finished with.

"And when do I get my drawer back?"

"Not yet. Please bear with me. You'll, get it back, I promise. But maybe with a different underside."

CHAPTER TWENTY-ONE

It took a while, but Prof Merckx eventually called when Robert was with Saskia.

"Robert. It's Roger Merckx. May I call you Robert?"

"Absolutely. How are you getting on?"

"We are done, as best as we can, and as much as we can do."

"And?"

"Well, the good news is that there's definitely a painting there, and it is a portrait, as you surmised. It's a woman. That much we can see."

"And the bad news."

"There is a lot of paint over the top, it is very brittle, so it will take some work to try and remove it."

"In your opinion though, is it enough to be investigating further?" asked Robert, knowing full well what his answer would be.

"Yes, I think so. It looks intriguing and I am happy to give you introductions to people who can help you more than me. What you have is not another painting over an old one, but nothing at all. Just brown paint. And you can't show any provenance, just a blue drawer and a supposition. That's not strong, you know."

"I know. But I'm sure it's worth it."

"Your call. You are free to come and pick it up at your convenience."

"I'll be there today," he said. "Is that OK?"

"Absolutely, I'm here all day."

"Thank you very much. I'll be there shortly after lunch."

"Fine. And I will be mailing you the full image when we get off the phone, so you can see what you have."

"I can't wait. My computer is right here in front of me."

Robert had his laptop ready, waiting patiently for the email, which in his mind seemed to take ages to come, but it was only fifteen minutes until he received a transfer link for a hi-res image.

"Eureka!" he yelled to himself and Saskia. "Take a look."

Saskia came around to look over Robert's shoulder. "Wow, that's a clearer image than we thought, eh?'

"Yep. That's got to be her. See, it's a head and shoulders and a round face, right? Rembrandt's Saskia had a round face."

"I need a drink," said Saskia.

"No you don't. We'll celebrate tonight. Why don't you come with me to Antwerp?"

"Yeah, let's do this together."

Robert and Saskia picked up their drawer from Prof Merckx, who pointed out that the underside had been separated from the drawer with a lot of care and that it should stay separate.

"Don't worry, I have no intention of putting it back. I will give it a new bottom as soon as I get back. My son wants his drawer back."

Once they were back in Amsterdam, Robert set about finding wood and giving the drawer a new lease of life, if only for peace at home, but he didn't deliver it immediately. He and Saskia embarked on some more serious research into restorers.

Their starting point was the Dutch Society of Restorers, which was a mine of information, and they eventually selected and contacted a restorer who went by the wonderful name, Lulu Winter. When they had her on the phone, she turned out to be an Austrian living in

Amsterdam. She didn't quite follow the provenance of what they had for restoration, but she agreed to take a look and see if it was even worth trying. There was no mention of Rembrandt.

The following day, Robert and Saskia headed over to meet Lulu in one of the old warehouses not too far away. It was one of those old canal warehouses which had been turned into apartments. Lulu had converted hers into a combination of studio and apartment. It was on the first floor, very large, with low ceilings where the only natural light came in from the back and front of the apartment. This would perhaps not have suited an artist, but an art restorer's tools are primarily bathed in intense artificial light.

Lulu greeted Robert and Saskia as they came up the stairs.

"Welcome. It's nice to meet you. I am curious to see what you have there." She pointed to the panel that Robert was carrying in a protective blanket. "I have also looked at the image you sent me via email. Interesting. Very interesting."

"We think so too," said Robert.

"Do you have any idea what it might be, other than a portrait? That much is clear."

"No," they lied. "We were hoping you would be able to help us." Neither Robert nor Saskia wanted to talk up what it might be.

Robert told Lulu where the panel came from and showed her pictures of a chest, not the blue one he had, but Saskia's twin. For the sake of this conversation, the original brown one would probably have a higher provenance value than one which had been painted blue. They also told Lulu they knew the chest came from the seventeenth century.

Once they had revealed the panel and laid it out on Lulu's workbench, both Robert and Saskia kept their eyes on Lulu, not the panel. They wanted to see her initial reaction. That was going to be key.

"Wow. I'm not sure about this. That's not an artist painting over it to use it as a background for a new painting. That's what we normally get. This is crude work."

"Yes, but it was done by an artist," said Saskia unthinkingly.

"How would you know that?"

"I meant to say it looks like it might have been done by an artist. It doesn't look that crude. The paint appears to be very old, and peeling, but done with style, no?" She knew she was bullshitting, but continued, "Can you determine how old the paint might be?"

"Well, there's not much to see yet, but I can see you've picked away at some parts and there is indeed something underneath. But how to get at it, that's the question. Or, even if we can?

"We like to be optimistic," Saskia said.

"Listen, why don't I make you a coffee and you sit over there while I have a quick look. I won't be able to do much, but I'd like a little time to study what you have, because you will also need some idea of the financial consequences. Right?"

"Absolutely. Yes, we understand this is going to be a lot of patient work. We just need to know if this is something for you and if you're interested."

"Oh, I know I'm interested. Give me a little time and we can talk."

Lulu mounted the panel at an angle on the multifunctional easel on top of her workbench and swung an arc light over the panel so she could get a closer look. She spent minutes like that, going over the paint and picking at it occasionally and very carefully with a scalpel. She naturally had very little to go on because she was not looking at a painting, just a peeling brown paint layer, following the contours of an X-ray image on a big computer screen next to her.

After a while, she joined Robert and Saskia on a seat next to her work sofa, where they were sitting.

"First of all, I'm glad you brought this to me, and I would like to explore it further if you are in agreement. But now I'm afraid I'm going to get a little technical, so please bear with me."

"We're not going anywhere," said Robert with a smile. "Please go ahead."

"Well, this is by no means going to be standard restoration work. We are agreed that there is something underneath the upper paint level, but before I do anything I need to get to the bottom of what I am dealing with—I mean that horrible peeling brown paint. If, as you say, you think it is very old, it may be very difficult, or even impossible, to separate the paint from the artist's work below. That will be especially true if it is oil based. However, I am hopeful that since there was never any intention to paint another painting on top, whoever painted over it chose to use a cheaper animal-based binder with the brown pigments. If that is the case, then we may be able to have a go at scraping away the upper layer. It does look brittle, which is a good sign."

"But how will you know what is best to do?" asked Robert.

"Basically, there are two approaches, non-invasive and invasive. As you can imagine, when we are researching paintings, we prefer to go for the non-invasive techniques, for example, the X-ray radiography for the imaging, which you have already done—and things like X-Ray fluorescence for identifying the pigments used. For what you're after at this stage, I'm afraid we are going to have to be invasive because we are not interested in the brown pigment, only in what is underneath it. So, I have to warn you now, if the paint can be removed, we do run the risk that there is some danger to the integrity of the original painting. I do need to make that clear. I hope it will be like peeling dried mud from a face mask, but I doubt it somehow."

"Thank you. So, if we get to the painting, we will likely still have a lot of work to do to restore it, right?"

"Yes, I think that's highly likely, but let's cross the first bridge first."

Robert didn't really want to think about crossing bridges but understood the priorities. Lulu went on to explain her fees, as well as what turned out to be an extensive contract that protected the rights of the owners, and the liabilities, or rather the lack of them, of the restorer. Robert and Saskia were warned that the work would take a while, but they were welcome to come and watch if and when she reached an advanced stage in the scalpel work. The very thought of a scalpel on their painting gave them the shivers, but they knew there was little alternative.

The next few days were spent resuming work and family life as best they could. For Robert, that meant more transparency at home as he started to find a balance between his life with Saskia and the needs of his family. These things are never easy, but the sense of overwhelming difficulty was slowly replaced by the common sense of finding solutions to each of their needs. The matter of the painting in the drawer never came up, quite simply because Belinda never believed in it in the first place. That could be another bridge that will be crossed later, if at all. Daniel also got his drawer back.

Lulu eventually called and invited Robert and Saskia over. It didn't take much to get them to stop what they were doing and head over to her place. She greeted them at the door as they bounded up the stairs.

"I can hear the enthusiasm in your steps," offered Lulu as she let them in.

"What did you expect? You sounded pretty upbeat on the phone."

They looked over at the workbench, but there was a linen cloth draped over their precious cargo.

"Take a seat," said Lulu.

"As you can see from my grey hair, I have been in this business for a while. It can be frustrating, and exhilarating. Your painting was both. Frustrating because it took a lot of very patient peeling and exhilarating because of what I think I see. I also think you know more than you have been telling me, so before I show you what I have, I would like to ask you to tell me more about the provenance or origins of what you have. I'm not naïve you know."

Robert looked at Saskia for help but didn't get any, apart from one of those looks that said, "what have we got to lose?"

"Well," said Robert, "I have tried this story elsewhere and if I tell you, I ask you to believe me... no... us, that it's true and it all happened. I fully understand that no one else will believe us, but you may now be the only person in a position to understand some of our logic, because I will tell you what's there."

"You know?"

"I believe so. A portrait of Rembrandt's first wife, Saskia, by Rembrandt van Rijn," Robert said with emphasis. He then proceeded to tell Lulu the whole story, admirably uninterrupted by Lulu.

"Holy shit," was the only thing that came out when Robert had finished. "How can I argue with that fanciful story? But I have to give you some benefit of the doubt, because how would you otherwise know what was there. But I can't use what you are telling me for any provenance."

"OK, but can we see it?" Robert said impatiently.

"I'm not entirely finished with the scraping, but there is enough to see." Lulu got up and guided them over to the painting.

"You were fortunate. The brown paint was an organic base, so it made life easier, and the two layers could be separated, but not without some damage. It was still enough to reveal a portrait, as you say, of Saskia. I am convinced of that. Rembrandt was well known for painting portraits of his wife, so I guess he regarded this one as one of his lesser efforts. In the seventeenth century maybe, but not now."

"Lulu, take the cover off," barked Saskia, but with a smile.

She did. It revealed a fairly large portrait of what was now a very familiar face to Robert and his Saskia. It was Mrs. van Rijn and it definitely looked like a Rembrandt, but in a poor condition. Her chubby face was lit on one side. The subject had her familiar pale features, and she also wore a black and yellow hat with a rim. The background was familiarly dark.

"Wow, wow, wow," said Saskia.

"You know what makes it?" said Lulu. "Look at the signature. That was one of his early ones and he didn't use it often. It says Rembrant, not Rembrandt. But he did use it. I am guessing this must have been one of his first attempts at painting his wife, if she was even his wife at this point."

"Again, wow, wow, wow. What happened there?" said Saskia, as she pointed to a part of the painting that had clearly suffered more.

"Yes, I'm afraid it wasn't all easy. This was a first for me, but it required more patience than it was difficult. I had to be very careful with peeling the paint back and it didn't work equally over the whole painting, as you can see. There are parts of the hat that have suffered badly. You can see that the intent was to make parts of the hat yellow and only some bits have survived. I think I can safely say that, because the brown paint did peel off, the painter didn't use a strong binder with the brown colour, so it might have been something like casein."

"And that is?"

"Let's just call it a milk base, which makes sense, as it is much cheaper and there was no need to cover the original in something expensive. But there is still so much work to do. So, we need to discuss next steps."

"And what do you think they should be?" said Robert.

"As I said, I don't know how I will ever be able to explain your story, nor do I think I'm even going to try. I still have trouble with it myself, but you both seem so convinced. I will leave it at that. It will be your story, not mine. The bottom line is that we have something to show, regardless of the weird provenance. I suggest we let the real experts take over, and that's not me. Still, to be honest, I would like to stay involved. I am a restorer, after all."

"OK, but what does that mean exactly?"

"Well, as you can imagine, the world of art restorers is a very small one. Intimate, even. A mysterious clique of sorts. Our first port of call has to be the Rembrandt Research Project, which is the gold standard when it comes to any assessment of a work by Rembrandt. Naturally, they are here in Amsterdam."

"You know the people, right?"

"Yes, but not that well. I can at least make the introductions and get us started. But I do repeat my request. You are the owners of the painting and the ball is in your court, but I would like to stay involved. When something like this comes along it can be dog eat dog and I don't want to be shut out after all my work. In a way it has also become my baby."

"We got you," said Robert. "Let's do the following: Saskia and I will leave you with the painting… it's better kept here… and we will go home and discuss it. Before we go though, can we speculate on who would want the panel, and what value to put on it?" And after a little pause, he added, "We know that's a loaded question."

"Robert, you know I cannot answer that with any certainty. There are still so many hoops to jump through to get it validated and restored. That in itself is going to take a long time and take my word for it, your story of provenance will fall flat—if you use it. And provenance counts for a lot."

"I accept that. We will need to give that a lot more thought."

"If this is a Rembrandt, then we all know his pictures go for millions. You will have no trouble seeing this in a bidding war at an auction, if it goes that far. But there will also be huge pressure on you to keep the painting in this country, so prepare yourself. Welcome to the intrigues of the art world. So, my answer to your question. If you are not rich already, you will be."

"I guess we have a lot to think about. Why don't we arrange to meet tomorrow and talk further, if that fits with you?"

"Absolutely. I'm as excited as you are. And my lips are sealed until I hear from you."

When they were outside Saskia did briefly worry Robert when she said, "Do you think it's safe for us to leave it with her?"

"The thought has occurred to me, but surely these people are to be trusted. Aren't they?"

"Hell, I don't know."

They had a lot to talk about in the evening over dinner. Robert cooked a simple pasta, accompanied by a complex salad with a mix that included nuts and fruit. The discussion was not just about the painting; there were still so many open issues about how their own relationship was to continue. The discovery of a Rembrandt also affected that, not because it was a Rembrandt, but what would happen if they sold it? And there was still Belinda and how far she should benefit, even if she didn't believe any of his story; and he did want her to believe. There's only one thing for it, he thought, invite Belinda to Lulu's and let her hear it straight from her. But he didn't mention that idea to Saskia, not yet.

Once they were finished with the meal, but not the wine, Saskia got up and moved around to where Robert was sitting. She leant close to him. "And what are you going to do with the money?" she teased. "On paper, it's all yours, don't forget."

"You're fishing."

"You bet I am. I want to know what's going on in that fuzzy brain of yours. It's running overtime. I may be wrong, but I doubt it." She gently laid her hands on his shoulders after holding two palms to either side of his head.

"Obviously not as much as you think."

"Really. These little grey hairs tell a different story."

"It's not that much, and besides, a little grey hair is a small price to pay for all this wisdom."

"Well, now you're going to have to pay another price," she said, standing to the side of him and unbuttoning her shirt, one button at a time and very slowly. "This day has done more for me that get me excited about paintings."

"Can I just watch?"

"I'd like that." Saskia continued, pulling the shirt from under her tight jeans. Everything was in extreme slow motion to allow Saskia time to give Robert a sip of wine as each of her garments disappeared to the floor. Robert's eyes remained fixed on Saskia the whole time, until neither of them could resist anymore and the thick rug on the floor became the closest substitute for a bed. Bed would come later. This was a celebration of their day, and their love for each other.

The new day was again warm and sunny, and Robert suggested they have breakfast at a café.

"I wonder how Henry is?" he started.

"What made you think of Henry?"

"I was at the front of the house and saw a horse go by, which is very rare in the heart of the city. Made me think of Henry."

"Maybe it is Henry."

"Wouldn't that be fun?"

"OK, let's go. I'm also keen to get back to Lulu and discuss our options."

"I'm going to take the coins with us to show Lulu. I know it doesn't mean a lot, but it might help her better understand. You never know."

"You're kidding. You're not going to run the risk of walking over a bridge with that coin. I won't let you."

"Agreed, one hundred percent. First, I'm not going to go over *my* bridge. I'm going to go over the footbridge. Have you got an old purse?"

"Yes, but why?"

"I'm going to put the coins in the purse, or anything with some weight, and throw it to you on the other side. Just to be on the safe side. It will look stupid I know, but that should work, right?"

"Sounds sensible. I'm not sure we're going to get anywhere with the coins with Lulu. But I sense that I'm not going to talk you out of it."

Not far away from Saskia's house was a small footbridge over the Brouwersgracht canal, aptly named 'Melkmeisje' bridge after one of Johannes Vermeer's most well-known paintings, *The Milkmaid*. They needed to cross this bridge.

"OK, you go across first and I'll throw the purse to you. And don't drop it into the canal," said Robert with a smile.

"You know, I'm tempted to do that, just to be rid of them."

"Don't."

Saskia crossed and then waited on the other side. It was relatively busy on the streets, mainly cyclists, presumably on their way to work or college. Robert didn't want to make a spectacle of himself, as if he was inventing a new canal sport, so he waited a bit.

As he was waiting, he saw the stooped figure of a man pushing a rickety old bike and walking in his direction. The bike was loaded with possessions and Robert immediately made the connection. As the man came closer, he could see the familiar features of a plump face, ruffled hair and a black beret. Robert was staring again, but this time it was directly at the street wanderer. He didn't say a word, he just waited.

"Can I have my coin back?" was all the old man said.

Robert just stood there, mouth open, looking intently at the man and his possessions. He didn't know what to say. The purse with all of the coins was in his hand. All he did was slowly and meekly extend his arm towards the unknown, but remarkably familiar man.

"Here. They're all yours."

"Thank you," came the reply, and he then walked towards the bridge that Robert was also about to cross. The old man then added:

"You know what they say. Yesterday is history, tomorrow is a mystery, today is a gift; that's why they call it the present." And he walked over the bridge towards Saskia and disappeared.

Acknowledgements

My sincere thanks go to the many literary, historical and art buffs who have helped me with research and read evolving drafts - my brother, Val Pirie, Lulu Welther, Ralph Lupton, Anita Olifiers, Cherry Locke, Rob Bout, Hugh Foley and more....